# SWEET BEGINNINGS

## A CANDLE BEACH SWEET ROMANCE

### NICOLE ELLIS

Cover art by: RL Sathers/SelfPubBookCovers.com

Cover typography by: Mariah Sinclair

Editing by: Free Bird Editing —

Serena Clarke and LaVerne Clark

❀ Created with Vellum

*For my Family. Thank you for believing in me and helping me reach for my dreams.*

**1**

_D_ahlia Winters shifted in the squeaky leather executive chair and crossed her legs. She stifled a yawn as the suited lawyer standing at the end of the board-room table droned on and on. The last time she'd been in a law office was to finalize her divorce. Unlike the dissolution of her marriage, this visit resulted from less happy circumstances.

Spring sunlight filtered through the newly green trees outside, reflecting off the window and creating a lacy pattern on the table. Dahlia regretted not bringing her sketchbook in to capture the moment, but she settled for drawing in pen on the lined notepad in front of her. She wished she were anywhere but in the Seattle area law office of Schmidt, Anders and James.

"Dahlia, heads up," her mother whispered, kicking her daughter's shins under the table with the toe of her high-heeled shoe.

Dahlia pulled her attention away from the window and scanned the room. All eyes were on her, from the paralegal and attorney at the end of the table to Great-Aunt Ruth's best friend, Agnes Barnes. What had she missed?

"Ms. Winters. Do you understand the terms of your great-aunt's will?" Larry Anders asked. He transferred his tablet to one hand while maintaining eye contact with her as he sipped from a glass of water. Condensation dripped from the glass as the seconds ticked away.

Across the table, Agnes's eyes bored into Dahlia, her thin lips pursed in disapproval. A tightly wound bun pulled at the elderly woman's facial features, giving her an impromptu face-lift and increasing the severity of her countenance. In front of her, tight, scripted handwriting covered a yellow legal pad. What had she written?

"I'm sorry. Can you please restate the terms?" Dahlia asked. Why was the lawyer asking her if she understood the terms? Her mother was Aunt Ruth's sole heir. She flipped over the first page of her notepad, tucked a strand of strawberry blonde hair behind her ear, and lifted her pen as if to take notes.

The lawyer half-smirked, half-frowned and made a show of scrolling back several pages on the document he'd been reading from on his iPad. His custom-tailored, pin-striped suit hung perfectly on his lean form as he moved a few steps closer to her. He'd probably never been caught daydreaming in his life.

"Ms. Winters. Your aunt has left you the majority of her assets, including her house and the To Be Read bookstore in Candle Beach, Washington."

Blood pounded in her head. She must have misheard him. She pushed herself back from the table and gaped at the attorney. "I'm sorry. Did you say she left me the house and bookstore?"

He nodded in assent.

She turned to her mother, Vanessa. "Why didn't she leave them to you? You were her closest relative." Ruth Wright and her husband, Ed, had raised Vanessa after her parents were killed in a car crash when she was a small child. Before Ruth died, Dahlia's mother had visited her in Candle Beach almost every weekend while she endured chemotherapy treatments.

Vanessa shrugged her shoulders under a crisply ironed white blouse. "You always loved the bookstore when we visited in the summers. I'm sure she had her reasons."

Dahlia scrutinized her mother's face. She didn't appear to be upset about the slight, although she must have expected to inherit all of Ruth's assets. She struggled to process the lawyer's words. The summers she'd spent in Candle Beach would always be special, but her life was in Seattle now. What would she do with a bookstore and a house in a town three hours away on the coast? Could she sell the properties?

With the money from the sale, she could travel to Paris and paint for a year, or backpack through Europe. Jeff, her ex-husband, hadn't managed to quench the travel bug that had bitten her at a young age, although he'd certainly tried throughout their three-year marriage. While she'd yearned to travel the world, his idea of a daring adventure was a one-week, all-inclusive Caribbean cruise for their honeymoon. He'd been appalled by the poverty and filth in some of the ports and refused to participate in any excursions off the ship. When Dahlia had gone on shore without him, he'd acted like a spoiled toddler.

Now, all her dreams of traveling the world could come true. Aunt Ruth's bequest could make them a reality. Exhilaration raced through her body, followed closely by a nagging feeling. Aunt Ruth had loved the bookstore. Could she really sell it to an outsider?

At the front of the room, the lawyer cleared his throat and put his tablet on the table. "There are however a few stipulations to your aunt's bequests. Firstly, you must keep the bookstore open for twelve months and it must be profitable at the end of that year. If you choose to sell the house or bookstore prior to the end of twelve full months, you are entitled to only fifty percent of the profits. Secondly, Agnes Barnes is to be the executor of these provisions. It is in her power to adjust the terms as she sees fit to best meet your aunt's wishes. All of Mrs. Wright's financial assets will be kept in trust for you and other than a stipend for basic living expenses, Mrs. Barnes will need to approve any expenditures out of that trust."

Dahlia leaned forward, twisting her hands underneath the table. She glanced over at Agnes, who glared at her. Unless the woman changed the terms, there wasn't much chance she'd be traveling anytime soon. She remembered playing cards with Agnes on visits to Candle Beach as a child. After Ruth's husband had died when she was only fifty-four, her friends, who called themselves the Ladies of Candle Beach, had been her rocks. In her great-aunt's memory, if Dahlia decided it made sense to sell, Agnes would be reasonable, right?

"If I sell the assets, who receives the other fifty percent of the proceeds?" Dahlia asked the lawyer.

He nodded to his left. "Mrs. Barnes is entitled to the remainder if you choose to not fulfill the full terms of this provision."

Agnes peered directly at Dahlia with a self-satisfied expression, and primly adjusted her green cardigan sweater. Dahlia turned away from her gaze. The chances of Agnes being reasonable were slim if she stood to inherit.

Okay, so she now owned a bookstore in an idyllic small town on the Washington Coast. When her mother had implored her to come to the will reading, Dahlia had hoped Aunt Ruth had willed her the Royal Doulton tea set that had been a daily fixture in her childhood summer visits to Candle Beach. Now she owned not only the tea set, but the house that came with it. The thought was daunting.

"I told your aunt she was crazy when she informed me she planned to give you the bookstore," Agnes said to her. "Candle Beach is a special place and the bookstore should be owned by someone who is a part of the community, not some outsider."

Dahlia sat up straight and her blood boiled. Agnes may have been right that she wasn't the best choice to own To Be Read, but it wasn't her decision. "I'm *not* an outsider. Candle Beach has been a part of my life since I was a baby."

Her mother smiled and leaned back in her chair.

"The other Ladies and I agree that you aren't the right fit," Agnes said. "We think you should sell the bookstore. Wouldn't you prefer to stay here in Seattle? Candle Beach isn't exactly a booming metropolis. If you sell the bookstore, half of the profits should be plenty to let you travel the world, at least for a short time."

"Aunt Ruth left her property to me. I'm going to do what is best in this situation." Unfortunately, she wasn't sure what was best. Did she have it in her to live in a small town and own a bookstore for the rest of her life? The thought of settling down made her sweaty and nauseous. She reached for the pitcher in the center of the table and poured herself a glass of water. She savored the coolness of the glass before drinking deeply.

The lawyer cleared his throat and her mother nudged her again.

"Dahlia, what do you want to do?" Vanessa folded her French-manicured hands together and leaned across the rectangular table toward her daughter. Behind her, a designer suit jacket hung neatly over the back of the chair. Dahlia knew that before her mother had come to pick her up for the will reading, she'd been in a client meeting in her role as one of the leading commercial real estate brokers in Seattle.

"I need to think about it." She pushed her pen around on the table. The pounding in her head eased and she relaxed her unconsciously clenched jaw. A faint glimmer of what could be mistaken as approval appeared on Agnes's rouged face.

"I'm afraid I need a decision by five o'clock. There is a purchase offer on the bookstore that expires today." The lawyer separated a document from the pile of paper in front of him and held it out to her, face down. "This contains all the details of the offer."

The digital clock on the wall opposite the door read three o'clock. Dahlia stood and accepted the document from the lawyer. "Is there anything else we need to go over today?"

He looked at the paralegal, who shook her head. "No, we have your contact information," he said. "But please call us as soon as possible to let us know your decision, so we can relay it to the prospective buyer."

"I'll let you know by five," she said.

The lawyer motioned to the paralegal. Without saying a word, she handed Dahlia a business card and a copy of Aunt Ruth's bequest, including the stipulations of the will. Dahlia palmed the card and shoved it into the back pocket of her jeans. She refrained from reading the real estate purchase agreement and folded it in half along with the stapled bequest, gripping the sheaf of papers in sweaty hands. The ultra-short time frame for the purchase offer immobilized her for a moment. Agnes brushed past her, almost knocking her over in the process.

Vanessa slid her chair back and stood, smoothing the hemline of the linen skirt that completed her suit ensemble. Her heels clicked rhythmically on the tile floor as she joined her daughter at the door with her jacket draped in neat folds over one arm. She put her free hand on Dahlia's back to guide her to the door. "I know this is a lot to take in, but Aunt Ruth wanted you to have the bookstore."

"Ms. Winters," the lawyer called out to her before she exited the room. "There isn't a huge demand for commercial real estate in Candle Beach. I don't know if another offer will come anytime soon. I suggest you seriously consider the offer currently on the table."

She nodded and followed her mother out, her mind humming with the decisions to be made.

∼

Dahlia walked to the car in a dazed state. She waited outside of the passenger side of her mother's gray Lexus long after Vanessa had unlocked the doors.

Vanessa rolled down the passenger side window and called out, "Are you going to get in?" She glanced at her gold wristwatch and tapped her fingers on the steering wheel. "I've got to get back to work, but I'll drop you off first."

Dahlia opened the car door, sat down on the buttery leather seat, and fastened her seat belt on autopilot. She stretched out her legs and reveled in the space on the passenger side. The old Toyota Corolla she'd owned since college didn't have nearly as much space for her five-foot-nine frame. The spaciousness of the car was wasted on her petite mother.

"Honey, are you okay?" Vanessa glanced sideways at her daughter while expertly turning from the side street onto the highway.

"I'm fine." She gazed out the passenger side window. In this part of the city, houses from the early twentieth century lined the streets, much like in Candle Beach. On one of the porches, two old women sat together at a table, drinking coffee. They reminded her of Aunt Ruth and her friends. The women had always treated her well, saving small treats for her as a child and cajoling her to sit with them to gossip when she grew older.

Her mood darkened as she remembered Agnes's harsh opinion of her, which apparently was shared by the other Ladies of Candle Beach. She'd failed her aunt. With this realization, tears spilled down her face, and she swiped them away with her hand.

"You're not fine," Vanessa said, her voice tinged with concern. "What's wrong?"

"I feel horrible. I didn't have time to visit Aunt Ruth in the last few years and only saw her once when she was going through cancer treatments in the city. Okay, the truth is, I didn't make time to see her in Candle Beach." She quieted and looked out the window again, not seeing any of the passing cityscape. "And now she's given me this amazing gift and I don't know what to do. I was obviously a disappointment to her and her friends." The tears fell faster and she wiped them away with a facial tissue from the travel box her mother kept in the car's center console.

"Honey, Aunt Ruth knew you were busy with your own

life. I know how much she appreciated your weekly phone calls." Vanessa signaled left, then merged into traffic heading onto the northbound freeway lanes.

"Why do you think she wanted me to have the bookstore and house in Candle Beach?"

"Maybe she thought it was time for a change for you."

"A change? My life is fine, I don't need a change." She squirmed. The seat that had felt spacious minutes before now felt as hot and confining as a coach seat on an airplane with broken air-conditioning. She reached forward to turn on the fan and directed the air vents to blow at her face.

"Dahlia, I say this as your mother, someone who loves you and wants the best for you," Vanessa began, shooting quick glances at her daughter as she drove. "You're thirty-two, divorced, and working at a travel agency that gives you fewer hours of work each week. You can barely afford that rat-trap basement apartment you call home. You talk about traveling, but the closest you get is purchasing airline tickets and hotel rooms for clients. You need a change."

Her mother had a point. After the headiness of being free of Jeff had worn off, she'd floundered in indecision about the future. The inheritance from Aunt Ruth would change her life for the better, no matter how she proceeded with the sale of the property.

"But what should I do? I don't know if I can run a book-store. What if I can't sell the bookstore after twelve months and then I've lost my chance? But if I sell now, I lose out on half of the money. And there's no way Agnes will agree to let me out of the terms of the bequest earlier, unless I want to give her half of the assets."

The decision was too immense. She focused on the candle-shaped, vanilla-scented air freshener hanging from the rearview mirror and took a deep breath of the calming scent.

The image of a candle reminded her of Candle Beach. She'd loved to go there as a child and through her teenage years, only stopping when she entered the University of Washington and had to work full-time during the summers. She remembered the bustling main street leading down to the marina, the pounding surf outside of town, and the lazy summer days spent lounging on a grassy knoll in the town square, eating blueberry ice cream. Although she had been a visitor to town, the kids who lived there year-round had been friendly because her Aunt Ruth was well-known in town.

She shifted in the seat and reached into her back jeans pocket, pulling out the flat white business card the paralegal had provided. She traced the number with her finger and took a deep breath. She knew what she had to do.

She couldn't even think about selling the bookstore without returning for a final visit. Aunt Ruth deserved that courtesy. "I'm going to make arrangements to see the bookstore and stay at Aunt Ruth's house this weekend." Somehow, after making the decision, she felt lighter and filled with a blend of excitement and curiosity about seeing Candle Beach after a fourteen-year absence.

"Honey, that's great." While stopped at a red light, Vanessa reached over and hugged her daughter with one arm. "I think that will be great for you and maybe bring some closure. Maybe you'll even like it enough to stay."

"I seriously doubt that. My life is here." From what she remembered about the town, it wasn't exactly big on nightlife or cultural experiences, two things she enjoyed about living in the University District. "But it will be nice to see the old house and maybe drop in on a few old friends."

She'd kept up with a few people from her summer vacations in Candle Beach through social media, although she wasn't close to any of them after so many years apart.

"And hey, maybe you'll meet a nice guy. You certainly aren't going to meet anyone at work."

She chafed at her mother's intrusion into her love life. With the average age of her travel agency clientele hovering around seventy, she didn't meet many prospective suitors at work. It didn't really matter. It had only taken a few years of marriage for her to see that she was better off single.

But a little male companionship wouldn't hurt. She missed snuggling on the couch watching TV, but she didn't miss fighting for control of the remote. And while their love life hadn't been mind-blowing, she did miss the intimacy she had once shared with Jeff. Getting to that point in a relationship with another man seemed implausible unless she relinquished her independence. Never again would she give up her dreams for a man.

"I'll keep an eye out," Dahlia said wryly. "But I'm fine on my own. I don't need anyone telling me what to do or how to live my life."

She'd spent too many years striving to be the perfect wife that Jeff required, too many years not following her own passions. When she'd expressed an interest in rekindling her high school love for art with a sculpture class, he'd asked her why she wanted to do something so useless. Back then, she'd dreamed of moving somewhere new and exciting after living all of her life in the Seattle area. Jeff had pooh-poohed the idea, saying his finance career was in the city and it would be foolish to move. She laughed. Candle Beach wasn't exactly an exotic locale, but right now it seemed her best prospect to get the life she wanted.

Vanessa pulled into the scrubby grass-and-gravel

parking spot outside of Dahlia's rental apartment. In Dahlia's opinion, the reserved parking spot that she didn't have to fight students for on a daily basis was the best part of the entire rental agreement. It certainly wasn't her actual apartment. Her car was in the shop for what seemed like the umpteenth time, but the mechanic had promised she'd have it back by Friday. She unclipped her seatbelt, gathered her belongings and got out of the car.

"I'm not saying I'm moving to Candle Beach," she said through the open car door. "With any luck, I'll be able to arrange for someone else to run the bookstore and I can manage things from here. If not, there's always the option to sell. The bookstore and house must be worth quite a bit. Fifty percent of the profit from selling them isn't anything to sneeze at."

Vanessa smiled at her daughter.

"What?" Dahlia asked.

"Nothing," she said with a glint in her eye. "Keep an open mind. I know you think you don't need anyone or anything to make your world complete, but something is missing in your life right now."

Dahlia sighed. "Goodbye, Mom." She pushed the car door closed.

Her mother pulled out of the parking space and circled the block. As she drove past the house, she shouted, "Keep an open mind!"

Dahlia waved and blew her a kiss. Then she trudged down the broken concrete steps to her basement apartment and stuck the key in the rusty lock, jiggling it from side to side. The door wouldn't open. This happened sometimes. She removed the key, blew on the lock and tried again. Nothing. She repeated the process and the key finally turned in the lock, releasing the door. *Third time's the charm*, she thought.

She entered the apartment and the door swung closed behind her, blocking out much of the sunlight. She squinted as she reached for the light switch. The living area windows, or rather what the landlord called windows, didn't illuminate much. Even with the single overhead light and the travel posters plastered on the walls, the room depressed her.

Her grumbling stomach reminded her that lunch had consisted of a cup of coffee at the law office. She opened the refrigerator to check what there was to eat. It contained only a bottle of ketchup, a jar of capers, and something fuzzy in the vegetable drawer. She plucked a paper towel off the roll hanging from a cabinet, gingerly removed what used to be a vegetable and disposed of it in the trash. She'd forgotten to hit the grocery store on the way home from work last night and her snack options were limited.

Grabbing a spoon and a jar of peanut butter, she flung herself on the old maroon recliner that dominated the small living room. She was starting to feel like a lonely old spinster. *A cat*, she thought, *a cat would be nice*. Someone to keep her company. She finished her fourth spoonful of peanut butter and dropped the dirty spoon into the sink before collapsing on her bed in the alcove. *On second thought, maybe no cat*. It was a slippery slope. One cat became two, then three, and soon she'd be a crazy cat lady. She jumped off the bed, grabbed her phone and dialed the lawyer's office.

## 2

*A* loud buzzing woke Garrett Callahan from the couch. He rubbed his bleary eyes and slapped his hand around on the coffee table until he found the vibrating device.

"Hello."

"Hey man," his friend Dustin said. "Did I catch you at a bad time?"

"No." He sat up and swung his legs over the edge of the couch. His back was killing him. He stood and stretched before looking around the room. Piles of paper and dishes covered the floor and coffee table. A half-consumed bottle of Coke sat on the end table next to an empty coffee cup. He'd been up late working and must have fallen asleep. "What's up?"

"I wanted to know how you were holding up after the news about Lisa."

"What about Lisa?" He propped the phone against his shoulder and carried a pile of dishes into the kitchen. He set them down next to the sink, being careful not to knock over the existing mountain of dirty dishes. As soon as he made this work deadline, he needed to get this pigsty cleaned.

"Didn't you get the invitation? She's getting married."

His gaze slid over to the six-inch stack of mail on the dining room table. He sorted through it, separating out bills and anything else that looked important. And there it was. A five-by-five-inch cream-colored envelope addressed to him in fancy calligraphy.

He ran his index finger along the seal to break it, nicking his skin in the process.

"Yeah, I've got it." He pulled out the card. A wedding invitation on heavy cream cardstock stared back at him.

*Lisa Ann Lewins and Daryl Charles Bagrin request your presence at their nuptials.*

He didn't read the rest of it.

Lisa was really getting married. He sat down on a dining room chair and stared at the invitation.

"Are you still there?" Dustin asked.

"Yeah, still here. Thanks for checking on me. I'm working on something at the moment, but we should get together next time I'm in Seattle, okay?"

"Sounds good. Talk to you later." The phone clicked off.

He returned his attention to the invitation. The thick paper rubbed against the cut on his finger and he winced. He stared at the drop of blood smeared on the paper. How had she managed to get engaged so quickly? He and Lisa had been on and off again for the last five years and only ended their own engagement six months ago.

He needed to get out of the house. He threw the invitation on the table, took care of a few necessities, then grabbed his car keys and camera.

He drove without a destination in mind. His car turned into the Pacific Ocean overlook south of Candle Beach as if on autopilot. He parked and hung his camera on its strap around his neck. This beach trail was his favorite and he hoped it would snap him out of his foul mood.

On the downhill trek, he had too much time to think. He and Lisa hadn't been right for each other. He knew that, but like the cut on his index finger, the news of her engagement still stung. Lisa was a sculptor, and he could count the number of times on one hand that she'd managed to make it to a date on time without getting caught up in her work. Their shared apartment had been covered in clay dust, and she seldom remembered to pay the bills.

After their final breakup, he'd vowed never to get involved with a creative again. He'd moved to Candle Beach and thrown himself into his work. When he decided to date again, it was going to be with a nice, reliable woman, maybe an accountant or a scientist, not a flaky artist. Between growing up with an absent artist mother and his relationship with Lisa, he knew better.

When he reached the beach, he shot a few photos of seagulls frolicking in the chilly April surf. Then he climbed back up the trail, pausing for a few minutes to compose a picture of the town of Candle Beach and the Peril Island lighthouse. Once finished, he lifted his face to the sun, taking in its warmth. This was why he'd moved to Candle Beach—to have the freedom to be out in nature within minutes of leaving his home.

His looming work deadline brought him back to reality and he hiked back up the hill. Near the top, a woman stood looking out toward town, the wind blowing her wavy hair into a mass of tangles. She turned to him and smiled, enchanting him with her big blue eyes and genuine smile. He knew he'd just sworn off women, but he felt a strong desire to meet her.

The sunlight glinted off the copper in her hair and without thinking, he lifted his camera to capture the moment. He snapped her picture and then stopped with the camera still up to his eye. Why had he taken a photo of a stranger? He released his grip on the camera. She must think he was insane. Still, something drew him to her.

The woman greeted him, but he fumbled trying to speak. She kept trying to make conversation, but all he could manage were a few uninspired words. She looked taken aback and waved goodbye to him before hopping into her car.

He watched her go, not knowing what had just happened. What had gotten into him? Although he'd never describe himself as a ladies' man, he usually had no problem conversing with women. Had Lisa's engagement affected him so much that he'd lost his ability to speak to women at all? He hoped the mystery woman was a tourist passing by and he'd never have to explain his actions to her.

∼

For once, the fates aligned. The mechanic had told Dahlia the truth about her car being ready by Friday, and the property manager in Candle Beach agreed to let her into Aunt Ruth's house. She planned to visit To Be Read first and meet her aunt's sales assistant. She had high hopes of enlisting her to manage the store for the next year after she returned home to Seattle. With the way things were going, she felt good about that prospect.

With her Toyota Corolla packed to the gills with clothes and everything else she thought she might need for the weekend, she set out on the three-hour drive to Candle Beach. Her mother often chided her for her tendency to overpack, but she never took the time to make a packing list, and just threw things in a suitcase. She shuddered at the thought of how little she would be able to bring on a trip to Europe or Asia. She reminded herself that the lack of luggage space would be worth it for the experience.

Stop-and-go traffic stalled her progress and it took almost an hour to get out of the city. With the windows up to avoid as much air pollution as possible, the lack of air-conditioning was stifling. As she inched by the towering downtown skyscrapers, her car surrounded by exhaust-belching semitrucks on each side, she had to admit the idea of sampling small town life for a few days sounded amazing.

She rolled the windows down as she broke free from the city traffic and cruised along on the open highway. Fresh spring air flowed into the car, bringing with it the scent of cherry blossom and recently mowed grass. The tires whirred rhythmically over the pavement, a pleasant sound-track for her westward trip to the ocean. She turned on the radio, but when only static came over the speakers, she popped in a homemade CD playlist her mother had dropped off the night before.

A song came over the radio—a group of men singing about California Girls—and it filled her with nostalgia. A smile stretched across her face. Her mom had always played the Beach Boys on the way to Candle Beach, telling her it was the best way to get into summer mode. Every time she heard one of their songs she was instantly transported back in time to their annual road trip to the coast.

Now she passed through other beach towns along the way to Candle Beach, some unchanged and some vastly different from what she remembered. The coastal commu-nities had been hit hard by the demise of the logging indus-try. She slowed down when she neared the drive-thru hamburger shack she and her mom stopped at on every trip to the coast. Weeds covered the parking lot and diagonal boards covered broken windows. Black letters hanging from the crooked reader board formed illegible words. She mourned the loss of the best blackberry milkshakes she'd ever tasted.

A few newer gated housing developments had popped up along the way. They were most likely meant for wealthy retirees from the city and not the broad majority of area residents. However, any new construction brought jobs to the community and indicated the economy may be on the upswing. She hoped that was the case.

Before long, she neared Candle Beach. She pulled off at a graveled roadside overlook, carelessly taking up two parking spaces in the almost empty lot. After stretching out the travel kinks, she chugged half a bottle of water and jogged over to the edge of the cliff. She removed her cell phone from her pocket and snapped a picture of the famed Candle Rock sea stack, the town's namesake rock formation, in the distance on the beach below. With the tide out, she could clearly see Candle Rock's base, or 'candleholder,' from which rose a rugged spire, carved out of rock by thousands of years of the erosive force of the sea.

The ocean roared and waves rushed against the sand, taking rocks and debris back with each flowing retreat. The receding tide left pools in the bases of the numerous sea stacks, but with school still in session, there were no children to explore their wonders. The salt-tinged air filled her nostrils, a welcome change from her customary intake of exhaust-polluted city air. Far out at sea, the Peril Island lighthouse perched alone atop a rocky outcrop surrounded by miles of ocean. A few ships sailed across the horizon, carrying cargo to ports near and far.

A hundred feet below her, a hiker picked his way up the steep trail that led to the overlook. She watched as he stopped to take a picture of Candle Rock as well, and then paused to scan his surroundings before aiming his camera lens at the lighthouse. There was something reverential in the way he adjusted the focus to best capture the rugged beauty of his subjects.

After photographing the lighthouse, the man turned his face to the sun and closed his eyes for a few seconds, basking in the afternoon rays. The sunshine illuminated his profile, although she was too far away to see his features. He opened his eyes and took a deep breath before composing a few more photos. She watched as he capped his lens and returned to the trail, disappearing from view. She felt an odd sense of voyeurism after witnessing his private reverie.

She forced herself to look away and leaned over the unpainted cedar railing to catch a glimpse of the marina a few miles down the coast. Fishing vessels and pleasure boats alike were tied up at the town's three long docks, protected by a small bay and rocky breakwater that held back the roughness of the open waters. A strong sense of homesickness for Candle Beach slapped against her like the waves on the sand.

Alone at the overlook, she allowed her mind to wander. Candle Beach had never been her home in the true sense of the word, but it had provided much-needed stability as she dealt with her parents' divorce when she was a pre-teen. Staying with Aunt Ruth the summer they separated had given her distance from the situation at home and provided refuge as she worked through her feelings.

Back in Seattle, she'd often awake to her parents fighting, covering her ears until she could no longer stand it. They'd always stop as soon as she entered the room, but the damage was done and her grades began to slip at the end of sixth grade. In Candle Beach, with her father at home and her mother commuting to the coast on the weekends, the nights were peaceful. Aunt Ruth's group of friends had welcomed the shy twelve-year-old into their circle, seeming to sense that she needed their friendship and a community to heal.

After such a long absence from the place, why wasn't she rushing to get there? Was she afraid that the romantic images she'd curated about the small town would be crushed when she returned as an adult? She pushed the thought from her mind. She would find out soon enough. She turned to leave, but a rustling off to the side caught her attention.

A man carrying a professional camera on a strap around his neck stepped through the sparse tree line. His dark, wavy hair rustled slightly in the wind and he was tall enough that she had to look up to see into his eyes—rich chocolate-brown eyes that a woman could get lost in. Hiking boots adorned his feet and his khaki cargo shorts revealed muscled calves.

This was the man she'd seen on the trail, the man who'd revered the spring day and the scenic beauty around him. A magnetic pull drew her to him, as though a spiritual connection had been made between them by her accidental observation of his intimate moment alone on the trail. Without meaning to, she took several steps in his direction. He glanced at her for a moment and then picked up his camera, uncapping the lens.

"Hello," she called out, and smiled at him. A gust of wind blew her hair into her face and she smoothed it back with one hand, while holding her phone with the other hand. The man remained entranced by his camera.

"Hello," he mumbled back after a few seconds, shuffling forward without looking up. He pointed his camera at her, and for a minute she thought he was taking a picture of her, before she realized he was reviewing the photos he'd taken. Her mother's advice to keep an open mind echoed through her brain. What did she have to lose?

"Beautiful day," she said, unaccustomed to the eagerness in her voice with her second effort at communication. Candle Beach had made her soft already and she hadn't even passed through the town limits yet.

"Yes," the man said. He looked up at her, appearing to truly see her for the first time. "It is a nice day." He smiled at her with the vacant smile you give to a stranger.

The connection she'd experienced had been one-sided. She blushed and gave him a slight wave before she turned away, speed-walking all the way back to her car. At least now she had a humorous anecdote for her mother.

She couldn't put off her arrival in Candle Beach any longer. The twenty-year-old car's engine turned over on the first try, and she studiously avoided looking at the hiker as she backed out of the parking space. As she exited the over-look, she allowed herself a peek in the rearview mirror. To her surprise, the man wasn't taking more pictures, but had turned to watch her leave. She didn't take the time to analyze his odd behavior and let her tires spit gravel as she sped away.

## 3

---

*A* mile before Candle Beach, the highway veered inland, tracing the far side of Bluebonnet Lake before edging back to the coast. Dahlia found herself caught up in the beauty of the lake and almost missed the turnoff. Her stomach churned as she drove the short distance from the highway to town. How had Candle Beach fared in the last decade? Had it been caught in the economic decline? If so, had she been foolish to pass up the only opportunity she might have to sell the bookstore?

In a few minutes, the speed limit decreased to 25 mph and she was driving on Main Street. It was as though she'd traveled back in time. Nothing had changed. The sandwich board outside the candy shop still offered a daily sweet treat, and the green-and-white striped awning over the café's sidewalk seating was the same as she remembered. Fuchsias and impatiens cascaded out of flower baskets hung from lampposts, and a wooden bench outside the bus station offered a spot for weary travelers to rest before the next leg of their journey.

Upon closer examination, a few things in town were

different. The grocery store a block off Main Street had been remodeled, doubling its size. She spotted a new gas station hidden away behind it. Evidently, Candle Beach had prospered in the last decade, even with a bad economy. Maybe there was hope yet to sell the bookstore after a year—if she chose to do so.

She slowed the car and then stopped to let an elderly man cross the street to the café on the corner. In the park in the center of town, small children sat on the swings licking ice cream cones, while their moms chatted with each other on a nearby bench. Through the car's open window, the aroma of freshly baked cookies wafted out of a storefront, reminding her she'd have to stop in and visit her old friend, Maggie, who'd recently purchased the Bluebonnet Café. A few cars waited at the four-way stop on Ocean Avenue, patiently waiting for their turn. It was a welcome change from the bumper-to-bumper traffic back home.

She continued driving down Main Street, stopping in front of an early 1900s era standalone brick building with a red awning shading the sidewalk in front of it. Gold lettering on the glass front window provided the name of the business—To Be Read. The facade of Aunt Ruth's bookstore was exactly as she remembered.

She found a parking spot between an aging minivan and a newer model VW Bug. She lingered in front of To Be Read's front door for a long moment before reaching for the door handle. Her hand wrapped around the round brass knob and her fingers tingled with the memory of turning it hundreds of times before.

The door handle turned with a squeak and a bell over the door announced her presence in the store. A woman in her fifties sat behind the desk. A bulky green cotton knit sweater did little to disguise her pleasantly plump figure.

Gold rings covered her fingers, including a particularly large diamond ring on her left hand. Rimmed reading glasses perched on her nose. The woman looked up from the mystery she'd been engrossed in and smiled at Dahlia.

"Hello, I'm Marsha. Can I help you find anything?"

"Hi, I'm Dahlia, Ruth's great-niece. The property manager, Gretchen, said you'd be expecting me?" She walked closer to the desk.

"Oh yes, of course." Marsha removed her reading glasses and let them hang on the chain around her neck. After placing a bookmark in the novel she'd been reading, she got up from her seat and came around to the same side of the counter as Dahlia. "It's nice to meet you. Your great-aunt was a dear friend of mine." She held out her hand in introduction.

Marsha didn't appear to feel as much malice toward her as Aunt Ruth's friend Agnes. Her handshake was warm and her smile genuine.

After shaking Marsha's hand, Dahlia swiveled around and took a longer assessment of the store. While at first glance it appeared the same as she remembered, the years had taken a toll on the store. The heavy red velvet curtains around the bay window had a year's worth of dust on them and the brocade-covered chairs scattered around the room had frayed seats and could use a coat of furniture polish. In the high traffic areas, the hardwood floors had lost their shine. Maintaining the store's appearance hadn't been high on Aunt Ruth's priority list in recent years, and rightly so.

"So what do you think?" Marsha asked. "Is it the same as it used to be?"

"It's beautiful," Dahlia said truthfully. She pressed her torso against the back of a wingback chair, her fingers wrapping around the carved wooden trim at the top. In between the chair and its matching mate sat a glass end table, the scene of many impromptu tea parties with Aunt Ruth. She half expected to see Aunt Ruth come out of the back room to greet her with a steaming cup of Darjeeling tea and a plate of Danish shortbread cookies. Without warning, tears welled in her eyes. Marsha reached out, drawing her into an embrace.

"We miss her so much too," she said, patting Dahlia's back.

She murmured a thank you to Marsha while squished against her pillowy bosom. After a moment, Dahlia pulled away from the hug and strode over to a stack of books, running her hands over the covers. "I didn't realize how much I had missed this place. I wish I'd come back sooner."

Marsha nodded solemnly. "Well, you're here now. Ruth would be so happy to see you here. She used to talk about you all the time, you know. We all heard about your adventures in the big city." In a quieter, more confidential tone, she leaned forward and said, "I'm so sorry to hear about your divorce, but it sounds like you're better off." She pulled her close in another squishy hug.

Dahlia had, of course, told Aunt Ruth about the divorce in their weekly phone calls, but she'd never divulged many of the gory details. She'd tried to keep the tone light for Aunt Ruth, knowing she was going through so much with her illness. Had her mother told Aunt Ruth and her friends about the particulars of her divorce?

Marsha released her. "The other Ladies of Candle Beach and I are so glad you've returned to town to run To Be Read." She beamed and reached for her purse under the counter. "The book on the desk in Ruth's office should explain everything you'll need to know. Please don't be afraid to call me if you have any questions." She secured the purse strap around her shoulder, picked her mystery novel up off the counter and walked out of the bookstore before Dahlia had a chance to react.

"Marsha?" Dahlia called out, but the door shut on her words and the older woman was gone. What had just happened? Did she just walk out on the job? Didn't she work for Aunt Ruth? Marsha said Dahlia could ask her for help, but she had no idea what her phone number was, or even her last name to track her down. And what was this book she'd talked about?

She shook her head and walked back to the small office that was walled off from the rest of the storeroom. Outside of the office, shipping boxes were stacked in tall piles, ready to be opened. Overstock books lined rough-hewn wooden shelves on every free wall. In contrast, inside the tiny office, everything was in its place and the room was free of clutter.

She paused on the threshold of the office. It felt strange to intrude on her aunt's private sanctum. Aunt Ruth had spent hours every day sitting in the feminine desk chair at the antique secretary desk pushed along the back wall. On a three-level corner bookshelf, her aunt's prized collection of Russian dolls perched on dusty shelves. She flashed back to all the times she'd sat on a rug in the corner of the room, playing with some of the heartier dolls while Aunt Ruth tallied up the day's receipts.

The writing surface of the secretary desk lay open; its numerous slots filled with documents, calculator tape, and mail. A printing calculator filled the back corner of the desk. There was no computer in sight. On the writing surface lay a navy leather-bound notebook. She picked up the notebook and turned to the first page.

Aunt Ruth's neat handwriting filled every page, prompting more tears at the familiar sight. The notebook provided a detailed account of what she'd need to know to run the store, from how to operate the old-fashioned cash register, to the inventory and order management system. She'd thought of everything. Dahlia closed the book, resting her hand on its cover.

Next to the notebook was a work schedule, written in the same tight handwriting she had seen on Agnes's notepad in the law office. It appeared Aunt Ruth's friends had arranged to cover all the open hours of the bookstore between them. Based on what Marsha had said, they expected Dahlia to run the store from here on out.

She had assumed Aunt Ruth had hired a salesperson to operate the bookstore when she became too sick to work, and that the salesperson had stayed on after her death. Apparently that wasn't the case. If there wasn't a salesperson, there wasn't anyone to manage the bookstore after she returned to her home in Seattle.

She sat heavily in Aunt Ruth's dainty desk chair. The chair had fit her petite great-aunt perfectly, but it cut uncomfortably into Dahlia's long legs. She had a sneaking suspicion that much like the chair, being a bookstore owner wasn't a great fit for her either. Maybe Agnes had been right and she should cut her losses and sell the store as soon as possible. She shook her head. Giving in to Agnes wasn't an option.

What was she going to do? She hadn't expected for there not to be reliable help already in place. Judging from Agnes's attitude about her ownership of and ability to run the bookstore, she couldn't expect much help from Ruth's friends, even though Marsha had acted friendly.

Was a weekend in Candle Beach long enough to hire a manager for the bookstore? She didn't know what the chances were of hiring help, but to keep the bookstore running, she needed someone responsible enough to manage the place in her absence.

~

It was near dinner time and there had only been a few customers, so Dahlia decided to close the store an hour early to take her luggage over to Aunt Ruth's house. The lack of customers concerned her. If this was a normal day's business volume, there was no way the bookstore would be profitable in a year.

After consulting the blue leather operations manual, she shut down the cash register and made sure the back door was locked. Lastly, she locked up the front door with the key hanging on a hook next to the desk and walked over to the property management company located on the next block. She hoped her old friend Gretchen was still at work, as her impromptu shift at the bookstore had made her later than she'd planned. Candle Beach Real Estate had the key for Aunt Ruth's house, so she crossed her fingers that even if Gretchen wasn't around, someone would be available to give her the key.

An employee had propped the door open to allow the spring air to enter. The fresh air in the bright, clean office space made her realize how musty the bookstore smelled. She knocked on the open door.

A woman with shoulder-length auburn hair looked up from her desk and waved. She clicked the computer mouse a few times in rapid succession and stood up from her desk.

"Dahlia, it's great to see you again." Gretchen Roberts hugged her and guided her over to the chair opposite the desk, before sitting down in her own desk chair. "Come, sit down. How are things going with you? I was so sorry to hear of Ruth's passing, although I must say I'm glad it brought you back to town."

Gretchen had been one of her closest friends during her summers in Candle Beach. They had shared secrets during many a giggle-filled sleepover and attended a few parties together as teenagers. The longer she stayed in Candle Beach, the more memories flooded back. She'd had many good summers here—why hadn't she made more of an effort to return once she started college?

"It's nice to see you too." She slumped down in the chair, suddenly exhausted from an emotional return and four hours of driving. "It's been a long day."

"I can see that." Gretchen raised her eyebrows as she took in her old friend's wearied state. "What would you say to dinner at the Bluebonnet Café?"

Dahlia sat up straighter. "That sounds wonderful. I'd planned to go to Aunt Ruth's house before eating, but I think dinner first sounds like a better plan." Her stomach rumbled in agreement and Gretchen laughed.

"Let me grab the key to Ruth's house and we'll head over to the café." She walked over to a peg board full of labeled key rings and grabbed one of the sets of keys. "Okay, we're good to go." She picked up her purse and windbreaker, and they left the office together.

~

Dahlia started to relax soon after the teenage waitress seated them at a table in the middle of the Bluebonnet Café's back room. In the front room, two domed bakery cases offered a surprisingly large array of pies for the evening crowd. From what she'd heard, they served excellent pastries, donuts and coffee cakes in the morning.

Maggie, the café owner and an old friend of hers, had created a welcoming dining room for any meal of the day, with comfortable chairs and glass-topped tables. Under each glass top, inspirational quotes and thought-provoking questions provided conversation starters for customers while they waited for their food, or perhaps endured a dull blind date. In fact, the eating area may have been too welcoming.

As she turned away from Gretchen to view the rest of the dining room behind her, she saw Agnes, Marsha, and about four of the other Ladies of Candle Beach sitting around an oblong table in a side nook. Agnes saw Dahlia and nodded in her direction. She considered pretending she hadn't seen Agnes, but gave in and returned the nod, before turning back to Gretchen.

Gretchen had placed her menu on the table and was sipping a steaming mug of coffee that the waitress had deposited on the table as soon as they sat down. "Do you know what you want to eat?" she asked. "I'm not sure why I even looked at the menu; I always get the same thing for dinner."

Dahlia hadn't finished reading the menu, so she randomly pointed at something on the left side of the page. "Eggs Benedict sounds good." Breakfast food was comfort food, morning or night.

Gretchen flagged down the waitress and they placed their orders. The waitress scribbled their requests on her notepad and jetted away to the kitchen.

"Maggie's done well for herself." Dahlia motioned around the café. "I remember when this was Gus's Greasy Spoon."

"She's put a ton of hard work into the business. After her husband Brian died suddenly a few years ago and left her with a new baby, she moved back to town to have support from her family. She started out as a waitress here and used her husband's life insurance money to buy the place from Gus when he retired. I don't think she's slowed down or taken any time off in the last three years." Gretchen stirred more sugar into her coffee. "Speaking of not slowing down, how's your mom doing? I saw her around town a few times in the last few years and I wanted to send a sympathy card when Ruth died, but I didn't have her mailing address."

"She's good," Dahlia said. "Busy and in demand at work as always. Sometimes I feel like she has an endless supply of energy. When I get back home I'll let her know you asked about her."

"Wait, what do you mean, *when* you get back home?" Gretchen set her coffee cup on the table. "I thought you were staying to run the bookstore. Isn't that why you wanted the key to Ruth's house?"

"No, I'm only visiting for the weekend. I'm going to stay in Aunt Ruth's house while I'm here."

Gretchen's eyebrows arched. "So what are you going to do about the bookstore?"

"I'm going to hire someone to manage the day-to-day operations. The terms of the will state I have to hold onto it for twelve months, at the end of which it must be profitable. I don't physically need to be in Candle Beach that whole time. Of course, I'll be here from time to time. I'm excited about taking some time off to get back into painting and I'd love to paint some seascapes." Dahlia could almost feel Agnes's eyes bore into her back.

"Who are you going to have manage the bookstore?" Gretchen asked. "With summer coming, everyone has hired their summer help already."

Dahlia's heart sank as she focused on what her friend

had said. "If no one in town is available, do you think I can get someone from the local area?"

"It's the same everywhere. We get most of our tourist dollars in the summer, so we prepare early for the onslaught of vacationers." Gretchen's eyes were wide and her lips turned downward in apology. "I'm sorry Dahlia, I think you'll have a hard time finding someone trustworthy to work full-time at the bookstore on such short notice."

For the second time that day, her hopes were dashed. The waitress delivered their food—eggs Benedict with extra sourdough toast for her, and a French dip for Gretchen. The food smelled delicious and the portions were plentiful. She ate a forkful of egg and English muffin, the hollandaise sauce exploding with flavor in her mouth. She'd just mopped up some liquefied egg with the toast and stuffed it in her mouth when a man walked into the café and stood waiting at the front counter. He turned to survey the dining room and she froze. It was the man she'd seen earlier in the day at the overlook. Before he saw her, he caught the attention of the teenage waitress who'd seated them. After a brief conversation with the man, the waitress disappeared into the kitchen.

Dahlia rapidly swallowed her mouthful of food and swiped at her face with the cloth napkin. "Gretchen," she hissed under her breath, hiding her face behind the napkin. "Do you know who that man is?" She nodded her chin in his direction.

Gretchen rotated in her seat to look toward the front counter. Then she turned back to Dahlia and said, "Oh, that's Garrett Callahan. He moved to town a few months ago. In fact, he's renting the cottage just down the road from Ruth's house. Rumor is he's a writer."

After the embarrassment of her first encounter with

Garrett, Dahlia had hoped he was a stranger she'd never run into again. Now, it seemed they were neighbors. The way things were going in Candle Beach, she really shouldn't be too surprised. Her cheeks flushed as she remembered how he had returned her eager greeting with a vacant smile.

Gretchen stared at her, an odd expression on her face. "Do you know Garrett?"

"On the way to Candle Beach I saw him taking pictures at the overlook. That's all," Dahlia said. She put a large enough forkful of food in her mouth to make further discussion impossible and cast a furtive glance over to the front counter. Garrett had received his to-go order in a white bag and was exiting through the door.

"Are you sure that's all it is?" Gretchen asked. "You seem awfully interested in him. Not that I blame you." She craned her head around to catch a glimpse of him as he passed by the café's picture window.

"When I saw him earlier, I thought he was a tourist. I didn't realize he lived here, that's all," Dahlia said. Gretchen nodded once with a disbelieving gleam in her eyes, but dropped the subject.

"Do you know where I should start to find a suitable manager for To Be Read?" Dahlia asked.

The waitress dropped off their checks and they pulled out their credit cards to pay the tabs.

"Your best bet is to ask the Ladies over there," Gretchen said, pointing to Agnes and her cronies. "They know everything going on in town."

"Probably not the best idea in this case. I'm not high on their list to receive a favor." Dahlia explained to Gretchen about Agnes's disdain for her, and her role in the terms of the bequest.

"Okay, well, the next best thing to do is to check at the

newspaper office. Adam, the newspaper owner, has a finger on the pulse of things here. He may know if someone is looking for work."

With the checks paid, they put their credit cards back in their wallets and stood to leave.

"Are you ready to go to Ruth's house?" Gretchen put on her windbreaker to guard against the evening chill.

"Yes." Dahlia rubbed her arms and wished she knew where one of the many sweatshirts she'd packed was, but with the car so crammed with everything, it could take a while to find it. She looked at her watch. "But you don't have to come with me. If you give me the key, I can let myself in. I know it's getting late."

"No problem." Gretchen handed her the keys. "I don't mind. It's not like I have someone to go home to. I'll stop at my house to feed my dog and then head over. There are a few things I wanted to go over with you there."

Aunt Ruth's house was only a few blocks away from the café and Gretchen's place, so Gretchen walked home while Dahlia drove alone in her car. Her passenger seat was too full for a passenger and she wanted to unload her luggage at the house.

It was only six thirty, but she was feeling the effects of the long day and planned to crash early that night. She didn't know what Gretchen wanted to tell her at the house, but she planned on asking her what needed to be done prior to listing it for sale.

## 4

*D*ahlia followed Ocean Avenue almost to the top of the hill, high above town. A block before her destination, she turned down a side street and ducked into the alley that led to Aunt Ruth's house. The two-story Craftsman cottage stood at the crest of the hill, offering commanding views of the town and ocean below it from almost every room. Aunt Ruth had often quipped that she could watch over the town like a queen in her castle. There was some truth to that statement as Aunt Ruth had been a cherished and respected pillar of the community. Until her cancer had reached an advanced stage, she'd been a member of the town council for as long as Dahlia could recall.

She parked her car next to the detached garage facing the alley. She assumed when Gretchen arrived after checking on her dog that they would meet at the front door. To save herself a trip back to the car, she grabbed a laundry basket piled high with clean laundry. Balancing it precariously with one arm, she pulled out her lone rolling suitcase, which was stuffed with even more clothes. She shut the trunk of the car one-handed and dragged her suitcase over the loose gravel alley space.

The white wooden back gate stood ajar. Aunt Ruth had preferred for the gate to remain closed when not in use, and Dahlia couldn't remember ever seeing it left open before. To close the gate, she repeated the same awkward one-handed maneuver and latched the gate with a practiced touch. She glanced down the oyster shell path before she walked toward the front door with the laundry basket blocking her view.

About four feet from the front gate, her right foot caught on an obstruction and she pitched forward. The laundry basket flew from her grasp and lodged itself into a lavender-colored hydrangea bush at the side of the path. Much to her surprise, instead of the sharp oyster shells she'd expected to land on, she found herself pressed against a solid object. A warm, muscular, and blue, solid object.

"Are you okay?" The object spoke, and Dahlia edged her head up to see her rescuer. She'd landed flat out on top of the man she'd seen at the overlook. Garrett, Gretchen had called him.

"I think so." She wiggled her extremities and, finding no injuries, rolled off of him onto the ground. He turned to his side, and pushed himself off the pathway with an athletic bounce, then held out his hand. She grasped it and a feeling of electricity traveled from his hand to hers. She stared into his eyes and heat crept up her neck. Their hands remained joined for a moment longer than necessary before she released her grip.

What had that been about? She'd never felt such an immediate physical attraction to any man before, much less one who couldn't care less about her. She turned to survey the path behind her. Next to her toppled rolling suitcase, the white handle of a rake stuck out over the garden path.

"You tripped me," she said to Garrett. Her ankle hurt and she leaned forward to rub it with one hand. It must have twisted in the fall.

"To be fair, you tripped yourself. I wasn't expecting anyone else to be here. Are you sure you're okay?"

She nodded yes. "I think I sprained it slightly, but it'll be better by the end of the night."

"Okay. Let me know if you need any help walking." His eyes rested on her rolling suitcase. "Where were you going anyways?"

"I own this house. I'm staying here tonight." She narrowed her eyes at him. "Who are you and why are you here?" She wasn't the intruder, he was.

"You're Ruth's great-niece? Dahlia?" His eyebrows shot up. "I hadn't heard you were in town." He held his hand out to her. "Let's start over. I'm Garrett. Ruth was a friend of mine and I've been taking care of her garden for her. I'm renting a house down the hill." He nodded behind him to a small seafoam-green cottage with cheery white trim a block away. Even from here, his gardening skills were evident in the colorful flower beds surrounding the cottage's front door.

The remnants of his cheeseburger and fries to-go meal rested in a white paper carton on the garden bench. He must have come straight here to work in the garden after picking up his order at the Bluebonnet Café. And judging by the sweat ringing the neck of his blue t-shirt, he'd been working hard before she arrived.

"Yes, I'm Dahlia," she said, shaking his hand. His grip was firm, but not overbearing. He was much friendlier than she'd expected based on their earlier encounter. She decided to give him the benefit of the doubt and assume he hadn't really seen her properly when they met at the overlook.

He plucked a pair of lacy pink underpants off a hydrangea bloom and held them up to her. "I believe these are yours?"

She looked at him in horror. Her laundry basket had scattered its contents across the bushes. She frantically grabbed for the most intimate items and hugged them to her chest, blushing furiously.

Garrett diplomatically picked up a few socks and put them in the laundry basket before handing it back to her. A zing passed from his fingers to hers as they touched on the handoff. There it was again! What was going on?

"Can we start over again?" Her face burned with embarrassment over the contents of the laundry basket.

He grinned an impish smile that promised a keen sense of humor. "Sure. Are we going to re-enact the falling on me thing again too?"

She tried to glare at him, but failed and started laughing instead. There might be hope for this guy yet. "I think we can skip that part." She corralled the other clothing items and placed the laundry basket on the ground.

"Do Agnes and the other Ladies know you've arrived? They've been anxious for you to move here," he said.

"I'm sure Agnes wasn't anxious for me to live here, probably the opposite. I met Marsha at the bookstore and I saw Agnes when I was in the Bluebonnet Café earlier, so I think the word is out," she said. "And I'm not here to live permanently; I'm only here for the weekend. I need to find a manager for the bookstore and check on the condition of the house."

"But Ruth said you'd be moving here after she passed."
He had a quizzical expression on his face.

"No, this kind of life isn't really for me." Or at least she
didn't think this was what she wanted.

Garrett's face twisted with a smile he hid unsuccessfully.
"What exactly is 'this kind of life'?"

"You know, for anyone who wants to see the world.
Candle Beach doesn't have much going for it in terms of
culture and excitement." Garrett's face darkened with her
words, and she tried to backpedal. "I mean, it's fine for some
people. Candle Beach is a great place to um... relax, or raise
a family, or..."

"You know, Ruth thought the world of you. She talked
about you all the time." He propped the rake against the
house. "It was her last wish for you to move here and run
the bookstore. Doesn't that mean anything to you?"

"I can't move here just because my great-aunt thought it
was a good idea. My life isn't here. I promised myself a long
time ago that I'd never again do something solely for the
sake of someone else's plans. Aunt Ruth knew that." Dahlia
felt a pang of sadness and hoped what she'd said was true.

"The bookstore is an important part of the community.
Have you seen what the economy is like around here?
Having the proprietor of a business operate the business
themselves is an essential part of what makes the Candle
Beach downtown prosperous. Do you think some random
person you hire off the street is going to care as much about
To Be Read as you would?" Garrett crossed his arms and
leaned against a fence post.

"Well, no, but it doesn't matter. To Be Read was Aunt
Ruth's dream, not mine." The man was exasperating. She
had a sinking feeling that she'd been right about him
all along.

"I get it. You think Candle Beach is a place for people with dull lives and you have no interest in finding out if your assumptions are true or if you might have a future here." He picked up his gloves and the almost empty hamburger box. "Life can't be exciting a hundred percent of the time. At some point, it's necessary to be responsible." He strode off without another glance, the garden gate slamming behind him.

Dahlia watched him go, her mouth agape. He'd seemed so nice, but then something had struck a nerve and he'd turned into someone else. Candle Beach may be a small town, but with any luck, she wouldn't run into Garrett Callahan again.

～

Dahlia was still reeling from the roller coaster of emotions she'd experienced when she gathered her belongings and trudged up the path to the front door. The day had gone from bad to worse and she fervently hoped she could get to bed soon. Tomorrow she would start afresh and figure things out.

As she rounded the corner and caught her first glimpse of the front of the house, her heart sank. Like the bookstore, the house was in much worse condition than she'd anticipated. Cracked paint and dirt caked the once white picket fence. Aunt Ruth's prize rosebushes and other flowers had been well cared for, but the wooden arbor they hung over had seen better days.

A wicker outdoor set took up half of the wide front porch. The cushions were missing, and without them the porch swing looked uncomfortable, so she sat on the steps to wait for Gretchen to arrive.

Five minutes later, Gretchen jogged up the hill. She leaned against one of the front porch pillars to catch her breath. "Whew. That's quite a climb. Sorry it took me so long. Reilly, my dog, had pulled a bag of flour off the counter and I wanted to get it cleaned up before I had white paw prints all over my house. Have you been waiting long?"

Dahlia got up off the steps. "No, not too long. I had a run-in with my neighbor Garrett in the garden. Correction, I ran into Garrett in the garden. He'd been weeding Aunt Ruth's flower bed and I tripped on a rake and flung myself into him." She didn't mention the minute she'd spent lying on his muscular chest.

"Ooh, tell me more." Gretchen opened the front door. "He's been quite a mystery man since he arrived in town a few months ago. He tends to keep to himself, although some of the Ladies know him through the garden club."

"There's not much to tell. We started talking about my reasons for coming back to Candle Beach and he got upset with me and left. He seems like an odd duck." She shrugged her shoulders. "I don't think he'll be coming around here anymore."

"Hmm," Gretchen said. "I wonder what happened." She reached inside the door and flipped the light switch on. They entered Aunt Ruth's living room and Dahlia was transported back in time. The room hadn't changed since she'd been there last. Aunt Ruth's recliner sat in one corner next to a comfortably overstuffed sofa. In front of the seating was a maple coffee table that Dahlia had cut her head on when she was four. Aunt Ruth had wiped her tears, bandaged her wound, and given her cookies and tea. It was hard to believe she'd never see her again.

Although dated, the interior of the house seemed in better repair than the exterior. In the kitchen, rose-covered wallpaper provided the perfect backdrop for a Formica table and a seventies avocado green stove and mismatched white refrigerator. Ruth hadn't cared what things looked like, always claiming function trumped form.

They took the stairs up to the small second bathroom and the house's three bedrooms.

A peek into the bathroom revealed fixtures in the same avocado green as the kitchen, an aging ceiling light and more dreadful wallpaper. As a kid, Dahlia hadn't given a second thought to the interior decor. Now, with an eye to selling the house, she could see it would take quite an investment of time and money to modernize.

"This is what I wanted to show you," Gretchen said, as they entered the room Aunt Ruth had used as a craft room. "When I checked the house last week, I noticed a possible leak in the roof. I called the law firm handling Ruth's estate, but they weren't able to authorize any repairs until you got here." A water stain had formed on the ceiling and there was evidence of water rings on the hardwood floors below. A bucket had been placed under the leak to stop any further damage.

"If you'd like, I can give you the contact info for a local roofing company. They can give you a repair estimate. I have to warn you though, all the contractors in town are going to be booked out for at least a few weeks with the upcoming tourist rental season."

The water had soaked the bottom of the basket where Aunt Ruth kept the yarn she'd used in her most recent crocheting project. Dahlia pulled the dry yarn out of the basket and placed it gently on the sewing desk. Aunt Ruth had been crocheting a turquoise and white blanket before she died. The crochet hook was still attached to the loop in the unfinished blanket. She blinked back tears. Aunt Ruth had been so full of life. It was unfair that breast cancer had taken her when she was only in her mid-seventies.

"Dahlia?" Gretchen's voice sounded far away. Dahlia looked up from the half-completed blanket.

"I'm so sorry, but there's more," Gretchen said, leading the way out of the room.

*What now?* Dahlia thought. Gretchen took her down to the basement and pointed out several spots where water had breached the cracked foundation, forming puddles on the concrete floor.

"This should be taken care of before you try to sell the house. It would never pass a prospective buyer's home inspection. I'm not sure how much it will cost, but here's the number of the contractor we use, Donald's Home Repair. Don might be able to fix the roof as well—you'd have to call him to find out." She handed her a business card.

"Anything else you'd like to throw at me?" Dahlia asked, half joking.

Gretchen regarded her old friend. "No, we can talk more tomorrow. You should get some rest."

Dahlia waved goodbye to her from the wide front porch, then retrieved the rest of her belongings from the car. After she had dumped everything in the middle of the living room, she stopped to think about where she was going to sleep. She walked up the stairs and stood in the entrance to the large master bedroom where Aunt Ruth had slept.

On the dresser, an antique hand mirror lay between numerous crystal perfume bottles, all on a crocheted lace runner. She picked up the hand mirror, remembering all the times she'd used it to pretend to be the witch from Snow White. The open curtains highlighted the magnificent ocean view. Under the window, a hope chest occupied most of the floor space. Blankets and linens were folded neatly at the end of the bed, but even though waking up to that view would be amazing, she couldn't bear to sleep in Aunt Ruth's bedroom among her prized belongings.

She turned and walked along the carpeted hallway to the room that had been hers when she came to stay in the summers. A double bed took up half of the room, but a window seat in the upstairs bay window made the room feel spacious. Dahlia had fond memories of sitting on the seat and gazing out the window with its view of town and peek-aboo view of the ocean. A few newer romance novels sat on the bedside table, evidence that her mother had slept in there during her visits. Vanessa could never resist a good romance.

After opening the window to let in the cool evening breeze, she lay down on the bed, atop the crocheted coverlet. Her eyes closed as her head hit the soft down pillow, and she told herself she would bring her suitcases up in a few minutes.

## 5

*S*unlight streaming through the open window woke Dahlia the next morning. She checked her watch with bleary eyes, dismayed to see it was after eight. Normally, waking up at eight a.m. on a Saturday morning meant she could sleep for a while longer, but now she was a business owner—at least until she could find someone to take over management of the bookstore. She groaned and swung her legs off the bed. After a quick shower, she had just enough time to stop at the Bluebonnet Café for a chocolate chip muffin and large latte. As she'd heard, the pastry selection was excellent.

She opened the store at nine on the dot. Business was brisk, with weekenders buying beach reads. She perused the operations manual in between customers. At noon, she flipped the sign over on the door to announce she'd be back in half an hour. She had to find someone to run the bookstore for her, so she needed to pay a visit to Adam, the owner of the town newspaper. Since it was Saturday, she wasn't sure if he'd be in, but she couldn't put the chore off.

She peered through the windows of the *Candle Beach Weekly*, but the lights were off, except for what appeared to be a light on in a back room. She was standing on her tiptoes to get a better view when a sound from behind startled her. She lowered herself to standing and turned around.

"Excuse me, can I help you with something?" A man carrying a box of donuts and a copy of *The Seattle Times* jangled a ring of keys, which he then used to unlock the door.

"Hi." She followed him inside. "I'm Dahlia, Ruth Wright's great-niece."

"Pleased to meet you, I'm Adam Rigg. I own the *Candle Beach Weekly*." He placed the donuts and newspaper on his desk before shaking her hand.

She'd assumed the newspaper owner would be older, but with his freckles and tousled, carrot-red hair she felt like she'd just met Dennis the Menace in person. Immediately, she was at ease with him. "You're much younger than I expected," she blurted out.

"I get that a lot. It works to my advantage, because people tend to tell me things they wouldn't divulge to anyone else. It's like I'm undercover in my own skin." He waggled his eyebrows devilishly at her and she laughed.

Then she eyed the newspaper pointedly. "A competitor's paper?"

"We only publish local news. I like to keep up on what's happening in the rest of the state and the world. What can I do for you?" He offered her the box of donuts and she selected a maple bar. Not much chance she'd have time for a real lunch.

"I'm trying to find someone qualified to manage the bookstore after I go back to Seattle on Monday. Gretchen

Roberts mentioned you might be able to help me find someone."

"Hmm. Did she?" He grinned and his freckled skin flushed. "She does tend to overestimate my talents. No one comes to mind at the moment. It'll be hard to locate someone on such short notice, but let me think about it."

Dahlia had hoped for better, but she wasn't surprised to hear him say he didn't have a good candidate for her either.

"So you're only in town until Monday?"

"That was the plan, but it appears I'll need to stay a little longer to find a new manager for To Be Read."

"We couldn't talk you into moving to Candle Beach?"

"No, I don't think so. Why?" She took another donut out of the box, grabbed a chair from an employee's desk and settled in with her unhealthy lunch.

"Always good to get some fresh blood in town. Many of us who grew up here have moved to bigger cities, and we could use more young people."

"Are you a native Candle Beach-ian?" she asked. She couldn't remember seeing him when she'd visited in the summers.

"Yes, I've lived here all my life." He must have seen her perplexed gaze. "You probably don't remember me because you came in the summers and I spent most of every summer with my grandparents in Idaho. Grandma was a teacher and had the summers off, so it was the best time to visit them."

"Ah, that explains it." The donut stuck to the roof of her mouth. She motioned at the coffee pot across the room. "May I have some?"

"Sure, it's fresh today, help yourself."

She poured herself a full cup of coffee and sat back down. She didn't usually feel so comfortable chatting with strangers, but something about Candle Beach relaxed her and made it a natural act. To be honest, she didn't have many friends in Seattle either, and it had felt good to converse with her old friend Gretchen and what she hoped was a new friend in Adam.

"So I'm assuming you've decided to keep the bookstore for the full year instead of selling it?" he asked.

"Does everyone in town know about the terms of Aunt Ruth's will?" The gossip mill in this town was amazing.

"It is a small town," he admitted. "News travels fast."

"Well, I haven't decided. I thought I could hang on to it for a year, but without a manager, I don't know if that will work." She leaned forward and wrapped her hands around her coffee mug.

"Have you heard about the new Book Warehouse going into downtown Haven Shores?" he asked, referring to the town about thirty minutes south of Candle Beach.

"No," she said. "What about it?"

"It might be something for you to consider. Bookstore customers might decide to make the drive to Haven Shores for a better selection now. Ruth always did a good job of promoting the store and making it a welcoming place for customers, but the competition could make it difficult to turn a profit by the end of the year."

Dahlia fell silent. Her trip to Candle Beach had felt like watching a chain of dominoes toppling slowly, one after another. Aunt Ruth's house was falling apart, she couldn't find a bookstore manager, and with a new competitor in the area, how would she afford a manager? What was next? If she couldn't make the bookstore a success, maybe she should sell it if the prospective buyer's offer was still on the table.

She looked up at the round clock on the wall and stood. "Thanks for your help and advice. I've got to get back to the bookstore, but I may be back to pick your brain again in the future."

"No problem. Let me know if you need anything else while you're in town." He held the door open for her. "Please say hi to Gretchen for me if you see her. She hasn't been around in a while." He smiled at her as she stepped out onto the sidewalk.

"I will, thanks again." She hurried off down the street.

$\sim$

Customers weren't exactly lining up at the door when Dahlia unlocked the bookstore and flipped the sign around to 'Open' again. She retrieved the lawyer's business card from her purse in the back room and phoned the law office. She found herself pacing the floor between the main part of the bookstore and the storeroom as the phone rang on the other end.

What if business didn't pick up during the week? There was no way she could turn a profit without an increase in foot traffic. She didn't have the skills to turn the business around. Selling now could be her best option if the buyer was still interested.

"Hello, law offices of Schmidt, Anders, and James. How may I help you?" the receptionist chirped, jerking Dahlia out of her thoughts.

"Yes, Larry Anders please. This is Dahlia Winters, calling about Ruth Wright's estate." She flipped the card between her fingers, creasing the crisp, white paperboard.

Larry's voice came over the line. "Ms. Winters. How may I help you?"

"I'm here in Candle Beach and I'm having trouble finding a manager for my aunt's bookstore. To be truthful, this whole thing is a mess." She took a deep breath. "I'd like to accept the offer on the bookstore and list the house as well. There are a few repairs that need to be made, but I can get a handyman scheduled while I'm in town."

"Ms. Winters, I'm sorry to say that the offer on the bookstore has been revoked," Larry said. "I did warn you that it was only valid until five o'clock last Wednesday."

Dahlia fell silent. If selling the bookstore was no longer an option, she had no choice but to make it profitable. At that moment, she realized she had no idea about To Be Read's or Aunt Ruth's financial status.

"Can you please provide me with more information about the bookstore's finances? And Aunt Ruth's house needs work. Are there funds to cover that?"

Larry gave her a brief overview of her aunt's finances and promised to email her a full list of assets. "Please let us know if you'd like us to put you in touch with a real estate agent to list the bookstore. If you decide to sell, you should put the properties on the market soon in case the economy worsens at a later date."

After promising to call him back with her decision, she hung up the phone. Then she went into Ruth's office and sank down in the desk chair. Things were worse than she'd thought. While Ruth's own finances were fairly strong, with enough money to more than adequately fund the house repairs and anything else she needed for the property, she had used Uncle Ed's pension to subsidize the bookstore losses for years. With a history of losses, finding another potential buyer would be even tougher. Sitting in her aunt's chair, she closed her eyes, hoping that somehow Ruth's spirit would tell her what to do.

Before she received any messages from beyond the grave, the bookstore doorbell chimed, alerting her to a potential customer. She rose from the chair, shrugged her shoulders back and walked into the main room. She'd sleep on her decision and call the lawyer back in the morning.

## 6

*T*hree months later, Dahlia straightened the *New York Times* bestseller that had toppled from the lowest tier of To Be Read's front bay window display and glanced through the window. The weather was considerably nicer than when she had arrived in April. After she'd been unable to find someone to manage the bookstore for her, she'd been left with no other option but to quit her job and move to Candle Beach. Moving out of her apartment had actually been a relief, and after donating her bedraggled furniture to Goodwill, everything that remained fit either into her car or in her mother's basement. Although she missed her friends in Seattle, over the last few months she'd grown close to her childhood friends, Gretchen and Maggie. For the most part, she was enjoying her time in town, however long it may be.

She pushed the curtain aside to see if the summer storm had cleared. The hot July sun had burned through the fog and clouds of the morning's rainstorm, and now shone on a glistening Main Street, brightening both the town and her spirits. But her joy faded when she saw the woman approaching the bookstore.

It was too late to hide, too late to pretend to be busy in the back storeroom. The elderly woman's lips formed a thin, determined line across her face as she beelined for the store's entrance.

Dahlia gazed longingly at the back door before steeling herself for the woman's arrival by molding her own lips into a forced smile designed to hide gritted teeth. The woman entered the store, making a show of wiping her spotless low-heeled pumps on the entry mat. The acrid scent of recent rain followed her.

"Why Agnes, how nice to see you." Dahlia's cheeks screamed with the effort of the pleasant greeting. It had never hurt so much to smile.

Agnes didn't bother with such niceties. She squinted her eyes and peered over her pointed nose at the mud-streaked windows. "I see you haven't managed to run Ruth's bookstore into the ground yet, although you haven't been spending much time maintaining the place."

Dahlia sucked in her breath and slowly counted to ten while exhaling. Of course Agnes picked up on one of the few parts of the store that wasn't squeaky clean. A coastal rain storm had come through around dawn and spattered the windows with dirt from the flowerbeds in front of the store. With a new shipment of James Patterson's suspense novels delivered soon after opening, Dahlia hadn't had time yet to wash the grime off of the windows.

Agnes circled the bookstore's perimeter, her eagle eyes taking in every book on the shelves that dared to edge half an inch out of line from the others. She made a point to tap one soldier back into formation and shook her head at the rest. It was a wonder they didn't spontaneously realign themselves with the sheer force of her disapproval.

Dahlia leaned against the door frame and waited for the siege to end. Ever since she'd made the decision to stay in Candle Beach until the summer was over and she could hire help, Agnes had been a thorn in her side. Every week, she came into the store and inspected it. Never once had she said anything positive.

"How is business? I don't see any customers in here." Agnes narrowed her eyes at Dahlia. "I hear from the other Ladies that they never see customers when they pass by."

"It's great." Not that it was any business of Agnes or her spying Ladies Club. The truth was, with the opening of the Book Warehouse in Haven Shores in June, what little repeat business she had from the full-time residents was trickling away. At this rate, there was no way the bookstore would make a profit in nine months. She had hoped the summer tourist dollars would help, but here it was, mid-July, and the fabled cash influx hadn't materialized.

A woman wearing flip-flops, cutoff jeans and a purple tank top with 'Baby' emblazoned across the front entered the store. A hint of aromatic coconut sunscreen hung in her wake. While the beachgoer perused the fiction section, Agnes disappeared into the back to do who knew what. Dahlia sidled up to the woman to ask if she needed help, but she said she was just browsing while her husband picked up their picnic lunch from the Bluebonnet Café. When the doorbell jingled, announcing the woman's exit, Agnes returned.

"Did she buy anything?"

"No, she was just looking." Dahlia crossed her fingers. "But she said she'd be back later with her husband." She hated to lie, but sometimes little fibs were necessary.

"If she came in here, she was interested in purchasing something. Every customer is a sales opportunity and you don't have many of those. Have you done anything to promote the store to tourists? Are you participating in the summer market?" Agnes asked.

"No, it didn't seem like an appropriate place to sell books." Dahlia had seen a flyer last month for the summer market, but she hadn't done anything more with it than place it in the recycling bin. The market operated in Candle Beach's town square every weekend from Memorial Day to Labor Day. The vendors offered mainly arts and crafts, like jewelry, handmade items and photography, but there were a few produce and other booths as well.

"*Hrumph*," Agnes said. "Ruth always had a booth at the summer market."

"Yes, well, I'm not Ruth." Agnes's constant disapproval ground away at the last veneer of Dahlia's patience and she stifled a scream.

"That's obvious." Agnes sniffed high in the air, flounced the hem of her knee-length black raincoat with a quick movement and turned toward the door. "I knew you wouldn't be able to make it. You should have sold when you had the opportunity. Ruth would be appalled at the state of this place."

"It looks exactly like it did when I took the daily management over from you and your friends."

Agnes glared at Dahlia, who shrank back involuntarily. "I told Ruth she should have left her store to your mother. At least she had the decency to come and visit Ruth during her illness. And she has the ability to stick with a responsibility, something you sorely lack."

A book cover facing out in the self-improvement section

caught Dahlia's eye and she impulsively picked it up. She thrust her selection at Agnes. "*How to Win Friends and Influence People.* Perhaps you'd be interested in this book?" False sweetness dripped from her voice. "I could sell it to you at a discount, since I can see this book would be helpful to you."

"Dear, you can't afford to be offering books at a discount." Agnes marched over to where Dahlia had selected the book and plucked another one off the shelf —*Saving Your Relationship: How to Compromise.* "Perhaps you could have used this book a few years ago," she said in a matching saccharine tone. "Maybe you'd still be married."

Her comment slammed into Dahlia with the force of a freight train. She turned for a minute, not wanting Agnes to see the tears that threatened to fall. She regained her composure and turned back around. Agnes waited expectantly, as if ready for active confrontation.

"You don't know what you're talking about," Dahlia said. "Not that it's any of your business, but I wasn't the problem in my marriage, Jeff was. I was the only person making compromises." Anger rushed through her veins, flushing her face with heat. "I won't let you or anyone else tell me what to do. I never asked for this from Aunt Ruth. I'm doing the best I can under the circumstances."

"Are you?" Agnes surveyed the room again. "It's not just your marriage that you couldn't keep together. You've been like this since you were a child. Always wanting to put only half the effort into something and then running out to play. Do you know how many times Ruth had to redo a task you'd been assigned when you worked at the store in the summers? Instead of stocking the shelves properly, you'd throw the books on the shelf and leave to go party with your friends."

Dahlia recoiled. Although true, Agnes's words stung and she didn't appreciate the trip down memory lane. "Ruth never mentioned it to me. I didn't know it bothered her so much."

Agnes had a talent for making her feel both furious and ashamed at the same time. Ruth had always given her permission to leave to hang out with her friends, but now she wondered if she'd taken advantage of her aunt's kindness.

"Ruth was so proud of this store. Until she fell ill, she kept the place in tip-top shape. You can't even be bothered to replace the cookies. How hard is that?" Agnes nodded at the silver cookie platter sitting on a lace doily next to the insulated carafe of tea on the side table. Only crumbs remained on the plate after two couples had herded their small children through the store. "And is that an ant I see on the cookie tray?"

Dahlia rushed over to the offending item. The only thing she saw besides crumbs was a tiny piece of gray lint that had caught on the edge of the platter. She brushed it off surreptitiously with her thumb while picking up the tray.

"No ants here." She dumped the crumbs in the garbage, reached under the counter, and brought out some replacement cookies. She set some on the tray, then added more in case another group of kids came through.

"I know I saw an ant." Agnes frowned at her as though she'd dumped an entire ant hill into the garbage. Dahlia shrugged and set the heaping tray of cookies down on the side table. As much as she wanted to throw Agnes out of the store, she refused to escalate the situation any further.

Agnes harrumphed again and scanned the store.

"I suppose it doesn't really matter. You won't make a

profit unless you put some effort into operating the store and I'm confident that won't happen. In nine months, ownership of the bookstore will transfer to me and I'll make the improvements to bring this store back to what it was when Ruth was in charge."

Dahlia couldn't help herself. She'd never heard this stipulation of the will. Maybe she should have finished reading through all the paperwork the paralegal had given her.

"Excuse me, what do you mean the bookstore will be yours in nine months?"

"It's quite simple, dear." Agnes tapped her umbrella against the carpeted floor. "If you fail to turn a profit at the end of the year, which you will, I get the bookstore."

It hadn't occurred to her what would happen if the bookstore wasn't profitable after a year under her management. Now, the older woman's motivations were clear. If the bookstore failed, Agnes stood to inherit. If she lost the bookstore, would she lose the house too? She wasn't going to ask Agnes. She made a mental note to call Aunt Ruth's lawyer when she had a chance.

"Well, don't worry about taking on that responsibility. To Be Read will earn a profit by the end of the year," she said. "I have plans for improving the store and increasing foot traffic." She didn't know how, but somehow she would create a plan to turn things around.

Agnes smiled. "We'll see about that."

Dahlia walked over to the door and opened it, hoping Agnes would take the hint. Thankfully, she did.

"I'll be back next Wednesday," she announced as she exited the bookstore. She opened her black umbrella and strode off down the street, the umbrella casting a shadow behind her in the full sunlight. With her black raincoat, severe hairstyle and an umbrella instead of a broom, she only lacked a pointed hat to complete her witchiness. Dahlia looked in the opposite direction, toward the waterfront, and saw a rainbow arc over Main Street. If only there was a pot of gold at the end of that rainbow. She was going to need it.

She turned to survey her surroundings again. Would her great-aunt really be appalled at the state of the store? She'd tried to keep things up, but it appeared shabbier than ever. The curtains had been washed, but some of the velvet had rubbed off in the process. Everything was dingy with age. Was it worth spending Ruth's savings to attempt to save the bookstore?

She didn't know whether to laugh at Agnes's antics or run into the back room and cry. Agnes's assessment regarding the bookstore's profitability had been correct. Dahlia had been reluctant to use her limited financial resources to make improvements to the store if she was going to sell it in the near future. Now, investing in To Be Read had become a necessity.

She went to the office and sat down in Aunt Ruth's swivel desk chair. The immensity of the task at hand hit her and the tears she'd held back during Agnes's visit erupted. Then her eyes caught on a picture of Aunt Ruth and she stopped crying. She owed it to her to try.

She spun around a few times in the chair to shake the away the sense of doom Agnes had brought into the store, and then dragged her feet on the floor to slow down. Through teary eyes, she picked up a pen and paper. It was time to get down to business.

But she didn't get far on her plans to save the bookstore. A few minutes after Agnes left, the bell over the front door chimed. She stood from the desk and set down her pen.

Wiping the remaining tears away with the sleeve of the black long-sleeved blouse she wore to combat the air conditioner's arctic chill, she straightened her posture and smoothed the blouse over her skinny jeans. Her watch read four-thirty. In an hour and a half she could close the store for the day. Ninety more minutes without breaking into tears. She could do that easily.

Or so she thought.

~

Dahlia paused in the doorframe between the back room and the public area of the bookstore. The newly arrived customer had his back to her, facing a display of Lee Child thrillers. She recognized his dark wavy hair and the scent of his spicy aftershave.

Of all the days, why did Garrett decide to come in today?

She pasted a smile on her face, brushed her hair back with both hands and called out a cheery hello. He swiveled to face her, a genuine smile on his face. In the three months since their first encounters, they'd made polite chitchat when they saw each other around town and during Garrett's weekly visit to the bookstore for a fresh supply of reading material. With all the books he bought from her, she wasn't sure when he found the time to write his own novels. That is, if the town's whisperings about his writing career were accurate. Unfortunately, their relationship hadn't progressed beyond a professional one, even though she kept hinting she'd be open to more.

"Hi, I was beginning to wonder where you were," he said.

"I was taking care of a few things in the back. What can I do for you?"

"I'm browsing. Looks like you got in some new titles."

She nodded. As happened any time she was in a room alone with Garrett, she felt a magnetic pull to him, but he didn't seem to notice it.

"Can I help you find anything today? Maybe the new Susannah Garrity novel?" She picked up a copy of the romance author's newest book, turning the title to face him. The book's cover featured a hunky Viking and a stunning brunette locked in a passionate embrace. Garrett took a look at it and stepped backward. His face flushed until it matched the red short-sleeved polo he was wearing over a pair of faded blue jeans.

Dahlia grinned at his reaction and replaced the book on the shelf. She'd never seen him so unsettled and she quite enjoyed it. "Or perhaps you've read that one already?" she teased.

"I think I'll stick with this book." He waved the thriller he held in one hand. Then he regarded her with concern. "Are you okay?"

"Of course, why do you ask?" Was Agnes's effect on her that obvious? She thought she'd managed to hide how shaken she'd been after her visit.

"You look like a raccoon." He gestured to her eyes.

She put her hands up to her face and ran her fingers over the telltale grittiness of smeared mascara and melted foundation. "I'll be back in a minute."

She ran back to the minuscule bathroom tucked away in a corner of the storeroom. A glance in the mirror confirmed Garrett's blunt assessment. Rivulets of mascara from her earlier crying jag streaked her cheeks. After she wiped the makeup off with toilet paper and lotion, she gripped the edges of the old-fashioned white pedestal sink and glared at her reflection.

"Get a grip, Winters. You don't need him to see you cry." Even with the pep talk, the woman in the gilt-edged mirror stared back at her with eyes filled with sadness and doubt. She inhaled deeply through her nostrils and spun away from the sink. She continued the deep breathing exercise as she walked through the back room, pausing before she rejoined Garrett.

From the doorway, she watched him pull out a book, read the back cover and then place it back on the shelf, all the while humming a cheery tune she recognized as 'Do Wah Diddy Diddy'. Her lips turned up into a glimmer of a smile at the off-key rendition of the song her paternal grandfather sang to her as a child.

When she returned to the sales floor, Garrett was holding a few more books in his hands than before she'd left. If taking a quick trip to the back room increased all sales threefold, she should consider using that sales technique more often.

"Sorry about that," she said. "I was dusting the back room earlier and splashed water over my face to get rid of the dust. Water and mascara don't mix well. Thanks for letting me know." She stumbled a bit on the white lie, but hoped he'd accept it.

"No problem," he said easily, but the concern hadn't faded from his expression. "I know we got off to a rocky start when you came to Candle Beach, but it's a small town. I hope we can eventually be friends."

She wasn't sure how to respond. Did she want to be friends with him? Something akin to electricity jolted through her, but met resistance when it hit her dulled emotions. She was too exhausted to figure out what that meant.

"And as a potential friend, I'd like to ask again. Are you okay?"

She tried to smile. "I'm fine." The reassurance sounded flat, even to her.

He put his books down on the counter and stood closer to her. "You don't look okay."

She couldn't hold back any longer. Her eyes filled with tears and her body lost strength. She bit the tip of her tongue to fight off the tears, but the defense mechanism failed and they slipped out, streaming down her freshly scrubbed face. She sagged against the front counter.

Garrett pulled her close and wrapped his arms around her. She melted against his chest with her hands on his shoulders. He pressed her tightly against him, her tears forming a wet spot on his shirt.

"It's okay," he murmured over her sobs, while patting her back. For a moment, she half believed him. His embrace comforted her and made her feel less alone. *I could get used to this,* she thought as she closed her eyes momentarily. Unfortunately, that realization didn't help with the situation with Agnes. As much as she tried to stop them, the tears continued to fall.

Garrett leaned back and stared into her eyes, then pressed his lips against hers. Before she knew what she was doing, she returned his kiss. His lips were soft but firm and she felt herself drowning in the sensation.

Her eyes popped open and she broke their embrace. What was she doing? She wasn't the woman on the cover of Susannah Garrity's most recent romance novel. She released her grip on Garrett's shoulders and stepped back.

"What was that kiss for?" Her voice sounded breathless and she felt a little dizzy.

"I'm not sure." His expression mirrored the surprise she

felt. "You looked so sad and I wanted to make you stop crying."

"Well, I guess it worked." She walked behind the counter to retrieve facial tissue to mop up her face. "I'd offer you one to dry off your shirt, but I don't think it's going to help much," she said, attempting to joke.

"Don't even worry about it, my shirt will be fine." He stood with his arms by his sides. "Seriously though, what's going on? Is there anything I can do?"

"Not unless you want to own your very own bookstore." She'd gained control of the tears and busied herself with organizing items on the sales counter. She was grateful to have the high counter between Garrett and herself. For two people who hadn't yet reached the friendship stage, they'd now had two decidedly intimate encounters. Without a barrier between them, she doubted her ability to resist the temptation to launch herself into his arms again.

He picked one of his book selections off the counter and rubbed his thumb against the fore edge, ruffling the pages. He looked up at her, a thoughtful expression on his face. "If you wanted to sell To Be Read, I'd be interested in buying it from you."

She looked at him, mouth agape. "Are you kidding?"

"No. I intend to make my permanent home in Candle Beach and owning the bookstore would fit in well with my plans. You may have noticed I like to read." He gave her a winning smile.

"Just like that? You really want to buy the bookstore?" She knew he enjoyed reading, but he'd never given any past indication that he wanted to buy To Be Read.

"Well, I'd given some thought to it when Ruth passed away, but then she wanted you to run the bookstore, so I gave up on that idea," he said. "But you don't want to be here or to operate the bookstore, so maybe this can be a win–win situation for both of us."

"What do you mean by that?" She thought she'd done a decent job managing the bookstore in the last three months. She'd followed Aunt Ruth's ordering instructions to a 'T', kept up on the ads in the *Candle Beach Weekly* and maintained Ruth's tradition of complimentary tea and cookies for customers, even if Agnes acted like things weren't up to par.

"Well, you don't seem to have a passion for the business," Garrett observed. "You made it quite clear when we first met that you didn't want to own it, much less be living in Candle Beach to operate it yourself." He swept his hand through the air, motioning from wall to wall of the bookstore. "Before the chemo treatments wore Ruth out, she always had this place spotless and her enthusiasm for the business infused the store. Now, it looks like you haven't put any money or extra effort into the place for months. You haven't made any attempt to make it your own."

His words stung. She'd given up her apartment lease and job in Seattle, squeezed most of her belongings into a room in her mother's basement and moved to Candle Beach to fulfill her aunt's wishes.

The overhead fan kicked on and she had to raise her voice to be heard. "I'm doing the best I can."

"I'm not trying to upset you," he said, one hand up in the air. A desire to placate her dripped from his tone.

"Well, you have. I gave up everything for this place. You have no idea who I am or what I want."

"You're right." He put his hand on her arm. "I shouldn't have said that."

She smiled weakly at him. Between Agnes's visit and his, her nerves were frazzled.

"I honestly didn't mean to offend you," he said. "It

seemed like you were forced into this situation and I thought there was something I could do to help. You know, if you want some help with the place, I could help you. Although I've only lived in Candle Beach for less than a year, I know a lot about how the town works." He laid the book he was holding on the counter. "How about I come back to get these later and we can talk then, okay?"

She nodded.

The door clicked closed behind him and she laid her head down on her arms next to his stack of books. The breeze from the vents blew past them, bringing with it the incomparable new book smell. She breathed deeply, spinning back through time to a childhood spent amid the wonders of To Be Read's bookshelves.

Aunt Ruth had cherished the bookstore. She'd spent hours every day making sure every detail was perfect and inviting, from the impeccably aligned books in the window display to the stuffed animals in the children's section. Dahlia remembered Aunt Ruth standing on a tall ladder, wiping the shelves with a fluffy dust mop and humming under her breath as she worked.

If Dahlia had thought Agnes's visit was tough, it didn't even compare to Garrett's. While she didn't want to admit it, his opinion mattered to her. His offer to buy the bookstore notwithstanding, he'd always seemed levelheaded and reasonable. She looked around To Be Read. She'd gone into managing the store knowing it was a means to an end. Owning the bookstore was Ruth's dream, not hers. Was it worth staying? Or was she better off cutting her losses and focusing on what truly mattered to her?

She busied herself opening boxes in the back storeroom and pricing clearance items. The monotony of alphabetizing books on the overflow shelves calmed her, and an hour

passed before she realized it was almost closing time. Unfortunately, no customers had entered the store since Garrett
left. But the time in the back had given her some distance
from Agnes and Garrett's visits and some clarity of thought.

If Garrett wanted to buy the store, maybe she should
let him.

## 7

*Her wavy strawberry-blonde hair glinted in the sunlight....*

Garrett swore under his breath and deleted the description of his novel's heroine for the third time. Every woman he described looked exactly like Dahlia. Since the first time he saw her at the beach overlook, he couldn't get her out of his mind. What was it about her that made her so irresistible? And of course, his inability to speak to her like a normal human being continued to be a problem.

He'd been in her bookstore several times a week for the past three months, hoping that at some point he'd be able to converse naturally with her. Today, he'd at least been able to talk with her, but he'd somehow managed to stick his foot in his mouth at the same time. And that kiss... He'd kissed her on the spur of the moment, but it was even better than he'd imagined. He'd thought he'd finally made progress on moving their relationship forward, but had his comments about the bookstore ended all of that? What had he been thinking, offering to buy the bookstore from her? He knew she'd made an effort to manage the bookstore by moving to

Candle Beach. So why did it come out so wrong when he spoke with her?

His eyes slid over to the wedding invitation pinned on his bulletin board. He'd RSVP'd yes to Lisa's wedding, but hadn't decided if he would really attend. Now he had to make a decision, as the wedding was the next day in Seattle. He leaned back in his desk chair and pressed his fingertips together in front of him. Maybe he'd get some closure by seeing Lisa married. It wasn't that he had romantic feelings for her anymore, but they'd been close for a long time. Seeing her move on might set him free to do the same. Her wedding was at noon, so he could easily make it out to Seattle and back in the same day.

∽

A few minutes after Dahlia broke away from shelving books, a harried, middle-aged man carrying a leather messenger bag entered the bookstore. Finally, a customer. Better yet, she'd never seen him before. The man made a loop around the outer aisles of the store, pausing for a moment in front of the plate of Danish butter cookies. Aunt Ruth used to swear the cookies made people more comfortable in the store and more likely to purchase books.

The man whipped out a clipboard and made a note on the top sheet of paper.

Dahlia approached him. "Hi, can I help you find something?"

"Are you Dahlia Winters?" He flipped through the stack of papers and withdrew one from the bottom of the pile.

"Yes, why?" She didn't recognize the man, but he somehow knew her name. Generally when someone official knew your name, they weren't coming to offer you a sweepstakes prize. After dealing with Agnes and Garrett on the same day, what more could be thrown at her?

"I'm Miles Linz from the Grayton County Health Department. We've had a complaint that you're offering food and beverages without a proper license." He nodded at the plate of cookies.

"I'm sorry, but I don't understand. I inherited the bookstore from my aunt a few months ago and I've carried on her tradition of offering tea and cookies to bookstore patrons. I didn't realize I needed a license to do so." She leaned against the front counter for support. "I'm not selling any food or beverages, they're free for customers." To the best of her knowledge, Aunt Ruth had never carried a food and beverage permit.

"I'm sorry ma'am, but offering food or beverage without a permit, whether charging for it or not, is a violation of the county health code." He handed her an official-looking piece of paper.

"What's this?" She scanned the page.

"It's a notice of closure for your bookstore. Until you have proper licensure, we have to shut down the establishment." He shuffled his papers around before placing the clipboard in his bag.

"Can't I just remove the cookies and tea? I mean, the cookies are out of a can, it's not like I made them in my home kitchen."

"I'm sorry ma'am, but we can't let you do that. You'll need to shut down." He appeared mildly apologetic. "Look, it's Friday afternoon and the county office in Haven Shores closes soon, but you can apply on Monday and they'll issue the permit then. As soon as you get it, you can reopen the bookstore."

"But the weekend is my busiest time. I can't shut down for the weekend."

He shrugged. "Sorry, but there's nothing I can do. Once we've been notified of a violation, it must be corrected before a business can reopen. As of now, you're closed for business." He walked toward the door, pulling it shut behind him.

Dahlia grabbed a handful of the offending cookies and poured herself a cup of tea before collapsing into the wing-back chair. The bookstore was far enough in the hole as it was. Closing for the weekend would put her even further behind.

Giving up and returning to Seattle had never sounded so good. With Agnes's refusal to act like a normal, sane human being, and Garrett's offer to buy To Be Read, she had all the reasons she needed to return to her old life. With the profits from selling the bookstore, if she traveled frugally, she could backpack through Europe for at least a year. Maybe there would even be money left over to see parts of Asia. This was her chance to be the world traveler she'd always imagined herself to be, and she had the opportunity to be free of the chains of everyone else's expectations.

But then there was Garrett. With the way he'd been acting, she hadn't expected him to kiss her. The kiss had been everything she'd hoped for—sweet and sexy at the same time. She wanted to get to know him better, but did he want the same thing?

She set her teacup down and leaned back against the fraying brocade chair, closing her eyes. She focused on the sound of her breath. Only the faint hum of the air conditioner marred the silence of the empty bookstore.

Aunt Ruth would want her to be happy, whether that meant staying in Candle Beach or seeing the world instead.

A slight breeze ruffled her hair and she opened her eyes. Surrounded by the furniture Ruth had chosen and everything she had loved, Dahlia felt as though her aunt were present in the room.

"Aunt Ruth?" she whispered. Her skin prickled, casting doubt on her beliefs about Ruth's wishes. "I don't know what I'm doing," she said out loud. "Please tell me what I should do." She half hoped that ghosts existed so she wouldn't have to make the decision on her own.

Another puff of air caused her hair to stand on end, until she realized the health inspector hadn't latched the door completely, allowing for drafts to enter the store. She rose to shut the door. She pulled it closed as Ruth had done so many times before, and the connection heightened the sense that her aunt was with her in that moment.

Dahlia wanted to make her proud of the woman she'd become. Agnes had been correct that she'd been flighty as a teenager, a trait which had persisted into her twenties. While she had never seen herself as the owner of a small-town bookstore, the idea was starting to gel with her and she owed it to herself to see if it was a good fit. Although her dream two years ago may have been to be a free-spirited traveler, that didn't mean it was still right for her now.

She assessed To Be Read with a critical eye, all the way from the front display window to the tea and cookies against the back wall. Reinventing the store would take a lot of work. Was she ready for it? Did she have money to fund the remodel? Did she even want to take on the project?

She wasn't sure how she felt about investing her time and money in the bookstore, but what she did know was that she wasn't going to lose the bookstore and let Agnes win. Garrett's offer to purchase the store tickled at her thoughts. Selling to him would be an easy way out of the whole mess. She could take the money and run, albeit only receiving half of what the store was worth.

But she didn't like that option, for two reasons. One, because Agnes would get half of the sales proceeds, and two, because she didn't want to give up on Aunt Ruth's wish for her to run the bookstore. She got up to take a closer look at the store's fixtures.

The layout of the front window display hadn't changed in the last ten years. Threadbare curtains framed the bay window, but their breadth obscured the view into the store. She had to retract the heavy velvet folds to clearly see the display. Books stood in tiered rows, facing the window for people on Main Street to view. While functional, the design didn't invite patrons to come in and check out the new books.

Closing her eyes again, she thought about what would entice her into a store. A pop of color would help and props would liven up the display. She envisioned sand buckets and toy shovels behind the newest beach reads, or a cookbook display with an apron and cast iron pan. She grabbed a pen and scribbled furiously. Should she replace the curtains? No, the windows should be bare. Expensive curtains weren't in the budget and letting customers see the rows of books inside at all hours of the day couldn't hurt.

Excitement bubbled through her body and she swiveled around, seeing the bookstore with fresh eyes. The stained welcome mat had to go and the hardwood floors needed refinishing. Although the fabric-covered armchairs held a lifetime of memories of teatime with Aunt Ruth, they'd seen better days. Her eyes lit upon the shelves of fiction books. She'd kept up on ordering the latest books, but the shelves and displays themselves looked dated.

She crossed the room to the fiction section. Behind it,

Aunt Ruth had used a small alcove to house a tall potted plant. She attempted to pick up the planter and then push it across the floor, but the plant thwarted her efforts. It was heavier than it appeared. She sat down on the floor, braced her back against the wall and used her legs to slide the plant out of the alcove. Then she stood to assess the newly open space. Without the heavy, dark foliage of the plant, new possibilities opened up for the alcove. In fact, there may even be room for two comfy chairs and a small table in between them. Perfect for kicking back with a cup of coffee and a pile of books to peruse.

Coffee. To compete with the chain bookstores, To Be Read needed a coffee bar. Not just tea and cookies, but a compact espresso bar offering coffee and pastries. As if infused already by a jolt of caffeine, she rushed across the room to the tea area. She took a few steps back and mentally measured the space. If she moved the children's section over a few feet, she would have enough room for someone to make espresso behind a short bar. If the health department was going to require a permit for food and drink, she might as well add in a serviced espresso stand. She picked up the tray of cookies and practically bounced over to the front of the store.

She flipped the sign in the front window to 'Closed.' Outside, Mrs. Mendelsohn and Mrs. Lee passed by, deep in conversation, most likely about the latest knitting pattern they'd discovered. The two women came in often to browse through the craft section of the bookstore. She felt an odd tug at her heart. A child across the street in the large town park waved at her and she returned the wave, smiling as she did so.

Without realizing it, she'd become a member of the community and Candle Beach had become her home.

When she'd first inherited the bookstore, Candle Beach had been a fond memory, but not a place where she'd want to spend a significant amount of time by choice. Now, three months later, she had friends, a business, and even a stray cat had wheedled its way into her home and heart.

She'd never have thought three months could make such a difference in her life. Much as she hated to admit it, her mother had been right. She had needed something new in her life. Whether this was merely a brief stop in her life's journey or somewhere she'd put down roots, Candle Beach was exactly what the doctor had ordered.

She carried the tray of cookies to the back room, munching one as she walked. Changes needed to be made in the bookstore, but first of all she needed to confront her old archenemy, the general ledger.

A bookkeeper had been maintaining To Be Read's accounts and she hadn't worried herself too much with the overall income and expenses, assuming that he would let her know if there were any issues. As he'd done every week, he had left her a profit and loss statement when he'd stopped by on Tuesday. She hadn't looked at it yet and to be honest, she hadn't reviewed the statement in over a month.

Now, she forced herself to open the file folder and dive into the details. What she saw was worrisome. Sales were worse than she'd expected to see and expenses were higher. She needed to come up with ways to sell additional books and make more money.

The building creaked and she turned around. No one was there, but the door to the hallway caught her eye. She walked through the door and into the small hallway, which was piled floor to ceiling with boxes. Thank goodness Agnes hadn't sicced the fire department on her as well.

After using a stepladder to remove the topmost boxes in

one stack, she moved the remaining books to the side, revealing most of a previously hidden door. In all the hubbub of taking over, she'd completely forgotten about the small one-bedroom apartment over the bookstore.

She reached behind another box for the knob, but it didn't turn. She shoved the boxes into the center of the hallway and pulled harder, but it was locked. Then she remembered the ring of keys Gretchen had given her. She retrieved them from her purse and inserted one of the unused keys in the lock. The second key she tried worked.

She opened the door gingerly, not sure of what she'd see or smell. A wave of heat barreled down the stairs to greet her. Aunt Ruth had installed air conditioning in the main store and back rooms to protect the books from humidity, but there was no sign of it in the upstairs apartment. To her surprise, while she was greeted by a musty odor, there wasn't any smell or rustling of mice. The stairs creaked with every step she took but they didn't show signs of wood rot. She flipped on the light switch at the top of the stairs.

When Dahlia was a small child, Aunt Ruth had rented the upstairs apartment to a widower, but after he died, she'd used it as storage. Sometime while Aunt Ruth was sick, someone must have moved all of the file and book boxes downstairs into the hallway and storeroom for easier access. Now, the dim light revealed dust bunnies hiding under a sheet-covered couch and an ancient TV, but the room was otherwise free of clutter.

Off to the side was a small galley-style kitchen with a two-burner stove and a full-sized refrigerator straight out of the seventies. She remembered the two closed doors led to a bathroom with a shower and a decent-sized bedroom. She walked over to the kitchen window and spread the fading lemon-yellow curtains to let in light. She opened the window too, exchanging some of the stuffy air for the cooler air of the summer evening.

With the aid of the natural light, she sat in one of the two vinyl-padded chairs accompanying the Formica-topped kitchen table and reassessed the room. This could work. The apartment could be rented for some extra cash, either as a monthly rental or as a nightly rental for the tourists. While not ideal for repeat business at the bookstore, she knew from Gretchen that Candle Beach's thriving tourist economy had created a high demand for vacation rentals.

Her spirits lifted and her mind spun with everything on her to-do list. She returned to Ruth's office and grabbed a notepad and pen to take notes. She needed to call the property management company and get the apartment cleaned out. She stopped for a moment, tapping her pen against the desk. Did she need to get Agnes's permission to rent out the apartment? Surely that was part of her inheritance and could be used to offset the costs of owning the building housing To Be Read. She decided it was better to act first and ask forgiveness later. Something had to be done to keep the store from going under.

By the third page of notes, her hand cramped and she stopped to rub her fingers and thumb. Buying a computer for the store needed to be a top financial and time priority. Ruth had ordered books directly from the publishers by phone and paper orders, and Dahlia had continued that tradition, but the contact at the distribution warehouse had told her that they were moving over completely to computerized ordering. It was time to modernize the store and bring it into the twenty-first century.

She dug into the files and reviewed the accountant's statements again, noting places to cut costs. To purchase a computer and remodel the store's furnishings, she'd need to take a hefty bite out of Aunt Ruth's savings. Was it worth it? She looked around Aunt Ruth's office—correction, her office now—and decided it was a worthy investment in her future. The largest Russian doll on the top shelf beamed down at her, and silly as it may have been, she knew she'd made the right choice.

*a*n hour later, Dahlia slid into one side of the dark, scarred wooden booth across from Maggie at Off the Vine. The recently opened wine and tapas bar had quickly become a favorite among her friends. She and Maggie pored over the menu.

"Stuffed mushrooms for sure. They were so yummy last time." Dahlia ran her finger over the description. "And how about the boneless Buffalo wings and prosciutto-wrapped dates?"

"Sounds good. I'm glad the new owners left some of the old bar food on the menu when they converted Beers Ahoy into a wine bar." Maggie closed her menu. The waitress came by and the two of them placed their orders. A few minutes later, Gretchen flew in the door and rushed over to their table, collapsing next to Dahlia on the bench seat.

"*Ahh*. It feels so good to sit down," Gretchen said, stretching her neck against the high-backed seat. "I haven't had a break since lunchtime." She flagged down the waitress and ordered a jumbo lime margarita.

"I don't remember Beers Ahoy very well, but this place is

a huge hit with the tourists," Dahlia said. "Any place that can lure tourists in helps all of us."

Maggie and Gretchen exchanged knowing looks.

"Now you're talking like a native of Candle Beach," Maggie teased. "Soon you'll be spouting off the tide tables with ease."

"This is my home now," Dahlia said. "Well, for at least nine more months. Who knows, the town is growing on me."

The waitress returned with their drinks, and Dahlia reached for her glass of Chardonnay and gulped half of it down. "I needed this."

Maggie raised her eyebrows.

"What?" Dahlia asked. "It's been a long day...too long."

Maggie grinned and pulled a piece of olive loaf from the bread basket. "Thank goodness for late-night happy hour. I love my café, but sometimes I just want someone else to make me food."

"I agree," Gretchen said. "I had fourteen nightly tenants come in today with issues with their rental houses. After figuring out the logistics of getting all the problems fixed to their satisfaction, I'm beat."

"Well, I had another weekly visit from Queen Agnes," Dahlia said. "As usual, the bookstore wasn't up to her standards."

"Yeah, I saw her come out of To Be Read this afternoon," Gretchen said. "She had the biggest grin on her face." She delicately licked salt off of the rim of her margarita before taking a drink.

All of Dahlia's enthusiasm for remodeling the bookstore faded with Gretchen's words and she removed her hand from the basket of mushrooms. She'd been about to select a plump one to dip in the blue cheese dressing but her rising anger kept her from eating.

"Agnes was smiling?" She wiped her hands on a paper napkin and swigged the remaining wine from her glass. "She spent half an hour in the bookstore telling me how inept I was at running the place and how disappointed in me Ruth would have been."

She grabbed the mushroom she'd eyed previously and stuffed it in her mouth to keep the tears at bay. The juicy mushroom exploded in her mouth, giving her something else to think about other than how much Agnes hated her. When she finished chewing, she said, "Agnes is a piece of work. She used to be so nice to me when I came here as a kid. I don't know what changed."

Gretchen leaned over to Dahlia on their shared bench seat and gave her a quick shoulder hug. "She's not normally this awful. The Ladies like to control things in Candle Beach, or think they have some control, but this is odd, even for them. I'm so sorry Dahl."

"Oh, and that isn't even all of it," Dahlia said. "A few hours after she left, I received a visit from the County Health Department."

"What do they have to do with a bookstore?" Maggie asked. "We get semiannual surprise visits from them at the café, but I wouldn't think they'd care about a bookstore."

"They objected to the cookies and tea. Something tells me I wouldn't have been on their radar if it hadn't been for a call from Agnes." She signaled to the waitress for another glass of wine. "They've shut me down until Monday when I can get a permit from the county. It's like nothing I do goes right. I should have sold when I could."

Maggie reached for a boneless buffalo wing and daintily dipped it in ranch dressing. "If it's any consolation, I've heard a couple of customers at the café saying how nice it is that you're here to manage the bookstore. I think you're doing a great job."

"But that's the problem, I don't think I am. Or at least not as much as I could be doing." She tapped her fingers on the wooden table. "Do you girls think there's more I should be doing?"

Gretchen squirmed in her seat and Maggie looked away for a second. Dahlia caught their hesitation.

"You do, don't you? What can I do to improve the bookstore?" She wanted to get their impressions before she shared her own ideas.

"Maybe spruce it up a bit?" Gretchen said. "I can help you find a place to install new carpet or polish the hardwoods. Maybe even paint?"

"Yeah." Maggie nodded. "I think that would help freshen things up and be more inviting for customers. After Ruth got sick, she wasn't able to perform more than basic maintenance on the bookstore, so there are a few things that could use help." She sipped her glass of Merlot. "Maybe you should participate in the summer market? There's still over a month left before it closes."

"Would that help? It didn't seem like a place to sell books." Dahlia grabbed a pen out of her purse and jotted some notes on a clean paper napkin.

"It's not so much the actual selling of the books, but more the visibility the bookstore gets from participating. When tourists and townspeople visit the market they'll see the To Be Read booth and remember they wanted to read the beach read du jour. You know how it goes—out of sight, out of mind. With the new Book Warehouse in Haven Shores, you need all the good publicity you can get."

"After Agnes left, I was thinking about some improvements I could make too," Dahlia admitted. "What do you think about expanding the tea and cookies into a full espresso bar with pastries? I could move the children's section over and put in a small coffee bar there. I need something to compete with the Book Warehouse."

"So you're going to compete with the café?" Maggie asked. She wrapped petite fingers around her long-stemmed wine glass.

"No, no, nothing major, just the espresso bar and some pastries."

"Dahlia, I'm kidding. We have plenty of business at the café. I think that's a great way to modernize To Be Read. It'll be just like the big chain bookstores. If you want, we can provide you with pastries. Our pastry chef is fantastic."

"Thanks Maggie, I'd love that." Dahlia drained her second glass of wine. The alcohol had begun to take effect and she felt the worries of the day melt away. She caught sight of Garrett sitting at the bar flirting with the pretty bartender. She looked away before he saw her.

The waitress came around to check on them. "Can I get you ladies anything?" she asked. "The kitchen is closing in half an hour, so it's your last chance to try some of the new Asian chicken lettuce wraps."

"That sounds lovely," Maggie said. "We'll take an order of the wraps."

"Can I get a jumbo margarita please?" Dahlia asked.

The waitress noted it on her order pad. "Sure. Anything else?"

Maggie looked at the two wine glasses in front of Dahlia that the waitress was in the process of clearing away. "Maybe another basket of bread?"

The waitress nodded and left.

"Agnes must have really gotten to you," Maggie said to

Dahlia. "I don't think I've ever seen you have more than two drinks in a night."

Dahlia shot a glance at Garrett, who was now engaged in conversation with the woman next to him. The woman, probably a tourist, had long, jet-black hair and exotic features. She kept tossing her hair back and beaming at Garrett. He smiled and laughed as he drank from a bottle of IPA beer. Dahlia's eyes kept drifting back to him. He'd kissed *her* today, so why was he flirting with another woman? Apparently the kiss hadn't affected him as much as it had her, which hurt to think about. Part of her hoped he'd notice her and come over to their table.

"It's not just Agnes," she admitted. "Garrett stopped by today too. He offered to buy the bookstore."

"That's great!" Maggie said. "You've been so stressed about it. Are you thinking about it? I'm assuming you're still on the fence since you're talking about a remodel."

"I don't think it's the right time to sell. Besides, if I wait until the year is up, I get all the money. If I sell now, I have to split it with Agnes."

"Are you sure this is what you want, Dahlia?" Gretchen asked. "You could sell the bookstore and walk away. Think of all you could see and do with the money. It wouldn't take long to convince me to take the money and run if I were in your shoes."

"Yeah, me too," said Maggie. "We'd miss you, but if I didn't have Alex to worry about, I'd consider selling the café. You don't have any responsibilities to tie you down. Maybe this would be best."

Dahlia bristled at Maggie's comment about her lack of responsibilities. She knew her friend hadn't meant anything by it, but it still hurt. Everyone lacked confidence in her ability to successfully manage To Be Read. She tried to brush it off.

"If it had been anyone but him, I might have considered it." She slowly buttered a roll and ate half of it, then washed it down with a swig of margarita. The sweet and sour blend struck her as a perfect metaphor for her current predicament. The bookstore was a blessing, but the possibility existed that she wasn't cut out to own a business.

"Ah, so the plot thickens," teased Gretchen. "I knew you had a thing for him."

"Not a romantic thing for him," Dahlia said. "We're acquaintances, that's all. Well, I thought maybe there was something more, but look at him." She nodded to where Garrett sat at the bar, still with the gorgeous woman. He didn't appear to have noticed she was there with her friends. "Truthfully, part of me doesn't want to sell. Aunt Ruth wanted me to have To Be Read. I wish people would start believing in my ability to run the place. Even Garrett thinks I can't do it. He offered to help me with the business because he feels sorry for me."

Gretchen and Maggie exchanged knowing looks.

"Of course. The only reason a hot guy could possibly be interested in hanging out with you is if he felt sorry for you," Gretchen said with a straight face. Maggie's face contorted as she attempted to stifle laughter.

"I already told you," Dahlia said. "I'm not interested in him. And he's not interested in me, only in the bookstore." She didn't mention his pity kiss to her friends or the way she'd melted against him when he kissed her.

"Uh-huh." Gretchen's eyes were full of mirth as she consumed the rest of her drink.

Their teasing made her feel uncomfortable. "I should get going." She threw thirty dollars on the table, grabbed her purse and looked pointedly at Gretchen. Gretchen stood to allow her room to slide out of the booth.

Maggie's face fell. "We didn't mean anything by it," she said to Dahlia. "Please sit down."

Dahlia glanced at the clock on the back wall. It was after ten and with the alcohol and a long day, she was bone tired.

"No worries," she said breezily. "I'm heading out early tomorrow to check out some furniture stores in Haven Shores. I'll see you guys later."

"Do you want a ride home?" Maggie asked.

"No, the walk home will do me good. I've been inside all day."

She took a few steps toward the front door, but stopped when she saw Garrett saying goodbye to the woman he'd been chatting with. He saw Dahlia out of the corner of his eye and waved to her. She swiveled in her tracks and opted to head towards the hallway to the back door.

～

Stepping out into the chilly coastal summer evening, Dahlia swayed and braced herself against the door. The third drink coursed through her veins. For someone unused to consuming larger quantities of alcohol, even the extra helping of bread hadn't soaked up the excess liquor. She took a deep breath of the cool air and walked unsteadily down the alley. On the plus side, unlike in Seattle, she didn't feel in any danger walking down a dark alley at night. Laughter and gleeful shouts floated out from the arcade and the aroma of the pizza served at the four-lane bowling alley filled the air.

Outside the back door of the hardware store, she stumbled on a piece of wood and toppled to the ground. After

determining nothing was broken except her pride, she
brushed her jeans off. Paint cans lined up against a brick
wall caught her attention. In the dim glow of the street
lamp, Dahlia read the word "Sample" on top of the cans.
The hardware store owner must have intended for them to
be picked up with next week's garbage collection.

On impulse, she grabbed the can handles of what the
sample splotches showed as aqua and burgundy paint. For
smaller cans, they were surprisingly heavy.

Instead of heading home as she'd told her friends she
would, she decided to return to the bookstore with her
newfound art supplies. After clumsily unlocking the back
door of the bookstore, she set the paint cans down. No
longer tired, she flipped on the radio to a rock station and
turned the volume up, getting into the party mood.

She looked around the bookstore. At the moment, she
didn't care about her official to-do list. She needed to make
her mark on the bookstore now. By morning, everyone
would see that she cared and could make the bookstore
hers. Looking around, she decided that removing the
curtains needed to come first. She strode over to the oppres-
sive curtains and ripped them from their hooks. The glow of
the streetlamp shone through the window and lit the bookstore for all to see. Satisfied, she dumped the curtains in the
garbage.

With the adrenaline rush from tearing down the heavy
drapes, she surveyed the store for her next project. The
music throbbed through her as she stared at the potential
coffee bar area. Jogging to the back, she retrieved some paint
brushes she'd seen in the cleaning supplies closet. She
brought the cans of paint and brushes into the main store
and placed them on the old end table in the seating area.

She cleared four rows of children's books off the shelves

next to where the teapot and cookies usually stood and stacked them on the floor. With the weight of the books removed, the bookshelf moved with ease across the hardwood floor. She moved the other furniture away from the wall. With a pair of scissors, she pried open the lid of the first paint can, dipped her brush into it and smeared the paint across the wall. She repeated the process until aqua paint covered the entire back wall.

She stepped back to admire her handiwork. Some paint had dripped on the floor, but the hardwoods needed to be refinished anyway. She flexed her fingers. Using a smaller paintbrush, she used some black sign paint and the burgundy paint she'd liberated from the alley to create a mural on the wall above the future coffee bar. Once upon a time, she'd been a budding artist. Now, the thrill of creation flooded through her, filling her with joy. She spun around to figure out what to do next.

Through her giddiness, she realized a man was peering through the front window at her. She stopped and stared at him. He waved and she realized it was Garrett. What was he doing there?

$\sim$

Garrett had been waiting outside To Be Read for over ten minutes. He'd tried knocking at the door, but Dahlia hadn't heard him over the bass of the music. Next, he'd tried waving his arms in front of the window, but she had her back to him and appeared to be deep in concentration as she manically drew on a freshly painted wall.

He finally got her attention, but from her angry stance, he doubted she was going to let him inside. He'd seen her in the wine bar with her friends, but she'd studiously avoided making eye contact with him. He'd chatted up the bartender to get information about Dahlia. She told him Dahlia had come in about once a week or so with her friends since they'd opened, but that she didn't usually drink so much.

She had occupied a spot on the fringes of his mind since the first time he'd seen her on the overlook. After discovering her free-spirited nature during their conversation at Ruth's house, he'd tried to stop thinking about her, but the feeling persisted. He'd purchased more books from her than he could ever hope to read in a lifetime, but until their kiss today, their conversations had never gone any further than polite chitchat. Offering to buy the bookstore to help her out had seemed like a good idea, but something had backfired.

Seeing her at Off the Vine with her friends had been a stroke of good luck. When she made a move to leave, he'd wanted to talk with her and explain himself, but instead, she'd turned around and walked towards the bathrooms. When she hadn't come back from the hallway for a while, he paid his bill and discovered she'd slipped out the back door. It hadn't been difficult to find her.

The music stopped and she opened the door, paintbrush still in hand. She scowled at him. "What are you doing here?"

"I saw you leave the wine bar and you looked upset," he said. "I wanted to make sure you got home okay."

"You looked like you were doing fine chatting up the bartender."

"She's a friend. And she was telling me about a trip she and her husband are taking to the Bahamas."

"Right." Dahlia gave him a skeptical look. "How'd you find me?"

"They could hear your music clear to Haven Shores," he said dryly. "Are you okay?"

She didn't answer his question. "What are you doing here?"

He pushed the door open and stepped inside. "I see you've been doing some painting." The aqua wall glowed in the harsh fluorescent lights. It wasn't to his taste, but perhaps it would be better in the daylight.

With the music off, she seemed to deflate.

"Maybe you should go home and sleep it off. You look exhausted," he observed.

"I'm fine." She narrowed her eyes at him. "You can let yourself out." She flicked the paint brush at him as she spoke. Splatters of wet burgundy paint fell on the hardwood floors. She swiveled and returned to the newly painted wall. Loud music filled the air again, cutting off all hope of communication.

Why was she being so hostile? He'd tried to talk to her, but it was like their kiss earlier in the day had never happened. He stared at her for a moment, then exited, letting the door slam shut behind him.

~

Dahlia woke the next morning with a crick in her neck. Where was she? She sat up and rubbed the sleep out of her eyes. A sofa, small kitchen table, galley kitchen. She was in the apartment above the bookstore. A lemony scent filled the air and she saw a half empty bottle of Citrus Fresh Cleaner on the table, along with a bucket and a few used sponges. Had a cleaning fairy come last night? And why was she in the upstairs apartment?

She stood and the room spun. Marbles bounced around in her brain like a rousing game of Hungry Hungry Hippos. She lowered herself back onto the couch cushion and leaned back. Memories were resurfacing. The drinks at the bar with her friends, the late-night visit from Garrett and the attack of the green-eyed monster, and then that bottle of Aunt Ruth's favorite port she'd finished off after he stormed out. No wonder her head throbbed. Clean glasses stood on the drying rack next to the sink, furthering her belief in the cleaning fairy theory. She filled a glass with water and drank deeply, quenching the cotton feeling in her mouth.

Next up was locating some aspirin for her headache. She had some in her purse downstairs, but that entailed moving. She plodded over to the stairs and gripped the railing as she picked her way down. At the foot of the stairs a dustpan and broom were propped against the door to the main floor. As she moved them over to open the door, images flooded in.

After Garrett left, she'd been in a frenzy, determined to make sure the bookstore would be ready to open on Monday as soon as she received her food permit from the county. She wasn't sure what that had meant to her in her alcohol-induced state, and now she was a bit afraid to find out.

Apparently she'd also delved into Aunt Ruth's cleaning supplies. Getting the upstairs apartment ready to rent for extra income was imperative if she wanted to keep the business afloat. She remembered scrubbing and polishing the rooms upstairs with the fervor of an electric toothbrush. Tomorrow every muscle in her body would ache, but at least she could check readying the rental apartment off of her list.

She pushed the door open and cringed. Without the curtains, light blared through the window and straight into her eyes. She rubbed her forehead and looked away. The aqua wall looked bare, but in her opinion, cheery, and definitely not something Aunt Ruth would have chosen. She eyed the open space. With a dark wood espresso bar, the black and burgundy coffee cups she'd painted on the wall would stand out and entice customers to wind their way through the store to the back. She smiled. She may not remember all of last night, but it had certainly been productive.

## 9

*G*arrett stared up at the wedding venue through his windshield. A boat? Lisa was getting married on a barge on Lake Union. For some reason that didn't surprise him.

He exited his car and walked slowly across the parking lot. The white barge was docked next to a boathouse, where he assumed the reception would be held. The salty breeze off of the lake tickled his nose, reminding him of Candle Beach. He had to admit the location was beautiful.

He took a deep breath and entered the boathouse. Wedding guests milled around the reception area, waiting for the ceremony to begin. He caught sight of a few of his and Lisa's mutual friends and waved. They waved back but continued their conversations.

"Sir?" a woman behind a table asked. "Would you like to sign the guestbook?" She motioned to the open book in front of her.

"Uh, sure." His collar suddenly seemed too tight. What was he going to write to his ex-fiancée on her wedding day? Had he made a mistake in coming?

He gripped the pen and stared up at the ceiling. Finally, he settled for a generic 'Congratulations' and signed his name. Not a great example of his writing skills, but the best he could do under the circumstances.

An usher signaled that they were now seating guests. He followed the crowd out onto the barge and took a seat in a wooden chair on the bride's side of the aisle. Around him, everyone else chattered in excited voices. He tried to appear happy, but his stomach tightened as they drew closer to the moment of his former love marrying someone else.

Music filled the air and the bridal party walked down the aisle. Lisa's fiancé stood at one end of the barge, along with the officiant. Finally, the crowd stood as Lisa crossed onto the barge. His heart beat faster as she neared her groom. He watched as the wedding couple stared into each other's eyes as they recited their vows and kissed. Then they walked down the aisle as husband and wife. He'd thought seeing Lisa get married would hurt, but he felt nothing. Nothing at all. Well, maybe relief that the moment was over and he could move on with his life. Definitely no regrets about not marrying Lisa.

He allowed himself to be carried along with the rest of the crowd into the boathouse. The wedding party had formed a reception line, but he decided to keep a lower profile. He'd gotten what he came for—a sense of closure that this part of his life was over. He had a new future waiting for him in Candle Beach—one that he hoped involved Dahlia. That is, if he hadn't royally screwed that up.

The catering staff had set up a light lunch buffet and he filled a plate, sitting down alone at a table. He didn't feel like mingling with any of the other guests. The drive back to Candle Beach was long and he planned to leave before the wedding festivities like dancing and cake cutting began.

Should he say something to Lisa before he left? He glanced over to where the receiving line had been, but it had disbanded. He finished his sandwich and pasta salad and pushed back from the table.

Someone tapped him on the shoulder. He turned to see Lisa standing in front of him in her wedding finery. She looked beautiful. He stood to greet her.

"Garrett!" She bent forward in her giant dress and wrapped her arms around him. He folded his arms around her instinctively. It felt familiar, but was like hugging a family member.

She released him and tilted her head back. "I'm so glad you came. It's been a while."

"It has," he admitted. "You look gorgeous."

She smiled. "Thank you. Have you met my husband, Daryl, yet? He's around here somewhere." She scanned the room to look for him.

"No, I haven't. But I'm so happy for you. I can tell you're perfect for each other." He smiled, both at her and in realization that he meant it. Lisa was happy and he could move on.

"Well," he said. "I'd better go. Not sure if you heard, but I've moved to a small town on the coast. It's a long drive home."

"I had heard that. Candle Beach, right? That's a beautiful area."

"Yes," he said. "Next time you're in the area, give me a call. I'd love to show you and Daryl around."

"We will." She hugged him. "Nice seeing you again." She turned and walked away. He watched her stop at groups of guests, beaming as she accepted their congratulations. Then he walked out to his car and started for home, knowing that he'd made the right decision to attend her wedding.

~

With her business shut down by the health department until she could obtain a permit on Monday, Dahlia decided to use her downtime to find ways to make her mark on To Be Read. The first stop on the agenda was the Book Warehouse in Haven Shores. The large bookstore had opened in June, but she hadn't made time to visit it yet. In all honesty, spending what little off time she had at another bookstore didn't appeal to her. But in the name of research, she was finally going to see it. She hoofed it home to change her clothes and take a shower before setting out for Haven Shores.

The orange 'check engine' light blinked on when she started her car's engine, and then flashed off. Annoyance pulled her brows into a frown, but before she could voice the curse that had formed on her tongue, it flashed off again. She debated putting off the trip to Haven Shores, but decided to not use it as an excuse to avoid her tasks for the day. She drove slowly through the fog that hung over the town. A gray mist shrouded the buildings and anyone who dared walk around in the pea soup. The weather forecast called for afternoon rain, but she hoped it would hold off until she had safely returned to Candle Beach.

Thirty minutes later, she pulled into a parking space at the side of the Book Warehouse. The parking lot stretched out behind the store for at least the length of two football fields. In front of her car, a shelving unit inside a wall of windows featured current mystery novels. Interspersed among the mysteries were artifacts straight out of a Sherlock Holmes illustration, like his famed deerstalker hat and cape. This was exactly the type of display she planned to create in To Be Read's front bay window. Turning away from the display, she rounded the corner and noticed people milling around by the front doors. She had expected the store to be open, but their sign noted they wouldn't open for another half hour. What was she going to do until then?

She turned away from the front door to check out her options. The shared parking lot of the Book Warehouse boasted a closed teriyaki shop, a shoe store, and a video games store—nothing that appealed to her. Across the street, the bright neon sign of an espresso stand beckoned. After her long night painting and cleaning, a cup of coffee sounded fantastic. She crossed over to the espresso stand and approached the walk-up window. No one appeared to take her order.

"Hello?" she called out.

A teenage girl poked her head out the window. The pink extensions in her platinum blond hair hung over the windowsill. "Oh hi!" she said, with the brightness of someone who'd been imbibing their own wares. "I didn't see you there. We mainly get cars coming through the drive-thru."

"No problem," Dahlia said, as she perused the menu. Concoctions like the Haven Shores Spiced Mocha (with a dash of hot cayenne pepper) would normally appeal to her, but a few hangover effects persisted and she decided on a plainer beverage.

"What can I get you?"

"A triple shot non-fat latte sounds good."

The barista told her the total and she paid cash, leaving a dollar tip in the glass jar on the ledge. She'd done her share of food service as a teenager and she always appreciated it when customers tipped her. The girl smiled and shouted, "Thanks" over her shoulder as she jumped over to the drive-thru side to help a customer who had just rolled up.

Dahlia sipped her drink, relishing the warmth that emanated from the cup. Rain drizzled down from the gray sky, and she covered her head with her purple raincoat's hood to keep her hair from getting frizzy. She walked down the sidewalk, aiming for the covered overhang in front of the distinctive S shape of what used to be a Safeway grocery store.

As she drew closer to the building, she realized it was now an antique store and flea market. Rain leaked through the seams of the metal roof protruding from the building. She pulled on the door's bar handles but they remained tightly closed. She peered through the window and saw displays of fine china, collectibles and furniture. An emerald-green, velvet-covered sofa caught her eye and she hoped the store would be open later in the day. A quick glance at her watch showed the bookstore would open in a few minutes, so she crossed the street to join the expanding crowd at the front door.

At ten o'clock sharp, a Book Warehouse employee unlocked the heavy double doors and stepped aside to allow the crowd to enter. Dahlia hadn't seen that much interest in a store since she went shopping with her mom on Black Friday the year before.

With more trepidation than she expected, she followed the mob into the store. High ceilings and bright lights told her she wasn't in Candle Beach anymore. Shelves of books and reading paraphernalia covered every available inch of space. Uncomfortable, yet stylish, aluminum and vinyl chairs stood next to small tables, discouraging customers from staying too long. Early birds had already claimed the overstuffed armchairs crowded into a few nooks on one side of the store.

She stopped at the cash registers first to ask a question. A man in his twenties stood behind the register. Large discs hung in his ears, dragging his ear lobes down towards his shoulders.

"Can I help you?" He managed to ask his question without looking up from the open comic book on the counter.

"I was hoping you could tell me where I might find the kids' books." She smiled at him in what she hoped was a winning manner.

"Against the back wall." He still didn't turn his attention from the book.

"Do you know if you have anything by local children's book authors?"

"No. I don't know." He sighed. "Ma'am, if you have questions, you need to go to the information desk. We can't look that type of thing up here."

"Okay, where is that?" Dahlia scanned what she could see of the store, but the high bookshelves obscured her view of the information desk.

He sighed again loudly, finally looking up, but not meeting her eyes.

"Past the self-help section, in the middle of the store." He gestured to the far side of the warehouse. "You can't miss it," he said, returning his gaze to the comic.

She left the front of the store and attempted to follow the man's instructions. There were too many people in the store to see the signs well and she soon gave up hope of finding the information desk.

The aroma of freshly ground coffee traveled throughout the store, luring shoppers into the corner café. She allowed herself to be snared in its net. The coffee from the espresso stand had woken her up, but she needed more caffeine to sustain her for the day's adventures. Her stomach grumbled and she selected a bacon and egg English muffin breakfast sandwich to eat from the pastry case. She sat down at one of the two-seater wrought iron café tables and nibbled her food while checking out the store. Even this early on a Saturday morning, business was booming.

From this viewpoint, she could see the fabled information desk. She watched as people used the self-service kiosks. Other customers lined up to ask for help from the single customer service associate behind the information desk's counter. None of the users appeared to be enjoying the experience.

She took out her pad of paper and started making notes. To Be Read didn't have a large in-stock capacity, but what they did have was a dedicated customer service associate, namely her. If she was going to beat the Book Warehouse, she needed to step up the personal aspect of the business.

Shoppers were gathered around one of the tables near the information desk, but she couldn't quite see what it contained. She finished her breakfast sandwich, crumpled the wrapper and tossed it in the trash. Sipping her latte, she made her way over to the crowd. The table held books by a popular local author and a sign on the table noted that the author would make an appearance at the Book Warehouse later in the day. Would author signings work at To Be Read? Could she get authors to come all the way to Candle Beach? She made a note on her notepad and moved on.

Colorful walls and an oversized mural of Curious George led her to the children's section of the store. The immensity of the space dedicated to children's books surprised her. She supposed it shouldn't have shocked her, as books for kids sold well at her store too. Parents needed something to keep their children occupied on rainy days when they couldn't go down to play on the beach.

A table centered between two statues of characters from Dr. Seuss books caught her attention. Typed signs proclaimed this to be the 'Local Authors' table, and different age ranges and genres of children's books were represented. She made a note of the authors, vowing to replicate the display in her own store. Tourists went crazy over anything 'local', and supporting local authors was a nice bonus.

The bright ceiling lights and the outside glare coming through the skylights hurt her eyes. She decided to end her reconnaissance mission and head for the exit. At the check-out, long lines wound around waist-high posts. A man carrying a cane shifted his weight from side to side, and a woman with two small boys struggled to keep them under control. The clerks behind the cash registers called out, "Next" in bored voices and the lines moved forward by a few inches. The twenty-something cashier who'd 'helped' her earlier had put his comic aside and was conversing with an elderly woman, a pained expression on his face.

Dahlia guzzled the remains of her drink, feeling the caffeine surge throughout her body. Tossing the cup in a garbage can next to the security detectors surrounding the double doors, she exited out into the parking lot. Almost every parking space was now occupied, and several cars circled around the entrance hoping for a closer spot. While she could see why people were attracted to the huge selection of books at the Book Warehouse, her small-town bookstore had two important factors that could keep the tourist dollars in Candle Beach: personal attention and a warm atmosphere.

As the doors closed behind her, she grew excited about

the possibilities for To Be Read. Even in summer, sunshine wasn't a guarantee at the coast. If she could make space to expand the children's section, she hoped to draw in more parents searching for something to hold their kids' interest when it rained. While their children checked out the kids' books and perhaps played with some toys, parents could grab a cup of coffee and relax into a comfy chair. She hoped that the longer people spent in the store, the more books they'd buy. But first, she needed to create the intended atmosphere.

New paint, a coffee bar and furnishings would be the first step to making that happen. Across the street, the antique store's 'Open' sign was lit up, and she decided to check out the store's offerings. With any luck, the green sofa would be on sale and she could pick up a few new pieces of furniture without having to dip into Aunt Ruth's savings account. Traffic had picked up in downtown Haven Shores, so she left her car in the Book Warehouse's parking lot and picked her way around puddles and potholes to get over to the antique store.

∾

Unlike the sense of dread Dahlia had experienced when she entered her competition's bookstore, exhilaration and expectation rushed through her as she paused in the doorway of the antique store. As a teenager, she'd haunted thrift and antique stores for the perfect retro dresses for school dances. As she grew older, she had continued shopping for her clothes at such establishments and discovered a love for collectible salt and pepper shakers.

The antique store owners had divided the sizable grocery store building into hundreds of individual compartments in differing dimensions. On one side of the store crafted items reigned, and the other side offered antiques. She made her way past a display of old football memorabilia to the green sofa she'd spotted earlier through the closed glass doors.

It was even more beautiful in person. The crushed emerald-green velvet upholstery dazzled in the sunlight. The tufted back highlighted the sheen of the fabric and the rolled arms provided a sense of fashion that modern furniture lacked. Curved dark wooden feet completed the art deco feel.

"Do you like it?" a woman asked. Hope and pride tinged her voice.

Dahlia turned to see who'd spoken to her. The woman appeared to be in her fifties, but had a carefree air about her. The beginnings of laugh lines had formed on her makeup-free face and a curtain of wavy red hair in a shade not found in nature hung halfway down her back. The woman smiled, and Dahlia felt as though she'd known her for her entire life.

"Yes, it's beautiful." The sofa perfectly represented her own personal style. She ran her hand over the upholstery, marveling at the soft, rich texture. Then she noticed the price scrawled on a white tag hanging from the left arm of the couch. Her heart sank. Buying the beautifully restored antique couch would cost half of her remodeling budget, and she still needed to refinish the hardwood floors, set up an espresso counter and buy another armchair.

"I recovered it and stained the wood myself," the woman said. "It's one of my best pieces, if I do say so myself." She held out her hand. "I'm Wendy Danville."

Dahlia shook her outstretched hand. "I'm Dahlia, nice to

meet you." She stroked the velvety sofa again. "I would love to buy this, but it's out of my price range."

Wendy waved her hand over the sales area and the light glinted off of the half dozen rings she wore. "These are all my creations. Maybe something else would work better for you? What are you looking for?"

"I recently inherited a bookstore up the coast in Candle Beach and I'm doing some redecorating." She gazed wistfully at the green velvet sofa. "This was exactly what I had in mind, but I'm open to other options."

"Ah, Candle Beach," Wendy said. "A beautiful area. I've got family up there."

"Oh, are you from this area?"

"No, I'm from here and there. I like to rent a workspace for a while and work on a few projects. After they sell, I'm off to the next place."

"That must be exciting, getting to see new places all the time." Wanderlust slammed into her, followed rapidly by acid churning in her gut. She'd thought she'd repressed the urge to travel, but now it reared up, ready to lead her on a merry chase. Doubt spun around her. Was she ready to settle down in Candle Beach, even temporarily?

"It is wonderful," Wendy said. "Well, most of the time. Sometimes it can be lonely. But if things aren't so rosy after a while in one place, I can move on to greener pastures. I don't like to stay in one place for too long."

Dahlia said nothing.

"Are you alright?" Wendy asked.

"I'm fine. As a kid, I dreamed of living somewhere else. I always thought when I grew up I'd be free to do what I wanted."

"What is it that you want?" Wendy asked. "You're young; you should go for your dreams."

"That's just it," Dahlia said. "I don't know what my dreams are now. My great-aunt left me her bookstore, and it was her life's passion, but I don't know if it's mine."

Wendy regarded her with eyes full of years of wisdom. "Keep an open mind and you'll find your path."

Dahlia's breath caught. Her mother had said the same thing when she had wondered whether to sell the store.

"Enough of that," Wendy said. "I didn't mean to upset you." She motioned to another piece of furniture in her space, a formal ruby-red brocade sofa with a matching high-back chair. "This set is stylish and would be a fabulous addition to your bookstore. What do you think?"

She stared at the red sofa, but barely saw it. The red set was beautiful, but she couldn't get the green out of her mind. She could see people sitting on it, relaxing with a cup of coffee. It was exactly what she wanted for the store. The trust Aunt Ruth had set up for Dahlia's living expenses provided enough for her basic needs and some wants. It would be tight, but she might be able to use some of those funds to pay for this sofa.

Wendy caught her hesitation.

"Tell you what. I'll sell you the green sofa for the price of the red set. I'll even deliver it to Candle Beach. How does that sound?"

"It sounds great, but why would you sell it for less?" It wasn't the shrewdest business question, but it popped out of her mouth before she could wrangle it back in.

"Like I said, I have family up there and I think it may be time for a visit. And I like you. I think your bookstore is going to be a success and I can't wait to see it when you finish the renovations."

"Okay, then. Thank you so much." Dahlia wasn't going to

look a gift horse in the mouth. "Can you deliver it by Monday?"

"Sure," Wendy said. "I'm thinking about moving on up there this week anyways. My space lease is up in a few days and I'm considering selling at the summer market in Candle Beach for the rest of the summer. A few of my customers have mentioned it. Do you know anything about it?"

"Your furniture would sell well," Dahlia said. "There's a ton of tourists there who own summer homes and they're always looking for new furnishings for their houses."

"What about lodging? Is there a cheap motel with rooms to rent?" Wendy asked. "I suppose I could stay here in Haven Shores, but I'd love to get out of the fleabag motel I've been staying at."

An idea formed in Dahlia's head. "I have the perfect place!"

"Really? What is it?" Wendy cocked her head to the side.

"There's a one-bedroom apartment over the bookstore. The kitchen and bathroom are small, but the bedroom is a nice size. It hasn't been used in years, but it's perfectly livable. I cleaned the whole place last night. There's even space in the back room of the bookstore for you to work on your projects." Well, there wasn't currently space, but she intended to remedy that. The boxes in the hallway needed to find a new home and there were piles of books in storage that hadn't sold since the eighties. It was time for them to go. "What do you think about a trade?" Dahlia asked. "The green sofa for two months' rent?"

"I'll take it. It's been a while since I had a place to cook. I was getting tired of TV dinners warmed up in the motel's microwave or dinners at the local greasy spoon." Wendy's eyes shone. "My horoscope said today would be a fortunate day, but I didn't expect this. Hey, what sign are you?"

Dahlia grinned. "Pisces, why?"

Wendy nodded sagely. "Ah, a water sign. That explains the rainstorm today. And my horoscope said I'd interact with a Pisces today. We must both be having a fortunate day."

Dahlia didn't believe in horoscopes, but to each their own.

"You can move in anytime." She plucked a pen and notepad from her bag, wrote down her address and cell phone number, and handed it to Wendy. "Just call ahead and let me know when you'll be there so I can get everything set up for you."

Wendy smiled, then took a red pen from her pocket and wrote 'Sold' on the green sofa's tag. "I'll see you tomorrow."

Dahlia managed to make it to the next section of the antique store before she danced a few steps. Something about the green sofa spoke to her and made her vision for the bookstore more real. In one of the collectible booths a few spaces down, she found a salt and pepper set in the shape of books. She took it as a sign that things would work out. After paying for the shakers, she left the store, feeling more positive than she had in a long time.

To celebrate her new purchase, she stopped at a cute little café for lunch. She sat by the window and amused herself by making up stories about everyone who passed by. Before she knew it, it was after one o'clock. Lollygagging was fun but there was still so much to do. She paid her bill and hurried to her car.

Next on her agenda was a paint store, where she spent a couple of painstaking hours picking out the perfect shade of aqua for the wall next to the one she'd already painted. In a furniture store, she selected an expensive dark wood bar to use as the espresso area. Her wallet screamed as her money flew out, but she was getting closer to making the bookstore seem more like it belonged to her.

~

After picking up groceries and other odds and ends, Dahlia eased her aching feet back into the car. She sat in the driver's seat and removed her wedge espadrilles to rub her toes. She hadn't planned on walking so much in Haven Shores.

The drizzle that had stuck around all day turned into a downpour, pelting her with droplets of cold rain. She shut the door, turned the ignition and cranked up the heat to defog the windows. The sky had darkened with the storm and she wanted to get home before daylight faded completely. The winding coastal roads weren't fun to drive in ordinary weather conditions, but in a thunderstorm, they were dangerously nasty.

About ten minutes out of Haven Shores, the engine light blinked on again, and stayed on. She groaned and pulled the car over into the entrance of an abandoned logging road. She turned on the emergency blinkers and popped the hood. Taking a deep breath, she opened the door and stepped outside, cringing as the icy rain hit her face. Her hair and clothes were drenched almost immediately. After checking the level of engine oil, she cursed and slammed the hood closed. The mechanics hadn't fixed whatever had caused the Toyota's oil leak, leaving her stuck now on an infrequently traveled two-lane road in the middle of a rainstorm.

One of the few cars she'd seen out on the roads passed by, waterfalls of rain lit up in its headlights. She assessed her options. She could walk back to Haven Shores, but walking over eight miles on a road without sidewalks during a storm didn't sound safe. Then again, hitching a ride wasn't safe either. Her throbbing toes reminded her that she wasn't wearing sensible shoes. Hitchhiking it was.

She stood next to her car, feeling like a drowned rat. A semi flew by going ten mph over the speed limit and she jumped back. She leaned against the trunk of her car, hoping someone would stop.

Then a car rounded the corner and slowed. She moved over to the passenger side, ready to jump in and lock the doors if needed. The vehicle halted and parked behind her with its headlights on. She pushed sopping locks of hair away from her face and held her hand up to shield her eyes. A man stepped out of the car.

When she saw who it was, she half wished it was a serial killer who had stopped.

## 10

"*D*o you need some help?" Garrett shielded his face from the rain with his jacket.

"No, I'm standing out here to see how long it takes before I drown." Dahlia folded her arms over her chest.

"Looks like you've already achieved that," he observed.

She got back into her car and closed the door. Garrett knocked on the window and pantomimed opening the door. She unlocked it and folded her arms across her chest as he sat down in the passenger seat. Her stomach twisted. Why was she being so rude to him? Surely her jealousy had settled by now. It had been one kiss. He was free to talk to whomever he wanted.

The tension in the air was as thick as Maggie's banana cream pie. Her stomach grumbled at the thought of pie. She'd opted to skip dinner in town in favor of making it back to Candle Beach before the sunlight waned. Look how that had turned out.

"Engine trouble?"

"Yes. Stupid mechanics didn't fix it and now I'm out of

oil." She stared straight ahead, not making eye contact with him. This was one more reason for him to think she was irresponsible. She knew she should have checked the oil levels herself, but she'd just had her car fixed three months before. The repair should have lasted longer than that.

"I don't have any oil with me, but I can give you a lift home."

"That would be nice," she said stiffly. "Thank you." She knew she'd been rude to him the night before and she wasn't sure how things stood between them.

"Sure, that's what neighbors are for." He looked at the bags of groceries in the back seat. "Do you need a hand with these?"

She nodded and they each grabbed a few bags and stuffed them in the trunk of his car before she darted in through the passenger door.

They sat in their seats, their drenched clothing dripping onto the cloth upholstery. Garrett turned up the heater, but she still shivered.

"You've got to get out of those clothes." He turned to check out the contents of the backseat. "Here, take off your shirt and put this on." He handed her a fleece zip-front jacket.

She looked at him pointedly and he turned toward his window. Then she peeled off her wet top and pulled the fleece over her head. The men's jacket engulfed her and fell in folds against the car's seat, warming her instantly despite her wet hair.

"Thank you." She leaned forward to catch the heat emanating from the vent.

Garrett turned in his seat and put his hands on the wheel. "Ready?" he asked.

She nodded, burrowing into the comforting warmth of the fleece's collar. The garment smelled like his aftershave, reminding her of how she'd felt with his arms wrapped around her. She surreptitiously took another breath of the tantalizing scent before pushing the collar down and busying herself with drying out her purse. He pulled out onto the highway.

"So what were you doing in Haven Shores today? Just grocery shopping?" The rain pelted the windshield and he increased the wiper speed.

"A few errands," she said noncommittally. She didn't want to get into her plans for renovating To Be Read.

"Have you given any thought to selling the bookstore to me?" he asked. "My offer still stands."

"I won't be selling." She gazed out her window and then over to him.

"Oh." He tightened his grip on the steering wheel. "So you'll be staying in Candle Beach?"

She breathed through her nose. Even if he wasn't interested in her romantically, he'd been nice to pick her up and the least she could do was be civil to him. "I'm planning on staying for the foreseeable future. Actually, I was out buying paint and other supplies to renovate the bookstore." Her hair was still dripping. She brushed a pebble of water off the fleece.

"Look, I think you may have misunderstood my intentions," he said. "I don't want to take your business from you. If it works out for you—great. But if you decide being a small-town bookstore owner isn't your cup of tea, come find me."

Dahlia remembered how she'd felt listening to Wendy talk about the freedom of not being tied down to any one place or job. Her head pounded. Thank goodness Candle Beach was only ten more minutes down the road.

"You think I'm flighty, I get that. And maybe I am, but I'm doing the best I can." She jutted out her chin. "I'm going to renovate the bookstore and make it a success."

"That's great. I'm happy you decided to stay here. And I never said you were flighty," he said in measured tones. "But I grew up with a free-spirited mother and I know how hard it was for her to stay in the same place." He glanced out the window at the angry ocean surf, pounding against the beach. "Heck, I must have attended twenty different schools before I left for college. I never had a chance to make friends or get settled. I vowed never to live like that again. That's why I want to put down roots in Candle Beach."

"I'm not like that," Dahlia said. "I'd never do that to my future children. But that's part of the reason I want to see the world now." Her heart flipped at the thought of future children and she wasn't sure if it was due to being scared about that image, or from the idea of giving up her freedom at that point.

"I'm sure my mom never intended for me to suffer from her actions, but she couldn't help herself. She's not a bad person, but the feelings of others don't rank high on her priority list," Garrett said. "What about your ex-husband? How did he feel about it?"

"We're divorced. That says it all." She looked up at the ceiling. This was the longest car ride of her life. They passed by the overlook where she had first seen Garrett. It seemed like a lifetime ago but had only been three months prior. "I spent my whole marriage compromising on things I wanted to do. After a few years, I'd had enough."

"So he never compromised on things he wanted to do?"

The window had fogged up considerably and he turned the defroster knob to full blast.

"Never," she said, without even thinking about it.

Had he though? She thought back to their honeymoon. Jeff had wanted to tour historic Boston, but she'd insisted on a cruise. He'd given in, although he was terrified of traveling outside of the U.S. When she'd wanted to take art classes, he hadn't seen the point, but he'd offered to take a photography class with her. She'd told him it was the sculpting class or nothing.

"Okay, so maybe it wasn't as bad as I thought at the time," she said grudgingly. "We still weren't meant to be together—we were too different."

"Different isn't always a bad thing," Garrett observed. He expertly piloted the car around what she knew to be Bluebonnet Lake, although in this weather she couldn't see it.

"It is when it keeps a person from getting to do what they want with their life," she said.

"But isn't that how a relationship should work? Two people should grow in their relationship and learn from the other's interests and dreams," he said as they pulled into town.

She leaned back against the headrest, deep in thought. Before she could respond to his comment, he'd parked in front of what she'd always think of as Aunt Ruth's house.

The rain had decreased to a light sprinkle by the time they arrived. She jumped out of the car and he pulled the lever to release the trunk so she could retrieve her groceries. He didn't get out or offer to help. She didn't know if that stemmed from a desire to allow her space or if he was irritated with her.

"Thanks for the ride." She closed the door and waved to him before dashing for the front door. He waited until she had the front door open and then he took off. She watched his tail lights trail away as he drove down the hill to his rental cottage.

It had been a crazy day. Or perhaps, as Wendy had said, a fortunate day. Only time would tell.

## 11

The next morning, after forking over all of her remaining cash to have the tow truck bring her car to the mechanic's garage in Candle Beach, Dahlia settled behind the desk she'd placed in front of the bay window in Aunt Ruth's old bedroom. She hadn't yet worked up the nerve to sleep in there, but she'd moved the hope chest over to the other side of the room and replaced it with a desk to allow her to work from home.

She opened up her aging laptop and tapped her fingers impatiently on the desk while her spreadsheet loaded. As soon as she could, she needed to purchase a faster computer for the store. She reconciled her bank account with the purchases she'd made the day before in Haven Shores and the estimate the mechanic had given her. The result was sobering. Without additional cash, she wouldn't be able to finish the renovation, much less buy a computer.

She pushed the laptop lid closed, resting her hands on the top for a moment as she gazed out the window at the wide expanse of ocean. The waves lapping at the sand had always given her peace in the past, seeming to wash her troubles out to sea. The magic didn't work today. Her thoughts swirled around her like the tide surging through a seastack.

She only had one option, and it wasn't pleasant. Agnes held the purse strings, and to get any additional funds Dahlia would have to request the money from her.

She pushed herself up from the desk and went down to the kitchen to make lunch. Wendy had texted that she'd be in Candle Beach by five p.m. and Dahlia wanted to get a few more things done around the bookstore before she arrived, including moving the boxes that currently blocked the hallway leading to the upstairs apartment.

She filled a kettle with water to make tea and opened the fridge to peruse the contents, but a steady plop, plop sound distracted her. She turned away from the refrigerator to ensure she'd turned the sink handle completely off. She had, but the sound of dripping water continued. Puzzled, she rotated in a circle to seek the source of the sound. Near the back porch, the ceiling sagged in an ominous, widening tan blotch. Beads of water hung from the off-color section and puddled on the floor below. The patch the handyman had installed had started to leak. He'd warned her that it would eventually fail and he wouldn't be able to keep fixing it. She needed a new roof.

The tea kettle hissed and she plopped a tea bag in a cup and filled it with the boiling water. While the tea brewed, she swirled the tea bag around in lazy circles. Yet another thing for which she needed to obtain more money from Agnes. Her appetite had faded. Renting the apartment out for additional cash wasn't even an option anymore. She'd traded two months of rent for the green sofa she had to have for the bookstore. Had it been worth it?

She wanted to say no, but when she pictured the antique

in To Be Read, creating ambiance and solidifying her own personal style, she knew it had been the right choice. But what did she know about Wendy? She'd said that she had family in Candle Beach, but Dahlia knew very little else about her.

She shook her head. What was done was done. Wendy would come to town soon and Dahlia needed to get things together before her new tenant arrived. First she needed to call the roofing company to schedule a roof replacement, and she had to get the money from Agnes.

After getting an appointment on the roofer's schedule, Dahlia called Agnes and arranged to meet her at the Bluebonnet Café at noon. She forced herself to walk down the hill to town. She'd rather go to the dentist and have a cavity filled than meet with Agnes.

At eleven thirty, she placed the last of the boxes against the far wall of the storeroom and surveyed the store. She'd moved loads of books into the clearance section and filled several carts with the unpopular books to be marked down when she reopened on Monday. The hallway was clear and she'd managed to create a moderate-sized workspace for Wendy to work on her furniture projects. She brushed the dust off her hands and tidied her hair in the small bathroom, before reviewing the profit and loss statements the accountant had sent over and a printout of her own spreadsheet detailing her projected expenses for the bookstore remodel. Ironically, for being close to broke, she'd never felt more organized and in control of her financial situation.

When she arrived at the café, she saw Agnes sipping coffee at a two-seat table near the back of the room. *She would probably melt if she sat in the sunlight,* she thought. She waved at Agnes, who simply nodded back to her. As she passed the waitress, she asked her to bring over a cup of coffee.

"I suppose you want more money," Agnes said as a means of greeting, as Dahlia sat across from her.

"Yes, I'm renovating the bookstore and what I need exceeds the monthly stipend I receive from Aunt Ruth's trust." Dahlia pulled out her reports and prepared to show them to Agnes.

"No," Agnes said. "I will not give you any more money."

"But you don't understand," Dahlia said. She pushed her spreadsheet across the table. "Look at what we still need." She pointed at a line item. "At the bare minimum, I need to get the floors refinished, and I'd really like to put in an espresso bar at the back of the store. After I get the proper permits of course," she added, looking pointedly at Agnes.

"You need to make the store work without spending so much money on it. Why, Ruth worked her whole life for that nest egg. You're going to blow it all at once." Agnes shook her head. "I've never met anyone less responsible with money.

Agnes's words stung. Dahlia had worked hard to prepare for this meeting and to develop a plan to improve the bookstore and put her own touch on it.

"You said you wanted me to put effort into the store. Well, I'm doing that. I've got the upstairs apartment ready to rent and I have plans. This is going to work."

"It's going to need to work with what you already have. Figure it out like an adult." Agnes stood and threw three one-dollar bills on the table to cover her coffee.

"Wait. The roof at the house is leaking again," Dahlia said. "Can you at least give me the money to pay to replace it?" The excited energy she'd had yesterday had all been drained out of her body and she hated having to beg for the money to replace the roof.

"Have them send me the bill," Agnes said. She turned and strode out the door without looking back.

Dahlia stared at the old woman's retreating form. Pure exhaustion swept through her body. How had she thought going to her was a good idea? More so, how had she thought managing the bookstore herself was a good idea? Agnes was never going to let her succeed. She had a vested interest in the bookstore failing. Aunt Ruth had trusted Agnes with her hard-earned money, and this was how she'd been repaid.

"More coffee?" The waitress held up the coffee pot.

"No, I'm good, thanks." The waitress left and she pulled a few dollars out of her purse to cover the coffee. She set the money under the sugar packet holder and left the restaurant.

She entered the bookstore and walked through to the back room in a daze. Feeling defeated, she sat in Aunt Ruth's desk chair and surveyed her surroundings with tears clouding her vision. How was she going to make this work? She remembered her grandmother's advice to sleep on problems, so she left a note for Wendy at the bookstore with her phone number and walked home to take an afternoon nap.

~

Sleep brought nothing but a nightmare about Agnes flying overhead on a broomstick, trying to steal books from the store. Dahlia forced herself to get out of bed after an hour and make coffee. She had to make a decision. Stay in Candle Beach, or return home? Fortified by caffeine, she called Agnes to concede defeat.

"May I speak with Agnes, please?" Dahlia asked in a manner more formal than necessary since she knew she lived alone.

"This is Agnes."

"This is Dahlia. I'm sure this news will devastate you, but I'm leaving Candle Beach. The bookstore is yours. I'll drop the keys off at the property management company later today." She blinked back tears, grateful that Agnes couldn't see her face through the phone line. "Please let the lawyer know when you're ready to settle my share of the estate."

Agnes was silent for a moment. "I'm sorry to hear this. Your aunt wanted you to have the bookstore." She hung up.

Dahlia held the phone away from her ear. Was that an apology of some sort? Or another insult? Agnes had sounded sincere, but she'd done nothing but make Dahlia's life miserable since she'd arrived in town three months earlier. She put the phone back in its cradle and stood. The mechanic had promised to have her car fixed by Monday so she could get the food permit from the county. At least she didn't have to worry about the permit anymore. Her to-do list was full enough already if she wanted to leave town by the next day.

She shoved her clothes into the first of her two suitcases and collected her toiletries from the bathroom. She didn't have any place to go, but she knew she couldn't stay in Candle Beach, not with Agnes there. Her mother would probably take her in, or even her father if he was in town. She had options. None made moving home with her tail between her legs sound any better than it was.

In the bathroom, she found Garrett's fleece that she'd hung on the towel rod to dry. The black jacket mocked her. She'd seen Candle Beach as a place to start over with life. From the moment she'd arrived in town, she'd been battered by rejection—from Garrett, from Agnes, and from life in general. She fixated on the jacket. It represented everything that had gone wrong. She pulled it down, causing the hanger to spin crazily and clatter to the tile floor.

She ran down the stairs and grabbed her keys from the rack by the front door, gripping Garrett's fleece as if her life depended on it. She may not be able to save the bookstore, but returning the fleece would give her a sense of closure with him.

She marched down the hill to his rental cottage, refusing to let the town break her completely. Even though things hadn't worked out in Candle Beach, the time she spent there had given her the space she needed to change her life. Maybe it was time to get a full-time job and more permanent living space back in Seattle. After living in Aunt Ruth's light-filled house with its expansive ocean views, the idea of moving back to a basement apartment with few windows gave her the creeps.

That reminded her—she needed to tell Agnes about the rental arrangement with Wendy. She was not looking forward to that conversation.

～

Dahlia stopped in front of Garrett's cottage to remove a pebble from her sandal. She'd never seen his home close-up before. It was a charming seafoam-green Craftsman bungalow, surrounded by a white picket fence. White dormers peeked from the roofline above a roomy porch. Candle Beach had been built in the early 1900s and this house must have been original to the town. It didn't suit him, or at least how she thought of him.

In the flower bed below the porch, marigolds and blue-bonnets swayed in the slight breeze. Fuchsias trailed down the sides of baskets hung from the porch ceiling. This cottage had been built at a lower elevation than Aunt Ruth's house, but still offered a stunning ocean view.

What was she doing? She wasn't here to admire the flowers or the view. She unlatched the gate and walked up the stairs.

She rapped on the door three times with her knuckles then cocked her head to the side to listen for the sound of approaching footsteps, but none came. Good. Without Garrett home, she'd be back to packing in no time.

The fleece dragged her arm down like a weight. It had to go. She tried the brass doorknob, which turned easily. Thank goodness for small-town naiveté. She opened the door with the intention of leaving the fleece on the first available surface.

It couldn't hurt to take a look around while she was there though, right? Once inside, she did a double take. *Whoa*. Any crocheted-doily-loving grandma would be at home in his lair. She'd assumed his style would be dark and contemporary.

That couldn't have been further from the truth. He'd left every curtain open, flooding the front rooms with sunlight. Purple African violets flourished in special clay pots on the windowsills and tall white bookshelves covered a full wall in the living room. In the corner of the room, she spotted a desk covered with papers. Rumors had circulated around town about what type of books Garrett wrote. Saul at the Bike Barn even had a betting pool going, with the general consensus being he must be a suspense writer with his quiet, mysterious persona. The computer's screen was dark, but in between a cup of tea and the keyboard lay a sheaf of printed manuscript pages. The neatly typed sheets drew her closer. She reached out her hand to pick them up, but hesitated. Should she look? Curiosity won out.

The header of each page provided the title and the author's name. She read it and laughed out loud. Her snooping had been in vain. She'd thought she'd found a piece of Garrett's next novel, but the manuscript didn't belong to him. He must have been reading it for a friend. Why would the reigning queen of romance want him to provide feedback on her work? Was he involved with her in some way? She set the papers back down in the same neat pile and in the process of doing so, accidentally jarred the computer mouse with her hand.

The screen flickered and lit up. The novel's title in the header, the same as in the printed draft, drew her attention. But the author had stopped typing mid-sentence on this draft. Her eyes widened. Was this Garrett's novel? Her lips twisted into an ironic smile. Too bad she planned to leave town. A secret this juicy would have been fun to hold over him.

A breeze flowed through the room, fluttering the pages. She glanced over her shoulder.

## 12

"What are you doing in my house?" Garrett asked.

Dahlia turned around to face him. Icy guilt shot through her body like venom, immobilizing her feet in place. "Uh..."

He looked past her at the illuminated computer screen. "I see you've discovered my secret identity."

"*You're* Susannah Garrity?" She couldn't keep the incredulous tone out of her voice.

"Guilty as charged," he said. "I don't usually tell people because my publisher likes to keep it under wraps. Apparently women don't think men can write about romance."

Dahlia turned pink. She'd made the same assumption. "I never would have guessed."

"What, you don't think I can do romance?" His eyes twinkled with mirth.

"It wasn't top of my list of genres I'd expect you to write."

"Well, I'll have to change your impression of me." He locked his eyes with hers, his gaze full of promise.

The ice in her veins warmed considerably.

"So what are you doing in my house?"

"I came to return your fleece." Her words tumbled out faster than she could think. "I accidentally bumped your computer. I didn't mean to invade your privacy." She crossed her fingers at the little white lie.

"You accidentally bumped my computer? Which was five feet away from where you left the sweater?" He looked pointedly at the fleece and then back to her.

She tried to edge her way out of the room, but he planted his feet in a wide stance in the entryway, his arms folded across his chest. She wasn't getting out of this one unscathed.

"I didn't mean to discover your pen name." She stared into his eyes, hoping he'd believe her. In truth, she hadn't been trying to uncover his secret identity, only the type of books he wrote. "It doesn't really matter. I'm not staying in town, so don't worry about me telling anyone else. Your secret is safe with me."

He stopped trying to hide his amusement behind a frown and dropped his arms to his sides. "What do you mean you aren't staying in town? You had all those plans for the bookstore."

"Yeah, well, those plans required money from Aunt Ruth's trust, which Agnes isn't prepared to let me have. Without the money, I can't remodel the bookstore and I can't make the business profitable or competitive with the Book Warehouse." She shrugged. "I'm out."

"Where are you going?"

"I'm heading back to Seattle tomorrow," she said. He stepped aside and she walked past him to the open doorway. "It was nice knowing you."

"That's it?" he asked. "You're just giving up on your life here? What do you plan to do back in Seattle?"

She hesitated at the door, curling her fingers around the

outer door jam.

"Come back in and we can talk about it." He leaned against the wall and gestured to the chair across from him.

"I don't know what I'm going to do in Seattle." She stepped back into the room and plunked herself down in the armchair. "All I know is that I'm failing miserably here and I can't change anything about the terms of the trust. Anything has to be better than that."

"Are you sure Agnes won't let you have money to remodel the store? There has to be a way to fix this," he said. "I haven't known her that long, but she never struck me as unreasonable."

"Not unreasonable?" Dahlia echoed. "She's more than unreasonable. She's downright antagonistic about anything to do with the store. She was Aunt Ruth's best friend, but she's taking the trustee thing too far. I can't get her to release any funds because she thinks she's protecting Aunt Ruth's legacy." She pushed herself up from the chair and paced between the coffee table and the front door. Her sandals slapped against the floor with every step.

"What she doesn't realize is Aunt Ruth's legacy is the bookstore and her role in the community. Which I'm trying to protect by making To Be Read a viable business again."

His gaze followed her, but he didn't say a word. She continued her diatribe.

"After Aunt Ruth died, I gave up my job and everything I had to move here. That counts for nothing with Agnes. I can't win. She hates me and will never see me as anything but a selfish teenager."

"It seems like you're running away," Garrett said. "Are there any other options to get the money you need?"

"No, there's not, and I'm not running away," she said. "There comes a point when no matter how hard you try, you can't make things better." She walked over to the door again. Why did he have to come home? If he hadn't returned, she'd be home packing right now, instead of having this conversation.

"If you change your mind, my offer to help still stands. I can help you brainstorm ways to increase sales at To Be Read. I used to work for a marketing agency and I've picked up a few useful tricks along the way. I'd be happy to help you."

She nodded. "Thanks, but I don't think I'll be needing your help." She tipped her head up to the side. "Actually, there is something," she said. "Are you still interested in buying the bookstore?"

"I'm open to that, but I think you're doing a great job. You've come a long way since I first met you." He followed her to the entryway. "But it's your choice, of course."

"I'll have the lawyer get in touch with you about buying the bookstore," she said. "Goodbye." Tears pearled in the corners of her eyes, but she eked out a smile and closed the door. The disappointment etched across his face would haunt her forever. She remained on the porch and allowed the pain to wash over her like the waves on the sand below. She didn't want to leave like this, not when she wasn't sure of her feelings for him. But she suspected they were growing toward something important if just the thought of not seeing his face again made her so maudlin. If she left, it would be the final nail in the coffin for them. She breathed in the familiar flower- and salt-tinged air before she plodded down the steps and back up the hill to Aunt Ruth's house.

She'd meant what she said to Garrett. She'd failed. This had been her chance to create a new life for herself as a business owner. Back home, she'd been an assistant at a travel agency, a part-time one at that. In the last three months, she had transformed into someone unrecognizable, but in a good way. Sharp pains knifed her stomach. Starting over wouldn't be fun.

She reached Aunt Ruth's house and nostalgia wafted over her as strongly as it had when she'd first returned to Candle Beach. Would she ever come back here again? Or would it only be a memory, a blip in her personal timeline? No doubt, Agnes would be quick to sell the house and pocket the proceeds. How was there not a 'For Sale' sign in the front yard yet? She'd conceded defeat to Agnes over an hour ago.

She entered the house and nestled in the thick cushions of Aunt Ruth's living room couch. Images of a lifetime spent in the house flitted across her mind like a movie, from jumping off the couch as a toddler, to late-night movie marathons with Aunt Ruth, all the way to more recent memories of girls' night gabfests with Maggie and Gretchen. A photograph of Aunt Ruth and Uncle Ed hung on the wall above the TV. Normally, Aunt Ruth's image comforted her, but today, she avoided it.

If she wanted to get things wrapped up at the bookstore by evening, she needed to finish the packing. She planned to leave early the next day for Seattle. The faster she got out of Dodge, the fewer questions she'd be asked about her future plans. With the exponential power of gossip in Candle Beach, who knew how many people would hear of her departure by morning. It didn't matter though. She'd made up her mind and no one could make her stay.

∼

Dahlia was ensconced in the back office of To Be Read when she heard knocking at the front door of the bookstore. The

'Open' side of the sign had been turned toward her, so it shouldn't be a customer. She peeked around the door to see who had knocked.

Darn it. She should have expected this. Gretchen and Maggie peered in through the window with their hands cupped against the glass. She tried to back away from the door before they saw her, but they spotted her and jumped up and down, waving their hands like crazed fans at a rock concert. She knew she'd eventually need to tell them she planned to leave, but she'd hoped to do so at the last minute. Confrontations terrified her, and she knew they wouldn't understand her reasons for leaving.

She dragged her feet all the way to the front door and turned the deadbolt.

Gretchen burst over the threshold, her eyes flashing. "When were you planning to tell us you were leaving?"

Dahlia sighed and opened the door wide enough to allow them to enter. "I decided a few hours ago. I haven't had a chance to tell you yet. News travels fast in this town."

"Agnes told the Ladies right after you called her and they spread it around town. Gossip doesn't keep for long here," Maggie said as she followed Gretchen inside. "For once though, I'm glad they did. Gretchen is right—were you going to tell us?"

Maggie's eyes misted over and motherly concern filled her face. Her son, Alex, was a lucky kid to have her for a mom.

"What happened?" Gretchen asked.

"Yeah. You were so excited at the wine bar on Friday night," said Maggie. "What changed your mind?"

Dahlia led them over to the seating area that she'd rearranged in preparation for the remodel. They sat down in the armchairs and Dahlia pulled the tall stool out from behind the front desk and brought it over to their circle. Her friends waited in silence for her to speak.

"I was excited." She perched on the stool and thought for a moment. Things had happened so quickly and she didn't know where to start. She had experienced a roller-coaster of emotions over the last few days. "I went into Haven Shores to check out the Book Warehouse and figure out how I could compete with them. I picked out new furniture for the bookstore and had so many plans for To Be Read."

She stopped to make a mental note. Talking about the sofa reminded her she still needed to explain Wendy's lease of the upstairs apartment to Agnes. She couldn't keep avoiding it and she hoped Agnes would be reasonable about honoring the lease. After promising the space to Wendy, she couldn't renege on the deal, even if she wouldn't be around for Wendy's tenancy.

"Everything got to be so expensive." She slumped on the stool. "I figured out I'd need to have Agnes give me at least five thousand dollars out of the trust to finish the remodel." She nodded at the back wall where she'd pulled the tea area away from the wall. "I'm guessing the coffee bar alone will cost several thousand between the additional plumbing and the bar itself. It would have been so cool though." That reminded her—she needed to cancel the furniture delivery. She gazed wistfully at the space. For a brief instant, the bookstore filled with the aroma of brewing coffee and the chatter of customers.

"Okay. So did she give you the money?" Gretchen said, shattering Dahlia's vision. She leaned forward in her seat to hear Dahlia's response.

"No," Dahlia answered. "She refused to give me anything. She said I needed to work with what I had already and that Aunt Ruth wouldn't have wanted me to waste money."

Maggie spoke up. Her voice shook and a slow fire burned in her eyes. "This is exactly what Ruth would have wanted. She knew how important the bookstore was to the community and it was her life's work. She would have wanted it to grow and for you to do what you needed to do to make that happen."

"That's what I thought too." Dahlia pulled a tissue out of her pocket and dabbed at her eyes.

"So what now?" Gretchen asked. "You're just giving up on it?"

Dahlia had no patience left. Garrett had questioned her about her reasons for leaving and now her friends were too. It wasn't her choice to leave. Agnes had given her no choice in the matter.

She looked at Maggie. "When you and Alex moved back to Candle Beach after your husband died, your family took you in and helped support you until you could get back on your feet."

Then she turned to her other friend. "And Gretchen, you moved back here after college, knowing there was always room for you at your parents' real estate company. Not everyone has family they can depend on when things get tough. My mother has her job in Seattle and I don't want to ask her for the money. I've been the screw-up daughter for too long. Getting money from Agnes was my only opportunity to make this work."

She regretted her outburst as soon as the words were out of her mouth. Maybe her friends weren't offended. But one look at them and her heart sank. Maggie's lips were pressed into a thin line and she had furrowed her brow. Her fingers twisted together in her lap. Gretchen stared at

Dahlia, her face stony as she traced a circle on the floor with her feet.

"It took a lot of hard work on my part too," Maggie said in a level voice. "I wasn't exactly lounging around at my parent's house, watching TV all day."

"That's not what I'm saying," Dahlia said. She put her head in her hands. She'd royally messed this up. How was she going to get them to understand her predicament? They'd both grown up in Candle Beach and had the support of the community. Everything for her seemed to be an uphill battle. She turned to Gretchen, who said nothing.

At last, Gretchen spoke. "You have us."

She rose from her seat and hugged Dahlia. Dahlia smiled faintly as she attempted to hold back tears. Having good friends was one of the things she'd miss the most about living in Candle Beach. She had difficulty staying in touch with people when not in frequent contact with them. If she wasn't careful, when she moved back to Seattle, they'd probably return to being nothing more than friends on social media.

Maggie got up from her seat as well and joined in the group hug. "Gretchen's right. If there's anything we can do, please tell us."

"Unless one of you has thousands of dollars lying around, there's not much you can do to help," Dahlia said.

"Sorry, I can barely make my rent as is," Gretchen said. "I wish there was something I could do."

"I could probably pull together some money, but the café has me pretty tapped out," Maggie said.

Dahlia shook her head. "No, I couldn't let you do that. You've got a kid to support. This is my mess and my decision to make."

Maggie nodded and relief passed across her face.

"Thanks, you guys," Dahlia said. "I'll miss you both so much."

They made plans to meet for breakfast the next morning before Dahlia left, then Gretchen and Maggie exited the bookstore, pulling the door closed behind them. Dahlia had never felt so alone, not even in the days and weeks following her divorce.

She walked back through the bookstore to the office and sat down in Aunt Ruth's chair, spinning around in a lazy circle while dragging her feet on the carpet. This couldn't be the end. Planning the bookstore remodel had filled her with joy and a sense of purpose. Had she made the right decision to leave?

She put her feet down flat on the ground. Living in Candle Beach had changed her. Wallowing in self-pity and doubting her abilities wouldn't help. There was still a lot of life left to live, even if it didn't involve To Be Read or Candle Beach.

She organized the financial files she'd created and straightened the desktop. When Agnes took over management of the store before she sold it, she wouldn't find anything to disapprove of in how Dahlia had left things.

She returned to the sales floor for a final look around. What would Garrett do with the store if he bought it? Would he continue with her plans for an espresso bar or children's area? What would his displays look like? Her eye caught on a Susannah Garrity book facing out from the shelf and she grinned. Who would have thought Garrett was a bestselling romance author? Even though she now knew his secret identity, he remained a mystery to her. She would have liked to stay in Candle Beach to get to know him better.

"Hello?" A woman's voice came from behind her. Dahlia

whirled around. She'd forgotten to lock the door after her friends left.

"We're closed," she called out as she walked into the front room of To Be Read. Where were these customers when she was open for business? Irrational irritation shot through her body, but faded when she saw the perky face that peeked around the open door.

## 13

"Oh, Wendy. You made it," Dahlia said.

"Sorry, the door was open. Should I come back later to see the apartment?"

"No, come in, you're fine. I thought you were a customer." She motioned for Wendy to enter.

She breezed in through the door and embraced her, a cloud of flowery perfume following in her wake. "Oh good, I was hoping you'd be here. I lost your phone number, so I couldn't call when I left Haven Shores. I'm so glad to see you and be here. Candle Beach is such a beautiful town." She beamed at Dahlia. She'd piled her red hair into a ponytail and looked even younger than the day before. "Where should I park the truck to unload my stuff?"

"The truck?" She looked through the open front door at the white panel truck parked outside the bookstore. It took up two parking spaces and stuck out into the street. A car honked as it swerved around the truck's back end. Parking for a large truck hadn't come up in their brief rental discussion. Why hadn't it occurred to her that Wendy would have a truck to transport her furniture? Delivery trucks didn't usually stick around town after dropping off their loads and finding parking in downtown Candle Beach for the over-sized vehicle would be tricky.

"Uh, you can pull it around to the alley to unload," Dahlia said. "I'll go open the back door." They'd deal with the parking issue later.

"Thanks!" Wendy bounced out of the bookstore, her ponytail bobbing behind her. Dahlia hoped she'd have half of her energy when she reached that age.

In a few minutes, Wendy had the truck parked next to the bookstore in the back alley. Dahlia watched as she exited the vehicle, pulled open the back of the truck and lowered the ramp.

"Do you need help?"

"That would be great," Wendy said. "Your sofa weighs a ton. They don't make furniture nowadays like they used to."

The two women edged the sofa out of the truck and into the store using a furniture dolly and a lot of elbow grease. Wendy moved the stool Dahlia had used earlier out of the way and lined the sofa up perpendicular to the two existing armchairs.

"It's beautiful," Dahlia said. The emerald-green velvet sofa lit up the bookstore and provided the charm she'd hoped for. Painful slivers twisted in her chest. Someone else would get to enjoy the sofa. Would the new owner keep it in the store?

Wendy brushed her hands off and looked around. "Quite a place you have here. I see you've been doing some painting." She motioned to the wall Dahlia had painted Friday night.

"Yeah, I wanted to add some color in here."

"I think it's fabulous. This place will look great when you're done."

She smiled, but her heart wasn't in it. How was she going to tell Wendy that she wouldn't be around to see the completion of the remodel?

"Let me show you to the upstairs apartment." Dahlia led the way to the back staircase and they ascended the steep stairs.

"Oh my, it's nicer than I expected." Wendy immediately ran over to the open window to check out the view. "I can see the ocean from here." Wendy hugged Dahlia. "I love it!"

She twirled around and clapped her hands like a child. She strode from room to room, the smile on her face growing wider with each step.

"I knew it was fate when we met," she exclaimed. She hugged Dahlia again. It should have been odd to be hugged by a stranger, but it felt natural coming from Wendy. Her exuberance was contagious.

"Do you have a lot to carry in?" Dahlia asked.

"Not too much. I try to travel light. Then I'm free to go wherever I want." They went down the stairs and out to her truck. Wendy grabbed a few bags from the truck and deposited them in the back storeroom.

"Where should I park the truck now that I'm done unloading?" Wendy asked.

Dahlia assessed the options. "There's a small parking lot across the street. Your truck should fit there."

Late on a Sunday afternoon, most of the day tourists would be on their way home, leaving parking spaces available. She crossed her fingers. Wendy thanked her and hopped in her vehicle.

Dahlia's good mood faded after Wendy left and she remembered her predicament. She entered the office and sat down in Ruth's chair. She pulled out her cell phone and dialed Agnes.

"Hello, this is Agnes."

Dahlia's spine straightened, as if ready to be scolded by a teacher. She couldn't say anything.

"Hello?" Agnes said again.

"It's Dahlia." She paused. How was she going to tell Agnes about Wendy? Finally, she blurted out, "I rented the apartment in trade for some furniture. The new tenant, Wendy, moves in today. She's really nice." There was no response from Agnes.

"Uh, she moves out at the end of September. Then you can do whatever you want with the space."

"I see," Agnes said. "I take it you still plan to abandon the bookstore Ruth left you? You know, she thought it would mean something to you."

What, so now Agnes thought she should stay? The woman confounded her. Dahlia's blood had reached boiling point.

"I'm leaving because you've straitjacketed me. I can't improve the bookstore, and without improvements, I can't compete with the Book Warehouse in Haven Shores. If you hadn't noticed from the financial reports, sales are down since the mega bookstore opened last month."

"Dahlia, I think—"

"You can disapprove of me all you want, but I'm leaving tomorrow. I hope you can make the bookstore successful." She hung up. She truly did wish for the bookstore to regain profitability. Ruth would have wanted that. But enough was enough. Agnes couldn't control her anymore.

Behind her, the back door clicked open as Wendy let herself in. She climbed the stairs with her two bags, her luggage knocking against the walls with every step.

"Let me know if you need anything," Dahlia called out to her.

"I will. Thanks again." The door at the top of the stairs banged shut.

Her residual anger toward Agnes made the office walls feel like they were closing in on her. She placed a key and a note for Wendy at the foot of the stairs, grabbed a sketchpad and left the store, locking the front door behind her.

Unlike the rainy day before, the weather was sunny and warm, a perfect July day. Dahlia passed through the middle of town on her way down the hill to the beach access, but didn't allow her thoughts to dwell on any part of the town. She paused for a moment at the overlook. It seemed like a lifetime ago that she'd stopped there and gazed at Candle Beach in the distance. And longer than that since she'd met Garrett. She shook her head to clear away any lingering thoughts of him and descended the stairs to the beach below.

The tide was out and she had to walk several hundred feet from the base of the stairs to the compacted wet sand. On impulse, she pulled off her sandals and flung them up to dry ground. She rolled the cuffs of her Capri pants up above her knees and sprinted into the water.

The freezing water rushed against her ankles and shins, splashing droplets onto her pants. The warm sun beat down on her as she waded in the shallows. Pebbles swirled around her bare toes as the waves flowed in and out.

Things had to get better, right? She'd find a job in Seattle and an apartment. Anything had to be an improvement over the place she'd lived in before moving to Candle Beach.

Near the creek that came off of Bluebonnet Lake, a small child ran amongst the waves, chasing a golden retriever. The girl's giggles carried over the roar of the ocean. Had she ever been as carefree as that child? She'd always prided herself on being a free spirit, but had she ever truly been free?

Although she didn't like to admit it, she'd always been chained to a job, an apartment, or a relationship that didn't bring her joy. Being in Candle Beach made her happy. She sat down in the dry sand and raised her face to the sun, basking in its warmth. Grabbing her sketchpad, she quickly drew the little girl, but couldn't quite capture her carefree attitude. She dropped the pen and paper to the ground and lay back to relax against the firm sand.

With the sand cradling her in its comforting embrace, her mind wandered to To Be Read. It was a pity that all her hard work would go to waste. There was still so much to do at the bookstore. But it wasn't her problem anymore. After the store sold, she'd be lying on a beach on the French Riviera instead of on the Washington Coast.

As much as she wanted to enjoy daydreaming about the future, she found herself dwelling on the store. *Darn it!* She'd forgotten to move a new carton of books out of the storage area to the 'to be shelved' area. The books would be mixed in with the old books and not be available for customers to buy.

She tried to push the thought out of her mind, but the concern over the buried books ricocheted around her brain until she had to act. She sat up, brushed the sand off her body, and retrieved her sandals. Being responsible wasn't all it was cracked up to be.

When she arrived at the bookstore, she unlocked the front door and stepped inside. Two women's voices drifted down the stairwell from the upstairs apartment. She tiptoed up the stairs and stopped at the top to listen. One of the voices was Wendy's. The other was even more familiar. At the sound of the other voice, tension spiraled up through her muscles, super-charging her nerve endings. She pushed the apartment door open.

～

"What are you doing here?" Dahlia leaned against the door-frame and folded her arms against her chest.

The women sat at the kitchen table, her mother with her back to the door. At the sound of Dahlia's voice, Vanessa turned around and smiled at her daughter.

"Dahlia," she said. "I'm glad to see you." She'd traded one of her many power suits for a matching turquoise yoga pants and jacket set. Her ensemble would allow her to blend in well with the tourist crowd.

Why was her mother in Candle Beach? Vanessa hadn't set foot in town since Aunt Ruth died. She'd talked about taking some vacation time over the summer, but a big opportunity had come up at work and she couldn't take the time off. Now she was suddenly in town?

Dahlia thought she knew why.

"Would you like a cup of tea?" Wendy gestured at the two teacups on the table. "I picked up some muffins from the Bluebonnet Café too. They look delicious." She held out a blueberry muffin sprinkled with chunky sugar crystals.

Dahlia's stomach rumbled. "No thank you," she said to Wendy, and turned to face the other woman. "Mom, what are you doing here?" Her eyes drilled holes into her mother's face as she fought to control her speech.

"I came to see you," said Vanessa. "Let's go downstairs." She nodded at Wendy. "Thank you for the drink and chat. It was nice to meet you."

Wendy smiled back at her and stood to clear the table.

Vanessa and Dahlia walked down the stairs in silence. At the foot of the stairs, Dahlia turned to her and asked again in a hushed whisper, "Mother, why are you here?"

"A little birdie told me you planned to leave Candle

Beach and sell the bookstore." Vanessa regarded her daughter shrewdly. "Is that true?"

Dahlia's shoulders slumped. How had she heard about this already? She hadn't planned to say anything until she was back in Seattle with another failure on the books. The long arms of the Candle Beach town gossip machine reached further than she had expected.

"Yes," Dahlia said. "I'm leaving town."

"But honey, you sounded so happy when we spoke on the phone yesterday. What happened?"

"Agnes happened."

Her mother shot her a quizzical look. "Agnes Barnes? What does she have to do with it?"

"She won't loan me the money to remodel the bookstore," said Dahlia. She picked up a stray book off a box and put it in a pile with some others to be shelved. "I don't have any savings to draw from and the monthly stipend from Aunt Ruth's trust isn't enough to cover everything I want to do. Without the trust money, I'm stuck. The way things are currently, the bookstore can't compete with the big box and online stores. My only hope was to create an inviting space for the community and cross my fingers that doing so brought in sales."

"Okay," her mother said slowly. "So Agnes wouldn't give you the money. Did you think of any other options? Maybe scale back plans?"

She took Vanessa's hand and led her into the main bookstore. She pointed at the area where she had planned to build the espresso bar. "Look, that's where the espresso bar would go. And over there—the children's area. And a new seating area here." Her enthusiasm built as she detailed her plans.

She flopped onto the new velvet couch and ran her

hands over the softness of the material. "I bought this from Wendy. Didn't she do a beautiful job reupholstering it?"

Her mother smiled and took a seat next to Dahlia. "She mentioned she worked on furniture, but she didn't say anything about this piece. It does seem to brighten up the bookstore."

"Not that it matters anymore." Dahlia leaned against the side of the sofa. "Do you understand now? This place needs some major work. Without it, To Be Read is going to go under—sooner rather than later. I don't see any way around it."

"You could have asked your father or me for a loan."

"I didn't want to ask you for money. I'm an adult. I shouldn't have to beg my parents for money."

"So instead you're running away from your responsibilities like a child."

"That's not what I'm doing." Dahlia stood and paced the seating area. "You know it's not."

"Well, from my point of view, that's exactly what you're doing," Vanessa said. "Things have gotten tough and you want to take the easy way out."

"I want to take my half of the settlement from the bookstore and Aunt Ruth's house and travel around the world. It's what I've always wanted to do. I'm not running away from Candle Beach or my problems, I'm following my dreams."

"You worked at a travel agency for years and you never took a vacation," her mother said wryly. "That indicates that travel isn't a huge priority of yours."

"That's not fair. I didn't have money to travel."

"If it was important enough, you would have found a way to make it happen." Vanessa's eyes met hers. "Look, you've been following this pattern for your whole life. When things get difficult, you run away and leave your problems behind.

You changed your college major four times because you didn't like what you had to do to graduate. You've worked countless jobs since you finally received your diploma." She paused, then said in a low voice, "When your marriage got too difficult, you didn't go to counseling or work on your relationship. You left at the first chance you had."

"You should talk. Your relationship with Dad during the divorce made me miserable," Dahlia said. "Why do you think I run? You were always fighting. Coming to Candle Beach for the summer was the only chance I had to get away from it."

"I admit your father and I didn't handle our divorce as well as possible. We were too focused on ourselves and not on you and how our fighting affected you. We thought sending you to Aunt Ruth in Candle Beach was the best thing for you." Vanessa stared at the floor for a moment and then gazed up at Dahlia. Tears glistened in her eyes. "I'm truly sorry we hurt you."

Dahlia was quiet for a moment. She knew her parents' divorce had been difficult for her, but until this moment, she hadn't realized how much it had affected her in childhood and into adulthood. "I know you didn't mean to hurt me," she acknowledged softly and offered a small smile.

Vanessa wrapped her arms around her. "I'm so sorry." She repeated and patted her back, just as she had when she'd been a child.

Dahlia relaxed against her and sighed. It had been a long time since they'd had a close mother–daughter moment.

After a minute, Vanessa pulled away and held her at arm's length. "So what do we do about the bookstore?" she asked. "Aunt Ruth wanted you to have it. We had many long conversations about you and to be honest, she was worried about the trajectory of your life. She thought this was the best thing for you—a chance to be a business owner and have a life of your own here in Candle Beach."

"Aunt Ruth was worried about me? I wasn't a last resort for her?"

Dahlia knew her mom had spent quite a bit of time with Aunt Ruth before her death, but she'd never really considered that they may have conspired together to leave her the bookstore.

"No honey, she wanted you to have it." Vanessa hugged Dahlia again. "So what do you think? Do you want to be a small-town bookstore owner?"

Did she? She wasn't sure. Her mother had been correct in her assessment of her tendency to run when things grew tough. Was her dream to travel another excuse? Or was it her true passion?

She looked around the bookstore and something bubbled up inside of her. Owning the bookstore had incited a feeling inside of her that she had never experienced before. Maybe a sense of pride, but definitely excitement for the future.

"So what do you suggest I do?"

"How much money do you think you need?"

She showed her mother the financials and her plans for the bookstore.

"You've put a lot of effort into this," she said, with a hint of surprise.

Dahlia shrugged. "I didn't want to be unprepared when I asked Agnes for the money."

Vanessa pulled out her checkbook and scribbled on a check. "Here you go," she said, handing it to Dahlia.

Dahlia hesitated for a moment. "This is more than I need."

"Remodeling costs have a way of exceeding the best of estimates. Remember my weekend patio project that turned into a full backyard remodel?"

She grinned. Her mother's projects had a tendency to explode in scope. "When do I need to pay it back?"

"You can pay it back if you'd like, but consider it a gift. I want to see the bookstore and you succeed just as much as you do." Vanessa smiled. "Remember, I grew up with Aunt Ruth and Uncle Ed. I know how important this place was to them. It was part of my childhood after my parents died and I came to live with them in Candle Beach, the same as it was a refuge for you when your father and I divorced."

Dahlia took the check and put it in her pants pocket. "Thank you, Mom. You have no idea how much this means to me."

Vanessa put her arm around her waist and pulled her close. "I'm hungry. That was a long drive and I haven't had anything today except Wendy's tea and a blueberry muffin. The Bluebonnet Café?"

"Sounds great. I'm famished too," she said. "*Ooh*, and you've got to try the new shrimp risotto special. Maggie's been trying out new recipes to attract the summer tourists."

"Sold. I'm a sucker for anything with shrimp." Vanessa followed her out the door.

As Dahlia navigated the few blocks to the Bluebonnet Café on autopilot, she mentally assessed her to-do list. If she wasn't going to leave town, she needed to make the bookstore profitable. Contacting Garrett occupied the top spot on her list. She planned to take him up on his offer to help promote the bookstore. Their last encounter had been awkward, but he was her best chance at success.

Making a go of To Be Read wouldn't be easy, but she knew she could do it. Now that she didn't need Agnes's money, things would run smoother. With that thought in mind, she pushed open the door of the Bluebonnet Café and held it open for Vanessa, determined to not let thoughts of Agnes interfere with a rare dinner alone with her mother.

he next morning, she retrieved her car from the mechanic and obtained her food and beverage permit from the county offices as soon as they opened. On the way home, she stopped by Garrett's cottage. She knocked on the front door and a thrill shot through her while she waited for him to answer. Now that she was staying in Candle Beach, the possibility of a relationship with him was suddenly very real. Butterflies rolled and dived, and she put a hand on her stomach hoping to quell them. Taking a deep breath and squaring her shoulders, she knocked again, but nobody came. She pushed on the unlatched door.

"Hello? Anybody home?" She poked her head in. He was sitting at his computer desk with headphones on, unaware of her presence.

"Hello?" she called again, louder this time. Should she leave? She didn't want to go, after working up the nerve to come back. He continued to tap away at the keyboard. She turned to leave, but stopped before closing the door. He had offered to help her develop a marketing plan for the bookstore. And this wouldn't be the first time she'd barged into his house uninvited.

She approached him and tapped on his back. He jolted and whipped his swivel chair around, almost knocking her over in the process. Then he pulled his headphones off.

"*Dahlia.* What are you doing here?" he asked. "I thought you'd be well on your way to Seattle by now."

"My plans have changed." She took a deep breath. "And I'm hoping you meant it when you offered to help me promote the bookstore."

He raised his eyebrows. "You're staying in Candle Beach?"

"Yes, at least for the time being. I'm trying to make a go of it."

A slow smile spread across his face. "Did Agnes give you the money you needed?"

"No, I was able to borrow it from someone else," she said. "So, do you think you can help me? I need to make the best effort I can to have the bookstore succeed."

"Sure. Let me finish up with what I was doing and we can make a plan of attack."

He gestured for her to sit on the couch, and she picked up a copy of *People* magazine and flipped through it while he wrapped up his work on the computer. She wouldn't have guessed him to be a *People* magazine reader. The man never failed to surprise her.

She was deep into an article about the newest singing sensation when she felt Garrett's hand on her left shoulder. His touch zinged through her and her spine straightened. She turned sideways to gaze up at him.

"Are you ready?" he asked. His brown eyes sparkled and his easy smile melted her heart.

"Uuuuh, yes. I am," she stuttered. What was it about his touch? *Get it together, Dahlia*, she told herself.

He sat down in the armchair across from her and leaned forward to grab a notepad off the table. "Let's see. The terms of the will state you need to make the bookstore profitable by the end of twelve months if you decide to sell, correct?"

"Yes," she said. "So I have about nine months left on the clock. But with the Book Warehouse in Haven Shores now, sales have worsened."

"So nine months. That's quite a bit of time to try out some different tactics." He scribbled on the paper. "I think the first thing you need to do is to increase your presence in the community. From what I've noticed about Candle Beach, most of the business owners are involved in town events or local government."

"So I need to run for mayor?" She laughed at the thought.

"No, no, nothing like that. But you do need to get involved. Have you thought about joining the summer market?"

"Everyone keeps telling me that. Do you really think it would help?"

"It's very popular with both locals and tourists. It's an opportunity to get both your name and the bookstore to the front of everyone's minds."

"How do you know so much about the town?" she asked. "I've been here three months and I know barely anything."

"I'm a writer." He shrugged. "I spend a large part of my day observing people and how they react to different situations."

"So you're saying I'm going to end up in your next romance novel?"

His face reddened. "I only use characteristics from

people I meet. I don't base full characters on anyone I know in real life." He cocked his head at her. "Are you going to tell anyone about my nom de plume?"

"Well, I'd considered telling the Ladies of Candle Beach. I'm sure they'd be delighted to spread the news around town that we have a bestselling romance author in residence." She fought against a smile that threatened to ruin her poker face

His eyes widened. "You wouldn't."

She laughed. He was fun to mess with. "No, I won't tell anyone." She traced an imaginary zipper across her lips. "Your secret is safe with me."

The rigid line of his shoulders relaxed and he leaned back in the chair, kicking his feet up on the table. "Okay, then. So where were we?" He checked his notes. "Have you considered an online presence for To Be Read? You're not going to be able to compete on price or inventory with the big box stores, but many people like to support local businesses. You just have to make it easy on them. I think an option to order books online and pick them up in-store would be popular. As a bonus, you won't need to maintain a large inventory without a guarantee of sales."

"I could do that." Her mind chugged through her ever growing to-do list. Now she needed to create a website as well as improve the bookstore itself. "Anything else?"

"How about a promotion for vacationers? I've seen the gift baskets they give the tourists who stay in the nightly rentals. You could put a discount coupon in their basket for them to redeem during their stay."

"I like it." She took out her phone and typed notes on it. "If I can get the tourists into the store, they'll be much more likely to buy something." She sat back on the couch and dropped her phone to the other cushion. "Whew. This is a lot." She glanced at her watch. "Hey, it's almost noon. Do you want to have lunch with me? My treat."

She peeked at him from underneath lowered eyelids. If he rejected her offer, she didn't want him to see her reaction.

∾

Garrett considered her offer, but before he could respond, his phone rang. He pulled his cell phone out of his pocket, frowning when he saw who was calling.

"Hello?" he said.

"Hi, honey. I'm in town and I thought maybe we could get together for lunch." His mother's voice sounded tentative.

"You're here? In Candle Beach?" He cast a glance at Dahlia. He badly wanted to go out with her to lunch, but he hadn't seen his mother in ages. She tended to drift in and out of his life on a whim. He mouthed "sorry" to Dahlia. She nodded.

"Yes, I'm here. Are you free today? I hear the Bluebonnet Café is wonderful."

He sighed. "I guess." His thoughts darkened. It was irritating how she always waltzed in and expected him to drop everything for her. But she was his mother and he hadn't seen her in a while. It wasn't that he didn't like her, but they'd never really connected. She'd always been so busy with her own life that she didn't have time for him.

When he hung up the phone, his mood had soured. "I'm sorry, I can't do lunch today. Something's come up. Maybe some other time?"

Dahlia's face had fallen, but she said, "Okay, no problem. Thank you for all your help." She rose from the couch and gathered her belongings.

He wanted to tell her to stay, to call back his mother and tell her he couldn't meet her, but he couldn't make the words come out of his mouth. He walked her to the door instead.

"You're welcome." He closed the door behind her.

～

Ever since they'd kissed, Dahlia had thought Garrett might be interested in a relationship, but he hadn't pursued it further. Now that she was planning to stay in town, she intended to take matters into her own hands. He'd looked as though he was about to say yes to her lunch invitation until he'd received the mysterious phone call. After that, he'd been distant and she hadn't known how to respond. Next time she saw him, she'd try again.

She called Adam at the newspaper office and found out from him that the Chamber of Commerce had the forms to fill out to join the summer market. When she got there, she was greeted by a friendly volunteer, who promptly handed her the forms.

"The deadline for this weekend passed yesterday, but you can request an exception. The contact for exceptions is on the bottom of the second page," the middle-aged woman said.

Dahlia thanked her and left the office. When she got back to the bookstore, she sat down at the desk to fill out the forms. She wanted to have a booth at the coming weekend's market so she looked at the second page for the person to ask for an exception.

Well, okay, this wasn't going to happen. She flung the paperwork on the desk and buried her head in her hands.

The contact was Agnes. There was no way Agnes would make any special exceptions for her.

But then she remembered what she had told her mother about making an effort to surmount obstacles. She picked up her phone and placed the call to Agnes.

"Hi Agnes." She hadn't told her yet that she planned to stay in town. How would she take the news?

"Dahlia," Agnes said. "I'm surprised to hear from you. What can I do for you?" She was surprisingly pleasant, and it gave Dahlia hope.

She took a deep breath and plunged in. "I'm staying in Candle Beach. I think I'm the best person to manage the bookstore and Ruth wanted me to be here." She paused. "As such, I'd like to join the summer market to promote the bookstore. And I'd like to start this weekend."

"I'm sorry, the deadline for that has already passed. You'll need to wait another week," Agnes said.

She mentally counted to ten before responding. "But that's almost two weeks away. I need to get started now. What can I do to make that happen?"

"I'm sorry," Agnes said again. "I'm not able to make an exception."

"Not able, or not willing?" she asked, her temper flaring.

"Have a good day, dear." Agnes disconnected the call.

Dahlia stared at her phone, tempted to throw it across the room. It seemed like every time she made an effort, Agnes was always there to throw a wrench in her plans.

Usually, she would have given up and moved on to the next thing. But this time was different. She was tired of Agnes pushing her around. She got up and stormed out of the bookstore.

～

Dahlia pushed open the glass door to the newspaper office. Good, Adam was in.

He circled a selection of text on a document and then put down his red pen. He smiled at her and removed his reading glasses.

"Hi." She sat down across from him at his desk. "Are you always here?"

"No, not always," he said. "Sometimes I sleep at home." His eyes twinkled at his joke, but from what she'd observed, it was close to the truth. "What can I help you with?"

"How'd you know I needed something?"

"You look like you're about to explode," he said. He offered her a maple bacon donut and a cup of coffee. "These will help."

"Thanks." She hadn't had anything to eat yet that day. After leaving Garrett's house, she'd gone straight to the Chamber of Commerce and then come to the newspaper office. She bit into the donut and the salty-sweet flavor filled her mouth, and for a moment, erased all of her troubles. "I want To Be Read to have a booth at the summer market."

"So you've decided to stay in town?" he asked, regarding her shrewdly.

"You already knew, didn't you?"

"News travels fast." He shrugged. "Sometimes I wonder why I bother to put out a weekly newspaper. Most things are old news by the time the paper goes out."

She smiled. "Only the really juicy gossip. I don't think the Ladies care much about real news."

"True," he said. "So what can I do to help? Did you already sign up for a booth?"

"That's the problem. I want to start as soon as possible, but the deadline for next weekend's market was yesterday. I tried to get an exception, but the person in charge of that is Agnes Barnes, and she refused."

Adam laughed. "So you need me to pull some strings?" He bit into a maple bar of his own while waiting for her response. A few crumbs stuck on his lips and he brushed them off with the back of his hand.

"Would you?" She had hoped he'd offer, but she wasn't sure he would. By the end of her first year owning the bookstore, she'd owe favors to half the town.

"No problem." He turned around and picked up the phone from the other side of his L-shaped desk.

"Hey Kirk," he said. "How are you and the family?" He covered the phone and smiled at Dahlia, nodding his head as the man on the other end chattered on and on.

"Say, I was wondering if you could possibly approve Dahlia Winters for a booth at the summer market? She was hoping to get To Be Read on the docket for next week, but she's having some trouble with Agnes." He laughed. "Yeah, she's staying in town. So she's all set for next Saturday?" He nodded again. "Thanks so much Kirk. Let me know if you need anything." He hung up the phone and held up his hands.

"It's taken care of. All you need to do is submit the paperwork directly to the Chamber of Commerce and Kirk will stamp it himself."

"Oh my gosh, thank you, thank you." She went around the desk and leaned down to hug him.

He awkwardly patted her back. "No problem."

"Is there anything I can do for *you*?" she asked.

"Well, you're friends with Gretchen Roberts, right?"

She nodded. She had a feeling she knew where this was going.

"Can you put in a good word with her for me?" He looked hopeful.

"I will." She turned to leave. "Thank you again. You have no idea how much this means to me."

She exited the office and did a little jump in the air. Finally, something was going right for her.

## 15

*A*fter she'd received her food and beverage permit and reopened the bookstore on Monday, she'd proceeded with her plans to remodel it. The handyman had promised to refinish the floors sometime that week and she'd made arrangements for him to install the espresso bar after it arrived the next week.

By Saturday, her first day at the summer market, she was feeling pretty good about things. Gretchen had volunteered to manage the bookstore for the weekend, leaving Dahlia to run To Be Read's brand new summer market booth. She leaned back in a metal folding chair inside the booth and surveyed her surroundings. On an average summer week-day, children and dogs ran amok across the grass of the Francisco Lorenzo Memorial Park, or as the locals called it, the Marina Park, for its location just above the town marina. During summer market weekends, canopied tents offering a variety of wares covered half of the park. This close to the water, the briny ocean air mixed with the blossoming white gardenias that bordered the park, creating an intoxicating seaside aroma.

Tourists and townspeople alike milled around the booths, hoping to find the perfect locally crafted accent piece for their home or to fill their basket with organically grown produce. Their chatter filled the area and shop owners smiled in anticipation of big sales. A nice sunny day like this could work wonders for their bottom lines. She hoped her sales would increase as well. Unfortunately for her, mixed in with the heavenly scent of flowers and salt was a hearty dose of the meaty odor of bratwurst.

Agnes had assigned her a booth at the far corner of the market, sandwiched between a recycling coalition and the local non-profit animal shelter, on a small offshoot pathway at the edge of the food vendors. On the plus side, she didn't have to leave her booth for long to grab lunch, but the location left much to be desired for a for-profit bookstore.

She straightened her display of bestsellers and stood as a tourist straggled over to her booth.

"Hello," the woman said. Her tone was bright, but there were dark bags under her eyes. "I'm so glad to see there's a bookstore in town. We arrived late last night and after I unpacked, I realized I'd forgotten to bring something to read while the kids play on the beach. If I have to spend the whole afternoon watching them bicker about the other child destroying their sandcastle, I'll scream." She frowned at the thought.

"Oh, no," Dahlia said. "Well, I can help you with that. What are you looking for? I have some mysteries, some local history books, and some romances here, but I have more at my bookstore, To Be Read. It's just up the hill." She held up a few books, but the woman waved them off.

"Oh, this one will be fine." She surreptitiously picked up the latest Susannah Garrity novel. Her children joined her and she flipped the book over to hide the steamy cover image.

"A very popular choice," Dahlia said. "You know, I've met the author."

"Really?" The woman's eyes widened and she handed Dahlia her credit card. "You met Susannah Garrity?" Her children tugged at her shirt, but she brushed them off, intent on hearing Dahlia's response.

"Yes, Susannah was very nice and accommodating. A pleasure to meet."

"Is she as pretty as her picture? She looks so glamorous." She had a far-off look in her eyes, as though imagining Susannah living it up at a cocktail party, surrounded by gorgeous men.

"Uh..." Dahlia said, flipping open the back cover of the book to see an image of a forty-something woman with lustrous auburn hair and full makeup.

Where did they get that photo? It definitely wasn't Garrett. She placed the book in a paper sack emblazoned with the bookstore's logo before answering.

"Yes, the author is quite attractive." She tried unsuccessfully to hide a smirk as she ran the customer's credit card through her point of sale system, but the woman didn't seem to notice her amused expression.

"Oh, I knew she would be." She accepted her bagged book and allowed her children to drag her away.

By noon, only one other customer had made a purchase. Most of the shoppers didn't venture off the main pathway unless they were stopping at one of the food booths. Agnes was winning again, which Dahlia didn't like. She opted to close her booth for lunch and made a stop at the Bluebonnet Café, armed with a plan.

∼

Dahlia's grin stretched from ear to ear when she left the Bluebonnet Café. She carried a half dozen bakery boxes back to her booth and pushed the stacks of books to one side of the table. She opened a box and the aroma of Maggie's freshly baked cinnamon rolls wafted out of the box. From one of the boxes, she removed a paper sign that read 'Desserts' and a handful of napkins. She hung the sign from the top canopy of the booth. Most of the food offerings at the market were savory, and people soon flocked to her booth for dessert. At least half of them left with a book as well. Ironically, having obtained her food license due to Agnes's complaint to the county health department was the reason for her success.

At the end of the day, she retrieved a caramel apple muffin she'd ferreted away in an otherwise empty box and unwrapped it while surveying the other booths. The sellers appeared exhausted, but an undercurrent of satisfaction reverberated through the aisles. She bit into the muffin, savoring the crunchy brown sugar topping and the slight tang from the juicy nuggets of apple buried in each bite. Thank goodness she'd hidden the treat. Every pastry box lay empty, save a few forlorn crumbs. The baked goods had been a rousing success, drawing patrons to her booth who wouldn't have visited otherwise.

She calculated her earnings in the bookstore's office and was pleased with the total. What would Agnes throw at her next? Whatever it was, she could handle it.

∼

For Sunday, Dahlia restocked her booth with a fresh supply

of pastries and books. The local history books had proven popular the day before, so she doubled her inventory of those. On the way to her booth, she passed Wendy's booth. A boldly lettered sign proclaimed her as a purveyor of hand-restored furniture and custom upholstering services. Wendy smiled and waved at her as she walked by with her armload of boxes containing books and baked goods.

After she set up her booth, she returned to see Wendy. She ran her hands across a striking carved oak end table.

"You can't afford it, remember?" Wendy teased her.

"Yeah, yeah." Wendy had a point. "But I already bought the best piece." She still loved how the green velvet sofa set the tone for the bookstore. Once her handyman installed the dark espresso bar over the next week, the store's remodel would be near completion.

"Hey, my son is stopping by this morning," Wendy said. "I'd like for you to meet him."

"Sure, I'd love to. I didn't realize you had a son here in town." Although Wendy had mentioned having family in Candle Beach, she'd been uncharacteristically secretive about them. Dahlia sat down in one of the matching blue-and-white striped high-back chairs. "When's he coming?"

"There he is now," Wendy said. She pointed at a man picking his way through the piles of inventory strewn throughout the aisles as the vendors set up their booths.

"Garrett Callahan is your son?" Dahlia asked. They didn't share a last name, so she'd never have put that together on her own. What were the odds?

"Yes, why?" Wendy cocked her head to the side. "Do you know him?"

"He comes into my store every week for more books." Had Wendy been the mystery caller?

Wendy laughed. "Sounds like my son. He always was a

reader. Oh, and he's a writer, you know." She put her hand up to shade the side of her mouth and lowered her voice. "Although, I can't tell you what he writes, but let's just say he's passionate about his work and is wildly popular." A proud mama smile lit up her face.

Garrett approached, wearing a noncommittal expression. "Hi, Dahlia. Wendy." He nodded at them.

"I've just learned Wendy is your mother," Dahlia said. "Did she tell you she's living in the apartment over To Be Read?"

"No, she didn't mention that last time I saw her, or say much about why she's here," Garrett said. "Wendy, are you staying in town for a while?"

"I've decided to stay at least a few months, maybe put down some roots. Dahlia's been kind enough to rent me her apartment until the end of September." Wendy eyed him. "Is that okay with you?"

"Of course." His wooden speech contradicted his affirmation. "It'll be nice to see you living in the same place for more than a week."

Wendy smiled faintly at him, in a very un-Wendy-like way. Then she wrapped her arms around him and squeezed. He stood straight, with his arms pressed to his sides.

"I'm so glad to see you again. You left so abruptly after our lunch on Monday," Wendy said.

Garrett's jaw clenched and irritation flickered in his eyes. "So what did you need me for today?"

Wendy didn't seem to notice his attitude and motioned to the panel truck parked behind the booth. "I need help moving the last piece of furniture. I thought maybe you could help."

"I can do that," he said.

Wendy pulled car keys out of her pocket and walked

toward the truck. Garrett turned to Dahlia. "Nice seeing you again."

Dahlia looked at him. She'd never seen him so on edge. Usually he gave the impression of being at ease in all situations, but something about Wendy had him rattled. "Nice seeing you too," she said with equal politeness. "Thank you again for your help with the bookstore. Maybe we could get together sometime this week to discuss some other ideas?"

"Yeah, sure." His expression softened. "Give me a call and we'll set something up."

"Garrett?" Wendy called from the back of the truck. "I'm ready."

"Coming," he said, shaking his head.

Behind him, the other vendors had cleared their wares from the aisles and people were gathering around the market entrance. Nearby, the kettle corn vendor had started the giant rotating vat and the sound of popping corn echoed throughout the marketplace.

"I'd better head back to my booth. The market's about to open," Dahlia said. "I'll call you soon."

"I'd like that." He smiled at her, then turned back toward his mother.

She watched as he made his way over to the truck. His muscles were tense as he strode through the grass and he held his head so stiffly she'd be surprised if he didn't have a killer headache later.

From Wendy and Garrett's interaction, she'd gleaned that they weren't exactly close. She remembered him talking about his mother when he drove her home after her car broke down. He'd mentioned his mother's flightiness and inability to stay in one place for very long. Wendy's history fit his assessment, but she did seem to be trying to make amends for past wrongdoings.

Was Garrett painting her with the same brush as his mother? That would explain why he ran hot and cold around her. Dahlia wasn't like Wendy and she didn't know how to make that any more apparent to Garrett. However, she wasn't about to change anything about herself to please someone else. She'd done that before and never would again.

~

A constant stream of customers kept Dahlia busy for the rest of the day. Maggie's pastries had drawn so much business that she had to order more after lunchtime. Maggie had discounted the second batch of sweets in exchange for having a placard advertising the Bluebonnet Café affixed to the edge of the table.

Dahlia packed up the remaining merchandise and tore down her canopy tent. She fought to roll the canvas around the folded tent poles and stuffed them into the too-tight bag.

*I did it*, she thought, as she cinched the drawstring at the top of the bag. The unsold books fit into a single box and the second batch of pastries had almost sold out. She slung the tent bag over her shoulder and picked up the boxes.

As she left the market, she stopped at the animal shelter booth. "I thought you might like these." She opened the pastry box to reveal a half dozen muffins and placed the box on the table.

"Thanks!" The female booth worker grabbed one as soon as Dahlia set down the box. "I saw people with these earlier and wondered where they were getting them from."

"You're welcome. Next week I'll remember to bring you a few earlier in the day."

The woman nodded enthusiastically. "We'd love that."

She offered the muffins to her male co-worker, who was stacking promotional materials in a box.

Dahlia lugged her cargo to her car and drove to the bookstore, exhausted but thrilled with another successful day. Participating in the market had been worth all the trouble she'd had getting signed up for the weekend.

She entered To Be Read through the back door and propped the tent bag against a wall in the storeroom. She walked into the main bookstore, where Gretchen was shelving a few books.

"I'm almost done," Gretchen said as she placed the last book on the appropriate shelf.

"Thank you so much for volunteering to help me on summer market weekends," Dahlia said. "I don't know what I'd do without you and Maggie."

"That's what friends are for," Gretchen said. She gave Dahlia a quick hug and stood back to regard her friend. "You look bushed. The store's closed, but I made a fresh pot of coffee. Grab a cup and put your feet up. If you aren't sick of Maggie's baked goods yet, there's a few left from this afternoon."

"Coffee sounds amazing," Dahlia said. She poured from the carafe into one of the mismatched mugs she'd bought from the thrift store and selected a cherry and cream cheese Danish. At this rate, she'd need to sign up for a gym membership soon. The only thing keeping the weight off was the amount of nervous energy she'd expended to make the bookstore successful.

"I think I'll join you." Gretchen grabbed a funky flowered mug and a donut, and plopped down on an armchair in the seating area. "The store was so busy, I barely had a chance to sit down all day. Whatever you're doing to bring in business is working."

"I'm glad to hear that," Dahlia said. "Whew." She sat on the green sofa and put her feet up on the coffee table. "I feel like I've been running around like a hamster in a wheel." She pointed at a tear in the sole of her sneakers. "Look, I've even got a hole in my shoe from all the running."

Gretchen laughed. "Seriously though, I think this is going to work."

"We'll see. We had the tourist business over the weekend. I'll have to run the numbers once we get a week of business on the books after the remodel. The espresso bar is going in this week, so the construction may put off some people, but I bet we'll get some townspeople in to see what's new in the store."

"Yeah, this will be the biggest thing since the wine bar opened."

"I hope so," said Dahlia. "I'd love to show Agnes how wrong she was about me." And Garrett too.

At the thought of Garrett, she scanned the room. "Is Wendy back yet?" She set her coffee cup down on the table.

"No, not yet, why?" Gretchen asked, leaning forward.

"I found something out today about her. Did you know she was Garrett's mother?" She ran her hand through her hair.

"Garrett? Your Garrett?"

"He's not my Garrett. We're just friends."

"Yeah, friends with benefits." She wiggled her eyebrows at Dahlia, who retaliated by throwing a cushion at her. Gretchen laughed and threw her hands up in the air to ward off the cushion attack. "Okay, okay, you're just friends. But you want to be more, right?"

"I don't know. I think so. He kissed me once, last week, but every time I think something will come of it, we argue or something else happens and it never does."

"Maybe I should start dropping hints to him. He came in here yesterday and seemed disappointed not to see you. I think he'd forgotten you'd be at the market."

"Anyways..." Dahlia said. "Wendy is his mother. Small world, huh?"

"I'd never have guessed. She's so bubbly and outgoing, and he's so..." Gretchen's voice trailed off. "Well, not a hermit, but definitely not an extrovert. But then again, he's a writer and all."

Dahlia smirked. She wanted to tell Gretchen about Garrett's secret identity. But she'd promised him she wouldn't tell anyone.

"Do you think it's strange that Wendy never mentioned him before?"

"Eh, you've only known her for a week. It's not like she forgot to mention she was a mass murderer or something."

"You're probably right," Dahlia said. Time to change the subject and turn the tables on Gretchen. "You know, Adam was a big help in getting my application for the summer market approved."

"Uh-huh," Gretchen said. "He's a nice guy. I've known him my whole life. Very dependable."

"Dependable is good," Dahlia said, watching her friend carefully.

"I guess." Gretchen didn't sound so sure.

"He asked about you."

"He did? What did he say?" She seemed more interested now.

"Adam wanted to know what you were up to and asked me to put in a good word for him. Gretch, he really is a good guy."

"I know, but he's not very exciting. I feel like I went to college to get away from everything in this tiny town and then I failed to launch and had to come back to work for my parents. As much as I love real estate, this hadn't exactly been my life plan."

"I know how that goes," Dahlia said. She threw her hands up in the air. "Who would have thought I'd be a bookstore owner?"

"Aunt Ruth," Gretchen quipped. Dahlia threw the other cushion at her.

A noise in the back room drew both women's attention.

"Hello?" Wendy called out.

"We're in here," Dahlia answered.

Wendy entered the room and Gretchen stood. "I'd better get home."

Dahlia nodded at her and thanked her again for her help. She locked the front door after Gretchen exited.

Wendy flopped down on the couch. "It's been a long day. Profitable though. I sold almost every piece. I'm going to need to hit up some garage sales and flea markets for some 'before' pieces."

"I had a great sales day at the market too. And Gretchen said the bookstore was full of customers today."

Wendy looked up at her. "Sorry about the awkwardness with my son."

"Don't worry about it. That seems to be a common feature of most of the interactions between Garrett and me."

Wendy's head jutted up and her keen gaze pierced into Dahlia. "How so?"

Dahlia squirmed under her scrutiny. "He seems to run hot and cold with me. One minute he wants to be friends, the next, he's racing out the door."

"I was afraid of that." Wendy frowned. "He has a habit of not letting people get too close to him. It's my fault. I wasn't the greatest of mothers to him."

"I'm sure you were fine," Dahlia said. She was getting increasingly more uncomfortable talking about Garrett.

"No, I wasn't there for him when he was a child. I was working on my business and thought I had to be moving around to all the flea markets and craft fairs to be successful. Not exactly a great way for a child to grow up." Wendy's usually cheery face had crumpled and tears shone in her eyes.

Dahlia walked over to her and patted her shoulder, unsure of the appropriate response.

"I can tell he has feelings for you though," Wendy said, swiping her eyes with a facial tissue.

"For me? Why would you say that?"

"I may not have been the mother of the year, but I can tell when my son is interested in a girl."

Dahlia stared at her. This conversation was growing stranger by the minute.

"You two must be pretty close if he's trying to push you away," Wendy said.

"I don't know about that."

"Time will tell." Wendy stood, yawned, and stretched her arms high over her head. "I think I'm going to head upstairs. This weekend has worn me out."

Dahlia said goodnight to her and sat down on the sofa, pulling her legs up underneath her. What was going on with Garrett? His mother, who barely knew him, seemed to think he was interested in her, so why were things so difficult between them? She leaned back against the sofa's curved arm, closed her eyes, and relaxed her shoulder muscles. She'd had a long day too. Enough thinking about Garrett.

The weekend at the market replayed in her mind. Although physically draining, she'd never experienced such a thrill as she'd received by selling books to customers and, most of all, outwitting Agnes.

She opened her eyes and looked at the bookstore anew. This could actually work. The local handyman had fit her into his schedule and had already refinished the floors. The dark wood planks shone with love and polish, and she'd finished painting the rest of the walls. Her espresso bar would be installed during the week and the remodel would be complete. Aunt Ruth would be proud.

Contented, she closed her eyes again and fell asleep on the warm velvety sofa.

## 16

When Dahlia awoke, the sunlight that had been streaming through the bay window had been replaced by a soft glow from the street light. She turned her head to the side to see the clock on the wall. It showed the time to be after ten o'clock. She'd been out for several hours. She swung her legs off the couch and sat for a moment before she gathered her belongings, exited the building and locked the front door.

On a Sunday night, the town was quiet. Most of the weekend tourists had left and those who remained were safely ensconced in their luxury nightly rentals. Lights shone in a few windows, and from farther down Main Street, music from the bar's jukebox trickled out the door.

She walked up the hill, relishing the stretch in her hamstrings after her nap on the green sofa. She hadn't brought a jacket to work because the day had been warm. Now, in the evening chill, she had to wrap her hands around her arms to keep warm. A soft wind blew her hair back and she breathed deeply. The cold braced her, making her feel grateful to be alive and fortunate to call Candle Beach her home.

As she passed Garrett's house, she glanced at the windows. Most of the lights were off, but a TV flickered in the living room. She hurried past, lest he think she was spying on him.

The built-up heat from the sunny day embraced her as soon as she entered Aunt Ruth's house. Her stomach grumbled noisily and she headed for the kitchen. She rummaged around in the fridge and found a brick of cheddar cheese, a bunch of grapes and some crackers. Maybe not the healthiest of dinners, but it beat her steady diet of pastries.

After being outside, the kitchen walls seemed to close in on her. A breeze came through the one window she'd left open during the day and the beautiful, crisp summer night beckoned to her. On a whim, she filled a bag with the food and a Diet Coke. She knew exactly where she wanted to go.

The darkness of the sand loomed before her as she picked her way down the moonlit steps of the beach access. As a teenager, she'd often snuck out of Aunt Ruth's house at night to gaze out at the ocean for hours, enjoying its sanctuary. She felt almost giddy as she sprung off the last step and jogged over to a beach log a few hundred feet from the base of the stairs. Except for a few herons pecking at something in the surf, the beach was deserted.

She climbed on top of an old gnarled log which was stacked on top of other beach logs and worn smooth in places by frequent exposure to the waves. After the excitement of her success at the summer market, and her confusion over Garrett's behavior, she welcomed the quiet. She enjoyed the stillness for a while, and then pulled out her food. Her mouth salivated as she bit into a red grape. She was hungrier than she'd thought.

"Do you have enough to share?" a man's voice asked.

She whipped her head around to see who had disturbed her solitude. Being alone at night on the beach had never scared her, but she was still wary of strangers. She squinted through the darkness to see who had spoken.

"Dahlia, it's me, Garrett," the man said. "Sorry, I didn't mean to scare you." He crossed the sand to where she sat and leaned against the log.

"Hi." Her heart raced and anticipation rose in her chest.

"I saw you from the top of the stairs."

"What are you doing out here so late?" She moved the food over to make room for him to sit.

"I come down here often at night. There's something so peaceful about being out here after everyone has left. It allows me time to think," he said. "I've come up with some of my best book ideas while sitting here in the dark."

She offered him the food and he used the serrated knife to cut a wedge of cheese, which he placed on a wheat cracker. He chewed the food and swallowed. "I've been working on a new chapter all day and I forgot to eat."

"Well, I wouldn't want you to starve," she teased. "Who would get the fair maiden out of distress?"

"You, or the main character in my novel?" he quipped.

She punched him gently in the arm. He caught her wrist and took her hand. Her skin tingled below his fingertips and her breath caught at her body's sudden reaction.

"Dahlia, I'm sorry about how I've been acting. I really am glad you decided to stay in town."

Her eyes met his and her stomach took a freefall from the intensity of his gaze. She put down the piece of cracker she'd been about to eat. Tension crackled between the two of them. "I'm happy I decided to stay too." She choked a little on a few crumbs, pulled her hand away from his, and took a swig of her Diet Coke.

"I'm sorry about this morning. I had no idea you knew my mother." He glanced out at the inkiness of the Pacific Ocean, deep in thought.

"We met in Haven Shores last week," she said. "She seems great."

"Yeah, well, you just met her," he said. "Wait until you've known her for a few weeks. Although not many people have the opportunity to experience that, as she has a way of flitting off after she grows tired of a place."

Dahlia shrugged. "She told me she wanted to stay until the end of September. She seems to like Candle Beach." She looked up at him. "Was that her who called while we were working last week?"

"Huh?" he said.

"While I was at your house," she said. "You received a phone call and seemed upset afterward."

"Oh, right," he said. "That was when she called to let me know she was in town and wanted to have lunch with me. I hadn't seen the woman in over a year and then she shows up and I'm supposed to jump when she says jump." He shook his head.

"I don't think she meant it that way," Dahlia said. "When I met her, she seemed excited to come to Candle Beach and see you. Well, I didn't know she meant you in particular, but she talked about having family in Candle Beach."

"I'm sure she was excited to come here. That doesn't mean the excitement will last and it won't be like every other time."

"You never know." Dahlia finished her handful of grapes and straightened up the remaining food. Her hand grazed his when she reached for the crackers. A familiar tingle shot through her and her heart raced. Her eyes met his and he smiled seductively.

"Look, I don't want to talk about my mother. I'd rather talk about you. I came down here because once I saw you in the moonlight, I couldn't keep away." He brushed a strand of hair away from her face, his gaze burning into hers. "And now I find myself not wanting to talk about anything at all."

Her breath caught as he snaked an arm around her and pulled her close, so close that she could feel the heat coming off his chest and smell his tantalizing aftershave. Was this really happening? She closed her eyes. Every second felt like a minute until his lips met hers. The kiss was every bit as magical as their first kiss in the bookstore. She melted into him, wrapping her arms around his neck. His fingers caressed the small of her back, sending shivers up her spine. They stayed that way for a moment and then broke away slightly. She opened her eyes and stared at him. Moonlight illuminated his face as he smiled in wonder.

"Remember when you threw yourself at me in Ruth's garden on your first day in Candle Beach?" He stroked her face.

"I didn't throw myself at you," she said. "I tripped over a garden rake. You just happened to be in my way."

He grinned at her. "I remember it differently. Anyways, you looked so cute and embarrassed when you gathered your unmentionables off the bush. I wanted to kiss you right then and there, but I had the feeling you would have thought I was crazy. And I wasn't sure I hadn't been spending too much time with my novel and somehow romanticized the situation."

She laughed. "I probably would have thought you were crazy if you'd kissed me then." She put her hand on his arm. "But I'm glad you did now." They kissed again and he took her hand in his. For a while, they sat quietly and enjoyed the peace together.

The evening may have been still, but the thoughts racing around in Dahlia's mind were anything but. If she hadn't stayed in Candle Beach, she'd never have had the chance to enjoy the success of the store or Garrett's touch. Her life would have been very different. She snuggled in closer to his embrace.

No matter how hard she tried to calm her thoughts, she couldn't forget the sadness on Wendy's face when she spoke about her son. Before she could help herself, she blurted out, "Maybe you could have a real talk with your mother while she's in Candle Beach and discuss everything in your past."

He pulled away from her and looked out to sea. She stiffened. What had she done? She hadn't meant to upset him. Well, in for a penny, in for a pound.

"She wants to make things better between the two of you," she said, watching him carefully. "Maybe you should give her a second chance..." Her voice trailed off as the expression on his face turned stormy.

In carefully measured tones, he turned to her and said, "My relationship with Wendy is complicated. Too complicated for you to understand."

"But you could try? People do change, you know."

"People don't change." He slid off the log and planted his feet in the sand.

She looked down to where he stood. "People do."

"No, they don't. Thank you for the nice evening, but I think it's time for me to call it a night."

She followed him with her eyes as he walked down to the shoreline with his hands in his pockets. He continued on down the beach until he became nothing more than a black streak highlighted against the waves glittering in the moonlight.

Her heart dropped into her stomach. The fullness of success she'd felt earlier had evaporated, leaving only a hollow pit in its absence.

What did he mean by "people don't change"? If he didn't believe that, what did he truly think about her? He'd once accused her of being flighty and compared her to a woman she'd later learned was his mother. Now that she'd decided to stay in Candle Beach, had his opinion changed? And if it had changed once, would it change again?

Just when she thought life had started to even out, it had suddenly become more complicated. She packed up the remains of her snack and trudged up the steep flight of stairs. She arrived at her house without even registering the rest of the walk. After stashing the food in the fridge, she flopped down on her bed. Sleep didn't come easily, and when it did, it was full of nightmares about growing old alone.

## 17

*T*he next morning, bleary-eyed and badly in need
of a cup of coffee, Dahlia stopped in at the Bluebonnet Café. Maggie was manning the cash register, never
seeming to lose her cool as the line continued to grow. In the
lobby and the main dining room, townspeople huddled in
groups, chatting about something. One woman pointed out
the window in response to whatever her companion
had said.

When Dahlia reached the front of the line, Maggie
handed her a to-go cup of coffee before she had a chance to
order. "Thanks. What's everyone talking about?"

Maggie brushed an errant curl away from her eyes and
stopped what she was doing.

"Oh, it's awful. You know how Wendy parks her truck in
the lot across from the bookstore?" Her eyes widened and
she leaned in toward Dahlia.

"Yeah, what about it? I told her it was okay to park there.
Did someone complain about it?" Dahlia wasn't surprised
that Maggie and everyone else in town already knew Wendy,

but even in Candle Beach a parking violation wasn't big news.

"Someone vandalized it," Maggie said.

"You're joking, right? In Candle Beach?" she asked, although she could tell from Maggie's expression that it wasn't a joke. "Do they know who did it?"

"Probably kids or some drunken tourists," Maggie said. "Do you want your usual?" She moved over to the bakery case and picked up the tongs as she waited for Dahlia to respond.

"No, I think I'll go with a sausage roll today. I've had enough sweets for a while. Can I get an extra cup of coffee and a Danish for Wendy? She probably hasn't had a chance to eat yet today. I feel so bad for her. That truck is how she makes a living." A thought occurred to her. "Oh no, did they get the furniture in it too?" Wendy had told her she'd sold most of her inventory at the summer market, but Dahlia would bet she'd left any remaining pieces in her truck overnight instead of unloading them. She handed Maggie her credit card.

"I don't know," Maggie said as she swiped the card through the reader. "I've heard bits and pieces from customers today, but haven't seen the damage myself. We've been slammed with business. Everyone seems to be out and about today." She sighed. "You know how things are in Candle Beach. Something like this is big news."

Dahlia nodded. "Thanks Maggie." She grabbed the bag of pastries and the two cups of coffee. "Hey, do you want to have dinner or lunch together sometime this week?"

Maggie smiled and nodded yes before greeting the next customer in line.

Dahlia knew exactly where Wendy parked her truck, but she wouldn't have needed to guess if she hadn't. A crowd of people had gathered around the truck and one of the two Candle Beach police cars was parked near it. Adam milled around near the police car, snapping pictures of the truck and the surrounding crowd.

When she grew closer to the truck, she gasped at the damage. The front windshield had been smashed and chunks of safety glass covered the pavement like glittery green pebbles. The perpetrator had slashed the two left tires and the truck leaned drunkenly to that side. Wendy stood next to a police officer, talking animatedly, but Dahlia didn't want to bother her.

She circled the truck. Other vehicles were parked near it in the lot, but none of them appeared to have been damaged. Wendy's furniture truck had been singled out. What was going on here? Did someone have it out for Wendy as a newcomer to town? Or was it completely random?

While she was deep in thought considering the possible vandals, Wendy tapped her on the shoulder.

"*Aah!*" She jumped and accidentally jostled the coffee cups she held in her hands. Drops of the dark brew splashed on the ground.

"Sorry, I didn't mean to startle you." Wendy's green eyes were dull and rimmed with red, and her bouncy curls hung in a tangled mess down her back.

"No worries." She handed Wendy a cup of coffee and a Danish and used a napkin to wipe off her hands.

"Thanks," Wendy said. "I came out to the truck this morning before breakfast to get some paperwork and I found this." She waved her hand at the broken glass. "I haven't had a chance to eat yet today. Thank you for thinking of me."

"Wendy, I'm so sorry. This is awful," Dahlia said, scanning the mess again. "Do the police have any clue who did this?"

"No, at least not that they're telling me. I know this type of thing probably isn't high on the police department's radar."

"Maybe not in a big city, but in Candle Beach, this is huge. This will make the front page of the *Candle Beach Weekly* for sure," Dahlia said. "Did you hear anything from the apartment last night?" She looked up at the apartment over the bookstore. The parking lot across the street was close enough that Wendy may have heard the glass breaking through the open window.

"No, I had headphones on and was listening to a new Tibetan meditation track," Wendy said. "I woke up feeling so relaxed, and then I found this." She frowned at her mangled truck.

"I'm so sorry. I feel responsible, since I brought you to Candle Beach and everything."

Wendy hugged her. "Don't worry about it, it's not your fault. These things happen." She added with false cheer. "And insurance will cover it, so everything will be fine."

"Did they get to your furniture in the back?" The back of the truck had been closed when she looked at it, but there appeared to be scratches around the lock.

"No, thank goodness, I'd locked it. The police said they'd tried to pry open the door handle, but they were unsuccessful. Someone may have scared them off."

"Well, that's one good thing," Dahlia said. "I know you've put hours into each of those pieces of refinished furniture." She used her foot to grind dirt into the cracked pavement of the parking lot. "Did you call Garrett about it?"

"I called him, but he didn't answer." Wendy's face fell. "Not that I expected anything different." She grabbed

Dahlia's arm. "Let's talk about something happier. Isn't your espresso bar going in today?" She guided Dahlia over to the bookstore entrance, and Dahlia unlocked the door.

"It is," she said. She flipped on the lights and smiled with pleasure when she saw the store. The floors gleamed in the daylight, creating a warm glow throughout To Be Read. "Do you want me to tell Garrett about your truck if I see him?"

"Nah." Wendy waved her hand in the air. "It's not a big deal. Probably better if he doesn't know."

"Okay." It seemed like a big thing to her, but she didn't want to get in between Wendy and her son when their relationship was already tenuous.

"I hope you have a wonderful sales day," Wendy said. "Now that the police have finished with the truck, I'm off to find someone to fix the windshield and replace the tires. And once that's done, I need to find some furniture in need of reupholstering if I want to have something to sell at next week's market." She waved goodbye and strode off toward the back room.

～

At six o'clock on the dot, Dahlia flipped over the sign on To Be Read's front window. The store was closed for the day, but she planned to work on some new book orders. Before she reached her office, someone rapped on the front door. She paused in the entry to the back room, trying to see from there if it was someone she knew.

"Dahlia, it's me," Garrett called out.

What was he doing here? After he'd stalked off at the beach last night, she hadn't been sure she'd see him again.

She crossed over to the door and unlocked it, holding it open for him.

He stepped inside and presented her with a bouquet of red roses. Her pulse quickened. Was he giving her another chance?

She inhaled their fragrant aroma and smiled. "Thank you."

"I'm sorry about last night. I was a jerk. I know you were only trying to help." He stared down at his feet. "As you may have noticed, things between my mother and I are a bit strained."

"I probably shouldn't have stuck my nose in your business either," she said. "Apology accepted."

"I was hoping you might want to have dinner with me tonight."

She looked over her shoulder toward her office. The orders could wait. "I'd like that. What were you thinking for dinner?"

"The Seaside Grill?" he suggested. "It's a nice evening."

"Works for me."

He reached for her hand and wrapped his fingers around her palm. His touch sent bursts of happiness through her body. She gazed at him for a moment as they walked down the hill toward the Seaside Grill. Candle Beach had brought some good changes to her life. A business on its way to success, and a new relationship.

At the restaurant, they opted to sit at one of the outdoor patio tables. A blue umbrella shaded them from the sun and a gentle breeze came off the water. After placing their dinner orders with the waitress, Dahlia leaned back in the wrought iron chair, enjoying the warmth and the view of the ocean.

"Are you glad you stayed?" he asked her.

Her eyes locked with his. "I am."

He smiled. "Me too."

They sat in companionable silence for a few minutes while looking out to sea, both of them enjoying the atmosphere and company. The urge to tell him about his mother's truck being vandalized kept welling up inside of her. She managed to quash it, but felt more and more uncomfortable about not telling him. She didn't want to jeopardize their new relationship by keeping it from him, but she didn't want to betray Wendy's confidence either.

"Penny for your thoughts." He reached across the table and put his hand on her arm.

She trailed her gaze back to him. "Sorry. I was thinking about everything I still want to do with the bookstore." Her stomach twisted. There it was, another lie. If Wendy didn't tell him about the break-in, she wasn't sure how long she could keep it secret from him.

"Is there anything I can do to help? I'm a little ahead on my editing and I'd love to help out."

He was being so nice that it completely tied her stomach up in knots. At this rate, she wouldn't be able to eat the shrimp pasta she'd ordered.

"I was thinking about painting the walls tomorrow. Tuesdays are slow at the bookstore and I'm going to close early. Are you up for it?"

He nodded. "I'll be there around four if that works for you."

"Well, thanks. I appreciate the help."

The waitress brought their food. He dug into his steak, but she couldn't do much more than twirl strands of angel hair pasta around her fork and take tiny bites.

"Do you not like your pasta?" he asked. "Would you rather have some of my steak and veggies?"

She smiled. He was so sweet. Why had she ever doubted this guy?

"No, it's good. I'm just not very hungry tonight. I'm sure the leftovers will make a great lunch for me tomorrow."

"Well, let me know if you change your mind," he said. "So how was your first summer market weekend?"

"It was great." She sighed. "You and my friends were right. I think it will really help promote the bookstore to tourists."

A self-satisfied grin crossed his face. "I'm glad."

He asked her more questions about the summer market and she relayed the story of the woman who asked about Susannah Garrity. As expected, he got a big chuckle out of it.

After finishing dinner, they walked up the hill to their homes. She paused in front of his cottage. "Thanks for dinner."

He put his hand on the small of her back, turning her away from his house. "You may live close by, but I'm still making sure you get home okay."

She wasn't going to complain. Being with him tonight had been wonderful and she didn't want it to end. They'd both been careful to avoid any talk of Wendy during dinner and she didn't intend to change that anytime soon. She'd learned her lesson to stay out of his personal business, and had decided that extended to not telling him about the vandalism of Wendy's truck. His mother would tell him when she was ready.

Soon, they were standing on her porch.

"Do you want to join me out here for a while?" she asked him. "The night is so beautiful that I don't want to turn in yet. I could make coffee or open a bottle of wine."

A slow smile spread across his face. "Wine would be nice, thank you." He followed her inside the house.

They returned to the porch with glasses of white wine and she snuggled up against him on the porch swing. There was something magical about being out in the evening with the sun down, the streets quiet, and the crashing of the waves on the beach. He put his arm around her, pulling her even closer.

～

The next afternoon, Garrett showed up at the bookstore ready to paint.

"Nice jeans." Dahlia laughed. She'd never seen him wear anything so disheveled. His denim jeans were covered with paint splotches and there were holes in the knees. His white undershirt wasn't any better, although it did emphasize his biceps, which she couldn't help noticing.

"What, you don't like my best Sunday clothes?" He waggled his eyebrows at her and she sighed in amusement.

"Let me change into my painting clothes." She closed the shop and went into the bathroom to put on her full-length overalls and a tank top. She tugged her hair back into a ponytail and checked out her reflection in the mirror. Not too bad. Although they hadn't been dating long, she felt more comfortable with him than she had with her ex-husband. There was something about Garrett that put her at ease.

She lugged the two large cans of paint she'd bought in Haven Shores back into the main room. It was strange to think that it hadn't been that long ago that she was still mad at him, although now that she looked back on it, him picking her up in the storm had been the turning point in their relationship. He'd made her realize that while she didn't need to bow down to anyone else's ideas for her future, there was room for compromise in any relationship. She set the paint down in front of him.

"So what colors do you have for us today?" he asked. "Chartreuse? Neon pink?"

She slugged him lightly on the arm. "Ha-ha, very funny." With a spackling knife, she opened up the paint cans, revealing the turquoise and baby-blue shades she'd selected. "I thought the tourists would appreciate the sea-like colors." She shrugged. "Plus, they'll brighten the store and offset the dark espresso bar nicely."

He nodded. "I like it. Where should we start?"

She pointed at the wall behind the cash register. "Here. Let's go with the turquoise."

They'd covered the floor with plastic and painted half the wall when she caught him eying her brushstrokes.

"What?"

He stopped painting. "Nothing."

"I can tell you want to say something. Spit it out."

"I wasn't going to say anything, but have you thought about blending the strokes more? It looks a little streaky in places."

She stared at him, her blood starting to boil. Was he really trying to tell her how to paint her own store? This was her project. To calm herself, she took a deep breath and stepped back. He was just trying to help. And from this angle, she had to admit, his side did look nicer. He may have a point.

"I'll try it. Thanks."

"No problem." He smiled at her and went back to work.

They finished painting the wall and she stepped back to

admire their handiwork. "Looks good. Time for a break?" she asked.

"Gladly." He set his brush down on the paint tray.

She gave him an evil grin and flicked him with paint.

"Really?" He wiped paint off his face, smearing it in the process.

"Uh, huh." She swiped the brush across his face, adding to his war paint.

"Oh, you did not just do that." He grabbed her arm that was holding the paintbrush and pulled her close against him.

Her eyes met his and her breath caught. The paintbrush dropped to the floor. He smiled and dipped her back to kiss her.

She put her hands on his shoulders, closed her eyes and allowed herself to get lost in the kiss. After a bit, he gently moved her back to a standing position. She stared into his eyes.

"Well, if that's my punishment..."

She picked up the brush and flicked him again. In response, he grabbed his paintbrush, doused it with paint and stroked her face with it as she bent down to get more ammunition from the can. She wobbled and toppled over, falling to the floor laughing.

"How do you like that?" He held his hand out to help her off the floor.

She yanked on his hand, pulling him to the floor beside her. "I like this better." She covered his mouth with hers.

∾

The next day, Garrett arrived ten minutes early to meet Dahlia for lunch at SushiGo, the new Japanese restaurant in town. They'd agreed on the time the day before, and he wasn't surprised that she wasn't there yet. But when twenty minutes had gone by and she still wasn't there, he tried calling her. No answer.

*Maybe she had the time wrong*, he thought. He shook his head to clear the negative thoughts. She wasn't Lisa and he couldn't let his past affect his future. And he did want a future with Dahlia. She brought out something in him that he hadn't felt in a while, a sense of joy in the everyday. Whenever she'd think of new ideas for the bookstore or talk about her friends, her whole face would light up and lift him out of even the foulest of moods. He hadn't realized how boring his life was until he met her.

But where was she now? He told the hostess he didn't need a table after all, and walked over to the bookstore. It was open and Gretchen sat behind the cash register. She waved him over.

"Hey, Garrett. How's it going?"

He looked around. "Good, but Dahlia was supposed to meet me for lunch. Have you seen her?"

Her mouth formed an 'o' and her eyes narrowed. She pointed to the new children's area. "Uh, she's over there."

Dahlia was balancing on a short ladder with a small paintbrush in her hands. On the wall in front of her, she'd painted a few woodland creatures and a meadow full of wildflowers. She swayed a little to the beat of the music playing through her earbuds, completely engrossed in what she was doing. A smile formed on his lips. He loved seeing her so happy. He stood to the side of the ladder so she could see him.

She pulled the earbuds out. "Garrett. What are you doing here? I thought we were meeting at noon." Panic filled her eyes as she glanced at the clock on the wall. "Oh my gosh. I had no idea it was so late." She climbed down from the ladder. "I'm sorry. I got so caught up in my drawing, I lost track of time. Can we still go?"

"That's okay. Are you ready?"

"Yes. Let me just tell Gretchen I'm leaving."

She was back in a moment and looped her arm through his. "Ready."

They walked to the restaurant and were seated immediately. He and Dahlia chatted easily during the meal, but he couldn't shake the niggling feeling that he'd been through this before with Lisa. She'd be so wrapped up in what she was doing that she'd completely forget to pay a bill she'd promised to pay or fail to remember plans she had with him. After a while, it took a toll on their relationship. He didn't want that to happen with Dahlia, but he wasn't sure how to stop it. He pushed the thoughts out of his mind and concentrated on the beautiful woman in front of him.

～

As she looked around the bookstore on Thursday morning, pride surged through Dahlia. To Be Read now reflected more of her personality, while retaining some of Aunt Ruth's as well. The brightly colored walls and emerald sofa melded perfectly with the rug Aunt Ruth had loved and the front window display invited customers to discover the perfect beach read.

Flying high on the success of the summer market weekend, Dahlia hadn't thought much about increasing weekday sales. She grabbed a legal pad off Aunt Ruth's desk to jot down ideas. What would draw people in? An ad in the weekly newspaper? A sale? Or maybe a contest of some sort?

All of those ideas had merit, but she wanted something to draw in people who were already shopping in town. Perhaps something outside the store that would increase attention. Maybe a sidewalk sale? She hadn't seen many around town, but knew they were popular in other places.

The piles of hard-to-sell books stacked up in the back room would work well for a sidewalk clearance sale. The idea gathered steam. If memory served her correctly, there were a few tables leaning against a wall in the storage room. She found the tables, dusted them off and set them up outside of the store. On the tabletops, she artfully arranged the clearance books. Now, to bring in more people. She tapped her finger against her chin. Candle Beach Real Estate used wooden sandwich boards to attract customers. She called Gretchen and arranged to borrow a few.

About twenty minutes later, Gretchen lugged two sandwich boards into the bookstore. "Here you go," she said. "What are you using them for?"

"I thought I'd put one up here in front of the store to attract attention and maybe one down on the corner. What do you think?"

"I think you're going to provide a lot of free advertising for Candle Beach Real Estate." She wiggled her eyebrows at Dahlia.

Dahlia laughed. "I'm going to make a sign on poster board and tape it to the sandwich boards. I want to advertise To Be Read's sidewalk sale."

"Good idea," Gretchen said. "Keep them for as long as you need. We have tons of them for open houses."

"Thanks. Now, back to the salt mines. I've got a ton to do."

Gretchen said goodbye and left, and Dahlia reviewed her to-do list. She wanted to promote the bookstore's sidewalk sale in the weekly paper. If she remembered correctly from Aunt Ruth's advertising notes in her master guide to To Be Read, advertisements needed to be in by Thursday morning to get in Friday's print run. She called Adam to confirm.

"Hi Adam. It's Dahlia."

"Good morning," he said. "What can I do for you?"

"It's not like I always need something, right?" She laughed. He was right. When she called or showed up on the newspaper's doorstep, she usually needed his help.

"I want to place an ad for this week's paper. Is it too late to do that?"

"No, you're fine. What size advertisement were you thinking about?" he asked. They discussed the ad sizes and she decided on a quarter page ad featuring the sidewalk sale.

"You'll have it by tonight," she told him. She hung up the phone and placed her palms flat on the table, sliding them forward to deepen the stretch. The day had barely started and she'd made considerable progress on her marketing plans. Garrett would be proud.

In between customers, she opened the new bookstore laptop on the front counter and researched website design before diving into creating one. She wanted to create a sales site where customers could purchase books through a secure website. Her long-dormant design skills popped to the surface and she was proud of what she accomplished in a short time. She also set up a few social media pages and included those links on the advertisement to give to Adam.

Mid-afternoon, she came up for air and went outside. She thought she'd sold a lot of books off the clearance table and the almost-bare table confirmed her suspicion. She refilled the empty spaces and took a deep breath. The fresh air renewed her energy and she started to go back inside to make final edits to the ad.

Before she could do so, Mayor Chester Raines, Marsha's husband, walked up to her.

"The town's been talking about your remodeling at the bookstore and I wanted to see for myself," he said.

"Wow, that's great. I'd hoped to get some excitement going about the changes," Dahlia said. "Let me show you the inside."

Mayor Raines followed her inside. As he viewed the bookstore, a slow smile spread across his jowly cheeks. "The floors look wonderful, and I love the new seating area," he said. "Ruth would be proud of you."

Her face glowed. She hoped he was right about Ruth. Part of the reason she'd taken on the big project was for her own benefit, but the other part was to honor her aunt's legacy.

He cleared his throat. "Unfortunately, I have some bad news for you."

She groaned. What now?

"The Candle Beach town code doesn't allow for sidewalk sales. As a tourist town, we try to portray a more pleasing image for tourists," he said. He looked down at the floor. "Dahlia, I'm really sorry. I know you're in a tough spot having to compete with the Book Warehouse and all."

"But that doesn't make sense," she said. "What about the benches outside of Hank's Grocery or the patio tables outside of the Bluebonnet Café?"

"Those are within code. Tables of this sort aren't. Perhaps you could move them inside the door?" He looked at her hopefully.

"But the whole point of a sidewalk sale is for it to be on the sidewalk."

"I'm sorry," Mayor Raines said. "We're required to ask you to remove the tables. I wanted to come by and tell you myself because I've heard so many good things about your remodel."

"Did someone report me to the town council?"

"Well, yes," Mayor Raines said. "We did receive a complaint. I'm not at liberty to divulge who that was though. You understand." He flicked his fingers against his hand and avoided eye contact.

"I think I have a good idea." Agnes had struck again.

"Someone will be by later to check and make sure the code is being followed. Thank you again for understanding, and keep up the good work here." He walked over to the romance novels and perused the selection. "While I'm here, I think I'll pick up a book for my wife."

"Let me know if you need any help."

He nodded and continued checking out the titles.

Dahlia returned to her laptop and stared at the ad she'd designed for the sidewalk sale.

*Not going to need that anymore*, she thought. She held the cursor over the 'delete object' button on the free design program she'd downloaded to create the ad, but she couldn't bring herself to click on it. She was getting sick of Agnes's efforts to keep her from making the bookstore profitable. First it had been the visit from the health inspector, and then the blatant refusal to give her the money she needed. When those tactics had failed, she'd tried to keep her from selling at the summer market and stuck her behind the food booths when she'd obtained a spot. Now this.

If she could get past those trials, she could figure out a way around this as well. Inspiration struck. But she'd need help from another friend.

~

"You want to do what with my patio tables?" Maggie asked. She efficiently sorted out the baked goods that remained after the morning rush and repositioned them in the glass bakery case, adding some freshly baked pies to the bottom row.

"I want to have baskets of books on the tables. They'd remain outside of your store, but I'd have books available for sale and people could walk down the street to To Be Read to purchase them." Dahlia fairly bounced in excitement. "It's a win–win. Your customers get to have reading material while they're drinking their morning coffee and I hook them and reel them in to the bookstore."

"Hmm," Maggie said, coming around to the same side of the display case as Dahlia. "It sounds interesting, but I'm still not sure."

"Here, let me show you." She picked up the rectangular basket of books she'd set on the floor and led Maggie out to the patio tables. Of the four tables, one was empty, and she placed the basket on the edge of the tabletop nearest to the brick wall. She pulled a small sign out of the basket and flipped it over to the side of the basket for customers to see. It informed them that the books in the basket were for sale and they could purchase them at the bookstore.

"But what if someone takes it without paying?" Maggie asked.

She shrugged. "These were extra books in my inventory that I was going to dispose of next week. If someone takes it without paying, I won't be out much money. But, if they decide to purchase it and come in to the bookstore, I may gain a new customer."

"Okay, works for me," Maggie said. "Let's try it out this week and see how things go."

Dahlia hugged her. "Thanks a million, Maggie. I'll go get the other three baskets."

She returned to the bookstore and made up the other baskets. This idea was going to work. She'd adjusted her ad to reflect the sale being at the Bluebonnet Café. She anticipated gaining new customers not only from immediate book sales, but from the free advertising she received having the baskets on the tables at the popular town hangout.

Someone knocked at the back door and she let in the handyman who would be constructing the espresso bar.

"Hi, Elvis."

"The bar's here, Miss Winters. Where would you like me to install it?" he asked.

She directed him to the area she'd cleared and showed him where to hook up the plumbing. "I'm already receiving compliments on the floors," she said.

He blushed. "Glad to hear it. I'll get started on this now."

"I'll be back in a few minutes," she said. She ran the other baskets down to the Bluebonnet Café. A middle-aged man was sitting at the table with the basket, already reading one of the books.

She felt confident she'd bested Agnes again and knew she could handle anything the older woman could dish out. She only wished she knew why she hated her so much. As far as she knew, she hadn't done anything to personally offend her, and Agnes couldn't possibly be holding a grudge for something she had done as a teenager.

The patrons at the other tables accepted her offer to place books at their tables and she rushed back up the hill to check on Elvis's progress.

~

Propped against the front door of the bookstore was a small white envelope. Dahlia picked it up and turned it over. Wendy's name was scrawled across the front in black ink.

Why was Wendy getting mail left on the welcome mat, and how many people even knew she lived above the store? Weird all around. She carried the envelope into the bookstore.

The construction zone at the back had fallen into shambles.

"How's it going?" She was afraid she wouldn't like the answer.

Elvis frowned at her. "You've got the wrong size pipes for this type of work. I'm going to need to replace the pipes in the wall all the way back to the bathroom intersection."

"Are you kidding? How much is that going to cost me?" she asked.

"It'll take me at least an extra day and with materials..." He screwed up his face as he calculated the total. Dollar signs flashed across his face.

When he named his figure, she had to sit down. The espresso bar project would be at least twice the total she'd figured. She looked over at the bar, which sat forlornly in two pieces off to the side of the front desk. There was no going back at this point.

"Okay, let's do it. I need to get this up and running before the weekend. I don't want customers seeing this mess and thinking we're closed." She gestured at the sawdust and tools strewn across the hardwood floor in the construction zone. Thankfully, Elvis had tied up rudimentary 'Do not enter' tape around the project so no customers could enter the area and be hurt.

She got up and strode into the back room, gripping Wendy's envelope. This would take some reworking of her plans. Thank goodness her mom had loaned her extra cash in case things went over the initial estimates. How had she known? She grinned. Her mother knew everything. Although she often joked about Vanessa being prepared for anything, she secretly hoped she'd inherited a portion of her talent.

After entering the new estimate for the espresso bar into her remodeling spreadsheet, she pushed the desk chair back and chugged water from the bottle on her desk. Things would be okay. It may have felt like one step forward, two steps back, but she was making progress. Next week, with the construction finished, this would all seem like a bad dream.

The envelope on the desk caught her eye. She picked it up and headed upstairs to Wendy's apartment. The door was closed. She knocked twice and Wendy opened it, with her unruly hair tied up in a knot. Her face was flushed and a yoga mat lay unfurled in front of the TV.

"Hey," Wendy said. "Sorry, was I too loud? I didn't think my downward dog pose barked that much." She chuckled at her own joke.

"No, I wasn't sure you were even up here." Dahlia held out the envelope. "Someone left this for you on the front door mat."

"Weird. I wasn't expecting anything." She took the envelope and ran her finger along the sealed seam to open it. She pulled out a plain white index card and read the few words inscribed on it in red ink. The color drained from her face.

"What is it?" Dahlia had never seen Wendy so pale.

"Nothing." She stuffed the card back into the envelope and dropped it in the recycling bin. With her back to Dahlia, she braced herself against the kitchen table and took several deep breaths.

"Wendy, who was that from?"

"Nobody. It's not a big deal. Somebody I used to know." She turned around, a fake smile pasted on her face. Fear quivered behind the edges of her smile.

Something wasn't right.

Dahlia plucked the note out of the recycling bin. Scrawled across the plain white index card were the words *I found you*.

She held the card up to Wendy. "Who left this for you?"

Wendy shook her head. "I don't know." She sat down in a kitchen chair and shrank back against the seat.

"We've got to tell the police about this," Dahlia said.

"Tell them what? That someone left a note for me at the bookstore?" Wendy sighed. "They've got better things to do than investigate a vaguely threatening note."

"What if it has something to do with the vandalism of your truck?" Was someone stalking Wendy? The older woman hunched over in her chair, hugging her arms against her body. Why was she trying to act so nonchalant about the vandalism and note? What was going on here? "You should tell Garrett."

"No!" Wendy said sharply. "There's no need to tell him. He already thinks I'm full of drama. This would only add fuel to the fire." She stood from the table, grabbed the note from Dahlia and ripped it into tiny pieces, which she dumped into the recycling bin. "It's nothing. Don't worry about it. Don't you have to get back to the bookstore?"

"Okay, but if something else happens, let me know. For the record, I really think you should tell the police. If nothing else, it will be on file."

Wendy nodded, and Dahlia forced herself to walk down

the stairs. Leaving Wendy alone and not notifying the authorities seemed wrong. She may have been correct that the police wouldn't do anything, but it wouldn't hurt to tell them. For now, she'd respect Wendy's wishes, but if anything else happened, she was heading straight for the Candle Beach police station.

## 18

*O*n Friday night, Garrett waited on the beach log until the fiery sun had sunk below the horizon and every tourist had vacated the area. He had planned a romantic picnic for Dahlia, one that would make any of his heroines swoon with joy. After waiting over an hour for her, he'd started munching at the goodies in the wicker basket. Now, only crumbs remained and the half bottle of champagne had been drained.

He dialed her number for the fourth time since he'd arrived at the beach spot where they'd arranged to meet. "Dahlia, I'm going home now. I'll talk to you later." He sighed. "I wish you'd been here, the sunset was beautiful."

He gathered up the picnic items and trudged back up the hill to his cottage. Things had been going so well between them and he didn't know what had happened. Had she forgotten they had plans? She had been late for their lunch date earlier in the week, but he didn't think she'd completely blow off a date. He'd tried to convince himself that her flakier tendencies were just part of her charm, but missing their date was sending warning signals to him.

∾

"You're still here?" Wendy's voice rang out from the entrance to Dahlia's office. "I thought you had a big date with Garrett tonight."

Dahlia's eyes shot to the clock on the wall. Ten o'clock? It couldn't be that late. She'd immersed herself in the online book catalogs, trying to catch up on the latest trends, and had been sucked in by the vast selection. She grabbed her phone. The battery was dead. She checked the time on her computer. It really was past ten.

"Oh my gosh." She wildly packed up her belongings and stuffed them into the laptop bag. "Garrett's going to kill me." He'd been so excited about taking her on a sunset picnic on the beach, and she'd ruined their date.

"I'm sure it'll be fine. Garrett's pretty easygoing about things."

She glanced back at Wendy and did a double take. The older woman's eyes were bloodshot and dark bags hung under her eyes. She appeared to have aged ten years since the note had been found on the bookstore's doorstep.

"Are you okay?"

Wendy waved her hand. "I'm fine. I just haven't been sleeping well. Go find Garrett."

Dahlia wanted to question her more, but she knew she needed to get to Garrett. "Can you lock up?"

Wendy nodded and Dahlia ran for the beach. She scanned the beach from the overlook, focusing in on what they called 'their' beach log, but it was empty.

When she got close to his cottage, every light was off. Her heart dropped to her knees, an acid feeling following it. She'd turned over a new leaf by taking responsibility for the bookstore, which she hoped he'd noticed, but now she'd let her work get in the way of their relationship.

As soon as she got home, she plugged in her phone. Her misery increased when she saw she had four missed calls and three voicemails from Garrett. In his first message, he sounded upbeat, asking her if she'd be there soon. In the next two, his voice carried defeat.

*Aagghh!* She screamed silently. She dialed his number, but no one answered. She rapidly texted an apology and waited. No response.

She waited up as late as she could, but eventually fell asleep on the couch.

∾

The next morning, the first thing Dahlia did when she woke up was to check her phone. Still nothing from Garrett. Her stomach churned. He must be furious with her for missing their date. She left for the Marina Park with her stomach still upset. How had everything gotten so complicated?

When she finished setting up her booth at the summer market, she set out across the lawn to Wendy's booth. After seeing her bedraggled state the night before, she wanted to check on her. When she reached the furniture booth, Wendy had her back to her.

"Hey," Dahlia said. "How's it going?" Wendy had added a few new pieces to her inventory.

She turned around. "Hi." She busied herself aligning a chair with an oak coffee table.

"Looks like you've been hard at work." Dahlia motioned to the new items.

"Uh-huh," Wendy said. "I haven't been sleeping well, so I've been working to curb the insomnia." She put her hands on her hips and surveyed her display. She looked as bad as she had the night before, maybe worse.

Dahlia hadn't known her for very long, but this seemed unusual for her. "Are you okay?"

"Of course." Wendy flashed a dazzling smile, reminiscent of her old self.

"Have you received any more notes?" She watched Wendy's face.

"No, nothing. I told you it was a random thing. Probably some kid playing a prank on me." She gazed out at the marina. "Beautiful day, isn't it?"

"It is. They're forecasting for high eighties today. Are you looking forward to the Founder's Day celebration next weekend?"

"Definitely. From what I've heard, this place will be buzzing with tourists. Maybe some of them will want to furnish their summer homes with my restorations." She wiggled her eyebrows at Dahlia.

People were starting to straggle in to the market, so Dahlia said goodbye and returned to her booth. Something was definitely amiss with Wendy. She hoped it wasn't serious. Later, she'd press her again, but for now, she needed all the sales she could get. The Founder's Day weekend sales had better be as good as she'd heard. Business had improved at the bookstore, but it was almost August and the majority of the tourist income would disappear after Labor Day.

Someone called to her from across the lawn. She looked up and waved at Garrett. He smiled and waved back at her. Her heart beat faster the closer he got. She felt awful about the missed date and had some apologizing to do.

"Garrett, I'm so sorry about missing our dinner date last night." She came around the booth and leaned against the table's edge. "I was working on some plans for the bookstore and I completely lost track of time. I tried to call you when I got home, but you didn't answer."

"I went to bed early. I left a few voicemails while I was at the beach, but you didn't respond." Garrett's smile had faded.

"My phone was dead and I'd left my charger at home. Do you think you can forgive me? I can't believe I lost track of time like that." She put her hand on his arm and searched his face. "I really am sorry. Maybe we can go out tonight instead?"

She thought she heard him sigh before he wrapped his arm around her and smiled.

"Well, I'm glad you were having such a good time with your planning. Tonight would be great. I have to head into the city early tomorrow morning for my flight to New York to see my editor, but we could grab dinner right after the market closes. Does pizza sound good?"

She breathed a sigh of relief and snuggled closer. "I love pizza."

He released her and looked up at the sky. "Looks like it'll be a nice day for selling books," he observed. "Lots of customers and no rain clouds in sight."

"Shoot!" Dahlia said. "I was going to go to Haven Shores yesterday and pick up some supplies for a new rainy day display for the front window."

"A rainy day display?" He arched his eyebrow.

"Yeah." She grinned. "I'm going to paint a rain scene on some wood and then put some rain boots and other items in the front window with some book suggestions for rainy days. I love getting to decorate the front window and change out the displays." Her elation faded. "I'll have to wait until

Monday now. Everything will be closed by the time I get done with the market today."

"I could man the booth for you for a few hours," he offered.

"Oh no, I couldn't ask you to do that."

"It's really no problem." He shrugged. "I used to help Ruth out once in a while at the bookstore's booth last year, and I'm familiar with mobile payment systems. I wasn't kidding when I told you I'd love to own a bookstore. Why do you think I became a writer?"

Well, if he wanted to spend his Saturday selling books, who was she to deny him that pleasure? She threw her arms around him. "That would be great. I'll be back in a few hours. Give me a call if you need anything, I won't be far away."

"Don't worry about it. I'll have all these books sold before you get back."

She eyed the stacks of books. "Good luck with that."

≈

"How did everything go here?" Dahlia asked when she returned. The pile of books had dwindled considerably.

"No problem. I didn't sell everything, but I did sell almost every copy you had of that local author's cookbook. A crowd of ladies seemed very interested in my description of how to bake the cranberry muffin recipe in the front of the book."

"Have you ever made cranberry muffins?" Dahlia cocked her head to the side.

"What? You don't think I could be a baker?" he teased.

"Well, have you?"

"No, but I flipped through the cookbook while I was

between customers. It seemed easy enough." He grinned at her and his eyes danced.

Dahlia laughed and kissed him squarely on the mouth. She could see why the ladies had bought anything he recommended. She sat down in the folding chair, her gaze straying to Wendy's booth.

It was empty. Dahlia's stomach clenched. Was Wendy okay?

"Where's your mother?"

"She sold everything and went home. Said something about a migraine coming on."

Dahlia breathed a sigh of relief and then remembered her predicament. Garrett hadn't mentioned anything about the vandalism of Wendy's truck, so he must not have seen Friday's edition of the town newspaper. This would be a natural lead-in to tell him about it and bring up the mysterious note.

"Garrett—"

"Excuse me," a middle-aged woman cut in. "Do you have any more of those Washington Coast cookbooks? My friends told me how wonderful the cranberry muffins looked." Her gaze was fixed on Garrett, telling Dahlia that the cranberry muffins hadn't been what the woman's friends thought looked good.

"I'm sorry ma'am, those were all we had." Dahlia smiled at her politely. "But I'd be happy to order you a copy."

"Oh, that's too bad. I was really hoping to get one today." The woman turned to Garrett. "Do you have anything else you recommend?"

Garrett stifled a laugh, but recovered quickly. "Sure, this book of local history is riveting. Did you know Candle Beach was founded in the early 1900s as a retreat from the city?"

"Wow." The woman looked at him in awe. "It's amazing it's still around."

"It sure is," he agreed. He sold her the book and the woman left, no doubt to tell all her friends about her conversation with him.

"You're a great salesperson," Dahlia said. "I may need to enlist your help at the bookstore."

"Anytime," he said. "I'll help you pack up and we can head straight from the bookstore to Pete's Pizza."

"Looks like I don't have much to pack up." She surveyed her inventory. "I can't believe how much you sold."

"What can I say, people trust me." He shot her an easy grin.

"Uh-huh," she said. She was going to miss having him around while he was in New York.

## 19

*A*fter dinner, Garrett went home to pack for his trip and Dahlia returned to the bookstore. She was determined to get her accounting in order to gain a better idea of her financial standing before the big Founder's Day weekend. She looked at the calendar hanging on the wall. Had the town actually been founded on the first weekend of August? If not, someone had created a smart ploy to separate tourists from their money, as Founder's Day weekend fell halfway between the fourth of July and Labor Day.

She heard Wendy banging around upstairs around eight, but didn't look at her watch again until after ten when someone knocked on the front door. She was about to go get it when Wendy hurried down the stairs and answered it. The commanding voice of Police Chief Lee echoed through the front room.

Dahlia peeked her head around the office door. Chief Lee stood near the front door talking with Wendy.

"Ms. Danville, I'm afraid there's been a break-in at your summer market booth."

Wendy was facing Chief Lee with her back turned to

Dahlia. Wendy wrapped her sweater tighter against her body and cupped her elbows.

"What do you mean, a break-in? Did they steal something?"

"We're not sure, ma'am. It looks like the perpetrators focused on vandalizing your wares rather than stealing them."

"My furniture." Wendy's voice lacked any emotion. She lowered herself to sit on a chair. Dahlia had a clear view of her face now, which was devoid of color. Her features had wrinkled and in that moment, she looked a decade older.

"What did they do to my furniture?" Her voice was suddenly full of a sense of urgency.

Chief Lee shook his head. "We'll need you to come to the booth and help us determine the damage and if anything was stolen."

"Okay." She stood. "Let me get some shoes on and I'll meet you there."

The policeman left the building and Wendy slowly climbed the stairs to her apartment.

Dahlia closed her computer and waited for her to return. When she heard footsteps come down the stairs, she walked out to the hallway. "I overheard your conversation with Chief Lee," she said. "I'm coming with you." She wasn't taking no for an answer. Her new friend had already been under so much stress and she wasn't sure how she'd handle this new issue.

Wendy didn't reply, but she hugged Dahlia and they walked silently out the front door. Dahlia ensured the door latched and locked behind them.

As the brisk night air hit them, Wendy seemed to come out of her catatonic state. Dahlia stopped her a few feet down the sidewalk. "Is there anything I should know? If there's someone from your past trying to scare you, I'd like to know. I can keep an eye out for anything suspicious."

She sighed. "No, I really can't think of anyone. Nothing like this has ever happened before."

Chief Lee had paused at the street corner to talk with someone on his cell phone. As they approached, he hung up. "I'm sorry about this, Ms. Danville," he said. "We'll do everything we can to catch the perpetrator."

The three of them walked to the Marina Park in silence. The cool, moist air kissed Dahlia's face. Being out at night invigorated her and combined with her anxiety over the condition of Wendy's booth, she felt wired and on edge. Muffled music came from the bar, but otherwise the town was quiet. The playground swings floated in the air as a breeze blew them from side to side, the only sign of life in the eerily empty park.

A police officer was guarding the entrance to Wendy's booth. Yellow tape surrounded the scene and the flashing red and blue lights had attracted a few bystanders. Dahlia, Wendy and the Chief ducked under the tent's canvas covering and Chief Lee aimed his flashlight on Wendy's merchandise.

Dahlia sucked in her breath.

The vandal had flung red paint over half of the furniture and used a sharp object to rip open the cushions of the reupholstered couch, sending tufts of spongy stuffing to the ground. A dream catcher swung drunkenly from the middle support of the tent.

Wendy's eyes filled with tears. "Who would have done this?" she said softly. She ran her hands over the furniture. Wet paint streaked her fingers like blood and she held them in the air, staring at them, but not seeming to comprehend the devastation wreaked upon her booth.

Dahlia put an arm around her friend, who continued to fixate on the red stains on her hands, as if avoiding the horror of the rest of the booth.

"How did this happen?" Dahlia asked Chief Lee. "I thought there were patrols of the summer market."

He hung his head, then looked up. "We have patrols, but there are only three of us to monitor the whole town. There was a report of a break-in over at the Lutheran church, but when we arrived, nothing was amiss. When Officer Diaz returned to the market, he discovered Ms. Danville's booth had been vandalized."

Dahlia looked over at Officer Diaz. He leaned against the patrol car, with his hands in his pockets, tracing circles in the dirt with the toe of his shoe as he snuck peeks at the group gathered at Wendy's booth.

"I apologize for this, but does anything look out of place, other than the paint and ripped cushions?" Chief Lee asked.

Wendy scanned the booth as if taking in the full extent of the damage for the first time. Her gaze caught on the dream catcher and any remaining color in her face drained out.

She pointed at the dream catcher. "That's not mine."

The police chief regarded her thoughtfully and then walked over to the offensive object. "This?" He poked it with a pencil. Charms on the dream catcher glittered in the lights of the patrol car.

Wendy nodded and the police chief used a plastic evidence bag to remove the dream catcher and string from the tent support pole.

"Does this look familiar?" He held the plastic-encased object up to Wendy.

"Yes." She trembled as he pushed it closer to her.

Dahlia narrowed her eyes at Wendy. "Wendy, do you know who did this?"

"I think so, maybe," she said. "I don't know." Her voice shook with fear.

"Ma'am, if you have any idea who did this, it's in your best interests to tell me," Chief Lee said.

Wendy breathed deeply. "Last year, I was working the Oregon Coast craft market circuit. There was a man there who wanted to date me. I went out with him once, but we didn't really click." She glanced down at her hands, as if just remembering the drying red paint. She rubbed her fingers together. "He didn't take well to me rejecting his advances. Nothing major happened, but I was tired of him pursuing me, so I decided to move on to Washington."

"And the significance of the dream catcher?" Chief Lee prodded.

"He sold dream catchers," Wendy said. "That was his thing. He was really into dreams and their meanings, as well as anything having to do with dreams. In fact, that was why he fixated on me. He'd had a dream of us getting married, so he was convinced that it was meant to be." She shook her head. "I'd never have gone out with him in the first place if I'd known he was so loopy. He seemed nice and normal at first."

"Can you give me his name?" Chief Lee asked.

"Dale Peters."

He wrote it down and asked Wendy a few more questions, which she answered.

Dahlia tugged at her sleeve and whispered, "Wendy, tell him about the threatening card."

Wendy deflated further.

"Ma'am? Is there something else I should know?"

"About a week ago, someone left an envelope and card

for me in front of To Be Read," Wendy said. "I didn't think it was a big deal, so I didn't call the police or anything."

"Do you think the vandalism of Wendy's truck and the note are related to this?" Dahlia asked Chief Lee.

"I don't know for sure, but I'll check it out. Do you still have the envelope and card?"

"No," Wendy said. "I threw them away."

Chief Lee made some more notes. "Thank you, ma'am." He flipped his notepad closed. "We'll look into this. For now, please be aware of your surroundings. We don't know where this man is or what he plans to do next, so it's best you aren't alone. Is there anyone you can stay with?"

Tears slipped down Wendy's face. "I can't go somewhere else. I've got to work on my furniture. Half of my inventory is ruined." She gestured to the destroyed furniture. "Founder's Day is next weekend. I have to have inventory for that. From what I've heard, it's one of the biggest sale days of the summer."

"I can stay with her at the apartment over the book-store," Dahlia said. She turned to Wendy. "If that's okay with you? I can sleep on the couch and keep you company." It wouldn't hurt her to spend the extra time at the bookstore. She had a lot of work to do before Founder's Day as well.

Wendy nodded, and relief passed across her face. "I'd like that."

"I'd prefer for you both to be off the bookstore premises, but it's better than nothing," said Chief Lee. "I'll have my officers patrol the area around the bookstore more frequently."

"Now that we've got that settled, when can I start cleaning up these pieces?" Wendy asked. Her color had returned and she seemed determined to move on.

A female police officer in her late twenties had been

taking pictures of the crime scene. She now stood off to the side, reviewing the shots she'd taken. Chief Lee glanced at her and she gave him a thumbs-up.

"We're about finished here," he said. "You should be able to get started in the morning."

"I'll be here at six," Wendy said. "Maybe I can rescue a few items and have them ready by the time the market opens at nine."

"I can help you," Dahlia said, but immediately regretted her words. As it was already midnight, six o'clock would be a miserably early wake-up time. The grateful smile on Wendy's face made her promise worth it.

"I'll walk you back to the bookstore," Chief Lee said. "Ms. Winters, do you need an escort back to your house to get things for tonight? I can have Officer Jenkins go to your house with you." He gestured to the female police officer.

"No, I'm fine." When she'd cleaned out the apartment, she'd found stacks of linens and blankets, so she knew she wouldn't need anything to stay at Wendy's apartment. Her favorite pillow would have been nice, but the extra sleep she'd gain by not going home first sounded even nicer.

When they arrived at To Be Read, Chief Lee searched the interior of the bookstore and the upstairs apartment. After finding nothing suspicious, he allowed them inside. "Make sure to lock all the doors and windows," he advised.

Dahlia felt like saluting him, but instead said, "We will, thank you."

She locked the door behind him and watched through the front window as he retreated down the sidewalk. His presence had provided a sense of security, but now she realized how vulnerable she and Wendy were alone in the bookstore. A beam of light strobed through the room, reassuring her that the extra safety patrols had begun.

She turned to Wendy, who had collapsed in one of the armchairs. "Are you okay? Do you need me to get you anything? A cup of tea maybe?"

"I'm fine," Wendy said, her voice quieter than usual. "I don't think I'm going to be getting any work done tonight though. I'll have to make do with the remaining furniture to sell tomorrow."

"Let's get to bed then." Dahlia checked her watch. They'd be lucky to be in bed by one. While she'd been a night owl in her college days, she now treasured every minute of sleep.

They trudged up the apartment stairs together. Wendy retreated to her bedroom and Dahlia pulled the extra linens out of the closet and arranged them on the sofa. Not the most luxurious of accommodations, but it would do. A breeze came through the open window, ruffling the curtains.

Had she checked the locks downstairs? The apartment window was high enough that no one could enter it without an extremely tall ladder, but she'd better check the back door. In all the excitement, she couldn't remember locking it.

She crept down the stairs, not wanting to wake Wendy. The older woman had fallen asleep immediately after entering her bedroom and her snoring filtered out through the closed door.

She double checked the front door and the small windows that opened on either side of the big front window. All were locked. In the back room, she pulled on the door to the alley to make sure it was tightly closed.

*Crash.* She whipped around at the sound. A few books had fallen off a precariously perched stack of books. Not surprising that they'd fallen, but the timing couldn't have been worse. The threat of Wendy's stalker was making her paranoid.

She went back upstairs and lay on the too-soft couch. Wendy's snoring and thoughts of the stalker kept her awake. The police needed to catch him soon, or she was going to be a nervous wreck.

## 20

*G*arrett stood on the sidewalk while the doorman hailed him a cab. His week in New York City had flown by. He'd met with his editor, who thankfully had liked the book he'd just finished and was interested in his next novel. He'd met a friend for dinner during the week and connected with a few old work colleagues. It had been a blast, but he was ready to get back to his life in Candle Beach—and to Dahlia.

The air in the city stank of exhaust, sweat, and who knew what else. More cars rushed by him in a few minutes than he'd see all day back in Candle Beach. How had he once lived here? And enjoyed it? That was another time in his life. Now, he preferred a much quieter life.

A woman selling jewelry down the street caught his eye. Her wavy red hair glinted in the sun, much like Dahlia's had the day he first saw her. Dahlia. As much as he'd tried to deny his attraction to her, she'd somehow managed to wriggle her way into his life. So what if she wasn't the boring accountant or scientist that he'd thought he wanted? All artsy types weren't the same as Lisa.

"Sir, I've got you a cab," the doorman said, scooting Garrett's bags over to the door of the taxi.

"Thanks." He smiled at the man and tipped him.

When they got to JFK, he paid the cab driver and stepped out into the milling crowd. He pushed his way inside the airport and scanned the signs for his airline.

After checking in and getting through security, he settled down in the waiting area for his flight. A man in his thirties next to him kept tapping his foot and checking his watch.

"Looks like we'll have a packed flight," Garrett said to him.

"I know. That's what I'm worried about." The man pulled out his phone. "My girlfriend was supposed to be here forty minutes ago. She said she lost track of time or something." He stood. "If she's not here soon, they're going to give her seat away."

"I'm sure she'll get here soon," he said as the man dialed on his phone.

Then the man hung up. Worry and anger were etched across his face. "Voicemail again. I swear, she's always late. It drives me crazy. And she can't even be bothered to answer the phone."

"I know the type," Garrett said. He opened the thriller novel he'd brought with him for the trip, but the words swam in front of his eyes. He'd been that man, both with Lisa and now with Dahlia. As much as he didn't want to admit it, Dahlia and Lisa were alike in many ways—ways that tended to annoy him. He closed the book and leaned back in his seat.

Dahlia missing their dinner date worried him more than he'd like and he'd watched her struggle with the organization and management of the bookstore. They were so different. He had to hand it to her though; she'd perse-vered through all the challenges Agnes had thrown at her. But was it enough? Was there really a future for them together?

A voice blared over the loudspeaker. "Flight 7886 to Seat-tle, now boarding."

He was going to have to make a decision soon.

~

Founder's Day came sooner than either Dahlia or Wendy would have liked. Although Wendy had made progress on rehabilitating the ruined furniture, she wasn't satisfied with her stock on hand. Dahlia had carefully chosen a selection of books for the tourists and had a full supply of muffins to sell, along with a commercial coffee urn.

"Whew, it's hot today," Wendy said. "You'd have been better off selling iced coffees."

"Don't even say ice." She wiped the sweat away from her forehead. Not even eleven o'clock and the heat was already sweltering. Usually the air coming off the water cooled the temperature to a comfortable level, but today the air remained motionless and the thermometer stayed firmly in the high eighties.

"Can't complain about the crowds though," Wendy said.

The warm weather had brought out record-breaking attendance for the Founder's Day celebration, and the summer market was in full swing. Later in the day, there would be a parade, town picnic, and nighttime fireworks.

"I think the whole town is out today." Dahlia scanned the crowds.

"Yeah, nobody wants to stay in their non-air-conditioned houses." Wendy sucked down half a bottle of water. "I'd better get back to my booth. I just wanted to see how you were getting on."

"I'm good. How about you? Have the police said anything about what happened last weekend?"

"No, nothing. He probably moved on to someone else. I couldn't have been the only person he ever dreamed of marrying."

"Probably not."

Wendy had seemed touchy about her stalker. Not that Dahlia blamed her, but considering Wendy lived above the bookstore, she felt she had a right to know what was going on. The day after the vandalism of her booth, Wendy had insisted Dahlia return to her own home. Dahlia had ensured that the police were still patrolling around the bookstore, but with no other threats to Wendy, had done what her friend asked.

"Oooh, a fish in the pond." Wendy eyed a young couple who were browsing in her booth.

"Hook 'em." Dahlia grinned. Although the town felt overrun with tourists, they were good for the bottom line.

She rearranged stacks of books and replenished her supply of local hiking guidebooks. They'd gone fast that morning.

"Ready for work," a woman said from behind her.

Dahlia stood from where she'd been kneeling next to a box of books on the floor. Her hair flew across her eyes and she brushed it back.

"Hey, Marsha. Thanks so much for helping me out today."

"You're very welcome. Chester has his mayoral duties at the parade and I just rattle around like the last coffee bean in the jar when we have these town functions." She lowered her bulky frame into the folding armchair.

"Well, I'm glad you're here."

Marsha took in the market and nodded with satisfaction. "Ruth would be proud of you, honey."

A smile quivered on Dahlia's lips. "Do you think so? Some of the things I've done with the bookstore aren't exactly what she'd do."

"Ruth would have done everything she could to hang on to the bookstore—which is what you're doing. She would be proud."

On impulse, Dahlia leaned down and hugged the elderly woman. "Thanks Marsha," she whispered.

"I miss her too, honey." Marsha blinked away a tear and busied herself straightening books on the table. "Now, let's sell some books."

"Will you be okay by yourself?"

"Of course, remember, us Ladies were running the bookstore before you came to town."

"Right." She laughed. She felt a strange sense of attachment to the offshoot of the bookstore. "Thanks for helping out. Maggie and Gretchen are both in the parade and I promised them I'd be on the sidelines to cheer them on."

"Go." Marsha smiled at her. "I'll be fine. Take pictures of any of the truly strange floats."

Dahlia wasn't sure what she meant by "truly strange", but smiled back at her and walked away.

The parade was scheduled to start at noon, so she found a spot on the curb along the parade route. The available seats filled up fast. Little kids with flags waved them in the air as their mothers fought a losing battle to apply sunscreen to their squirmy offspring.

She breathed in the warm, salty air. This was home. She knew she'd made the right decision to stay in Candle Beach, even though she may lose the bookstore anyways if it wasn't profitable at the end of the year. At least she'd have tried.

Around her, the crowds stood and cheered as the first of the parade floats rounded the corner onto Main Street. The first float was a gigantic chicken, advertising the Homestyle Restaurant.

"Bawk, bawk," cried the chicken, or rather the young man dressed as a fowl who waved from the float. She pulled out her cell phone and snapped a shot. Behind the chicken float, a group of baton-twirling dancers pranced along. The girls beamed as they came down the street. Next to her, a woman who must have been the mom of one of the dancers took photos in furious succession.

On the next float, a miniature house sat on a bed of imitation grass. She leaned forward to take a photo and realized it was the float for Candle Beach Real Estate. As it rolled past, Gretchen leaned out and waved at Dahlia as she threw candy to the kids along the way.

Dahlia grinned and waved back at Gretchen. This was way more fun than the parades in Seattle she'd gone to as a kid. Why hadn't she attended the Founder's Day parade during all those summers she'd spent in Candle Beach? She'd probably thought she was too cool for such things.

After a few more off-the-wall floats, including one carrying the mayor dressed in early twentieth-century garb, the Bluebonnet Café float appeared.

The float was decorated with an array of live plants and a few of the patio tables adorned with food from the café. Dahlia's stomach grumbled at the sight of Maggie's delicious food. Maggie had dressed her five-year-old son Alex as a chef, his costume completed by a white chef's hat. He waved from an enclosed box at the front of the float, looking too adorable for words. Maggie stood behind him waving at the crowds, who cheered as she went by.

The parade rolled around the corner toward the end of the route. Dahlia stopped at the Bluebonnet Café and grabbed a cheeseburger and fries to go. She wasn't sure how long Marsha would want to stay at the booth and she didn't want to abuse her generous offer to man the booth while she watched the parade.

She managed to snag a seat on an empty park bench and was halfway through her burger when Gretchen tapped her on the shoulder.

"Oh my gosh, those smell awesome." Gretchen ogled the fries.

"Want some? They gave me too many."

"Not going to say no to that offer. I haven't had anything to eat since early this morning. You'd be surprised how much work those parade floats are."

"Yeah, not going to let Garrett talk me into one of those, no matter how good they are for business," Dahlia said.

"Garrett?" Gretchen raised an eyebrow and bit into the fry.

"He's been helping me with To Be Read."

"Helping with the bookstore? Is that what they're calling it now?" Gretchen grabbed another fry and wiggled her eyebrows at Dahlia.

"Yes, helping me promote the bookstore." She picked her soft drink up off the ground and took a long swig of it, hiding her face from Gretchen's keen eyes. "Okay, we've been out on a few dates."

"I knew it! So how have things been going with him?"

"Good I think. I don't know. It's complicated." She put the takeout container down between them on the bench. Gretchen took it as an offer of the remaining fries.

"Complicated how?"

"He's been burned before by women in his life that weren't reliable. And you know me, I'm not always the most organized person in the world. I'm not sure if that's an issue for him, but I really like him and don't want to lose him." She shrugged. "With all that's going on, I'm trying not to overanalyze it."

"What's going on? More than just the bookstore stuff?"

"It's Wendy." Dahlia took another sip of her drink. "You know how her truck was vandalized a few weeks ago?"

"Yeah. Did they ever catch the person who did that?"

"No." She gazed out over the park at the children playing soccer. "Did you see the story in the *Candle Beach Weekly* about the break-in at her market booth?"

"No, I've been slammed at work. How am I just now hearing about this? Did the Ladies go on strike?"

Dahlia laughed and then fell silent. "It happened late at night, maybe they were all asleep. Adam covered it for the paper though, so I'd be surprised if it wasn't making the rounds of the gossip circuit." She frowned. "Someone from her past is stalking her. Well, they were. Chances are they've left town now."

"Does Garrett know?" A stray soccer ball rolled over to them and Gretchen threw it back to the kids.

"No, that's the problem. He's been in New York since the break-in. He doesn't know and Wendy doesn't want to tell him. I should tell him, right?" She slumped on the bench. "But then I'm betraying Wendy's trust."

"True, but maybe you shouldn't see it as breaking Wendy's trust, more like protecting her." Gretchen looked thoughtful. "I know if my mom was in trouble, I'd want to know." She glanced at Dahlia and they both laughed.

Chances were the very proper Mrs. Roberts wouldn't ever be in trouble.

"So you're saying I should tell him?"

"I can't tell you what to do, but if it were me, I would." Gretchen checked her watch. "I've got to get going. I promised to help set up the fireworks seating area. Do you want to meet Maggie and me tonight to watch the fireworks? She's going to let Alex stay up to watch them."

"Thanks, but Garrett's supposed to be back today. We made plans to watch the fireworks together." With everything going on, watching a fireworks display would take her mind off of things.

Gretchen left and Dahlia gathered up her lunch. Marsha would be wondering where she was.

At the far end of the park, a group had gathered for a series of events. From the pile of burlap sacks stacked near a picnic table, Dahlia gathered that there was a sack race on the agenda. Currently, teams of children and adults were carefully balancing eggs on spoons as they crossed the grassy lawn. Cheers erupted from the crowd as a winner appeared. Dahlia had fond memories of egg races as a child, but she couldn't help but wonder if she'd ever get to experience that with a child of her own. Why was that even occurring to her? She'd never had maternal urges in the past, but something about seeing Maggie's son earlier in the parade and the joy on these children's faces struck a chord.

She shook her head. There would be plenty of time for that in the future. Thirty was the new twenty, right?

## 21

*D*ahlia sat back in her chair and guzzled water. She'd had a long stream of customers at the booth...not that she was complaining. She heard footsteps behind her and someone wordlessly wrapped their hands around her eyes. Panic ripped through her body. Had Wendy's stalker come after her now?

She yanked herself out of the attacker's grasp and whipped around to face them.

"Whoa," Garrett said, holding his hands up in the air. "Are you okay?"

"You scared me." She placed her hand over her chest. Her adrenaline-fueled heart rate decreased to a normal pace as she relaxed.

Garrett kissed her cheek and her heart rate shot back up. "Sorry about that. I just got back into town and I wanted to see you."

"I'm glad you did." She wrapped her arms around his neck and kissed him. Having him gone for a week had made her realize how much she cared for him.

"How's business been?"

"Great."

"I stopped by Wendy's booth. It looks like she's been selling a lot," he said. "Not much inventory left. She said she was going to close up soon. Something about another migraine."

"Well, she didn't have much furniture to start with this week." The words popped out of her mouth before she could stop them.

"So business has been good for her?"

"Uh, yeah. Business has been good." Guilt washed over her. Wendy had begged her not to tell Garrett about the man stalking her. Since he'd left for New York the morning after the booth was vandalized, Dahlia hadn't needed to worry about telling him. Until now.

Should she tell him? If it were her mother, she'd want to know. But she'd promised Wendy. Garrett's close proximity to her and her guilt over the secret she kept from him made her stomach twist.

She eased around to the other side of the table, a safe distance away from him.

"What's wrong?" He peered into her eyes.

She avoided making eye contact with him.

"Dahlia, what's going on?" He stepped back and stared at her.

"Nothing." What was she supposed to say? Wendy was an adult and didn't need to report to anyone. But she knew how much Garrett hated people keeping secrets from him. She took a deep breath. "Are we still on for watching the fireworks together tonight?"

"Yeah, sure." He stared at her again. "I'll pick you up at nine."

∼

Garrett had stopped at the summer market before returning home to drop off his luggage. As soon as he'd reached Candle Beach, he knew he wanted to see Dahlia. The flight from New York had been long and full of conflicting thoughts. He knew he cared for her, but was that enough?

After he'd surprised her at her booth, she'd been cagey, almost as though she were hiding something from him. But what, he didn't know. He reached his car parked at the edge of the Marina Park and tugged on the door handle.

"Hey, Garrett," a man said, jogging up to him.

"Adam, hi." Garrett fiddled with his keys. The flight had been long and he wanted nothing more than a hot shower to wash away the day's grime and confusion.

"Glad to see you back in town. And I bet your mother is too. I'm sure she's worried about what's going on."

"What do you mean, what's going on?" His relationship with Wendy was still strained, but he'd just seen her at the market and she hadn't seemed concerned about anything.

"The vandalism of her truck and her market booth." Adam looked at him funny. "Didn't your mother or Dahlia say anything to you about it?"

"No, they certainly didn't." Fury circulated through his veins. What was going on? "Is Wendy in danger?"

"Nah, I'm sure she's fine. They think it's some ex-boyfriend of hers doing it." Adam shrugged and shuffled his feet. "I'm sure he was just blowing off steam and is long gone by now. Sorry, man. I covered the story for last Friday's edition of the paper and I figured you knew about it."

"No." Garrett couldn't manage any more than one word without blowing his top at the wrong person. How could Wendy and Dahlia have kept this from him? He wasn't surprised that his mother hadn't bothered to say anything. She probably didn't even think about being in danger. But

Dahlia? She should have told him. He may not have the best relationship with his mother, but he still cared about her safety.

"Here." Adam reached into his bag and handed Garrett a newspaper. "All the details of the vandalism at her booth are in here."

"Thanks." He took the newspaper, crushing it in his hand. "I've got to get going." He jerked his head toward his car.

Adam nodded. "See you later."

When Adam was safely out of sight, Garrett scanned the newspaper article. How had Dahlia not said anything to him when he'd called her from New York? He stalked back to her.

She saw him and her face lit up. "I didn't expect to see you so soon. Did you forget something?"

"Did I forget something? Don't you mean you and Wendy forgot to tell me something?" He held up the newspaper and stabbed his finger at the picture of Wendy's booth on the front page. His voice shook and he felt heat rise above the collar of his button-down shirt.

Dahlia blanched. "What do you mean?"

"You knew some nut job vandalized my mother's truck and booth and you didn't say anything?"

Dahlia stared at him like a deer caught in the headlights. "Wendy didn't want me to say anything." She came over to him and put her hand on his arm.

He brushed it off and stepped back. "So?"

"I didn't think it was my place to tell you," she whispered.

"What if he'd attacked her instead of only destroying her booth?" He felt the vein in his forehead pulse with every word.

"But he didn't." Dahlia's face crumpled and her eyes were bright. He hated seeing her cry, but he couldn't stop himself from yelling.

"What if he came after her at the bookstore? And if he found you there instead of her? You both could have been in danger. I should have known about this. I could have protected you both."

Their conversation had drawn curious onlookers. He lowered his voice. "I expect this kind of disregard for safety from my mother, but I expected you to be different." He paused and regarded her. "I guess I shouldn't have, all things considered."

"Garrett—"

"No." He ran his hand through his hair and stared up at the sky. "This isn't going to work. I've got to go." He turned away from her and stomped off.

~

Dahlia watched him go, her bottom lip quivering. She knew she should have told him about Wendy. She smiled weakly at the few people who'd been watching their argument. They avoided eye contact and shuffled away as though nothing had happened. She slumped in her chair and gazed toward the ocean without seeing it.

Had Garrett just broken up with her? She'd thought they were in a good place, and now this.

"Hey, Dahl. You okay?" Maggie approached her and rubbed her upper arm. She carried a bouquet of roses and some fresh raspberries from the market.

Dahlia blinked back tears and tried to focus on her friend. "No."

"Oh sweetie, what's wrong?" Maggie placed her purchases on the table and hugged her.

"Garrett broke up with me," she blubbered.

"What? Why?" Maggie leaned back and scanned Dahlia's face.

"He found out about Wendy's stalker."

"So? I don't understand. That's not your fault."

"Wendy asked me not to tell him about her truck being vandalized and then the furniture being destroyed. So I didn't tell him." Dahlia swiped at her face with the back of her hand. "Maggie, he's so mad at me."

"I'm sure he'll get over it." Maggie pulled a facial tissue out of her pocket and offered it to her.

"I don't think he will. He said it was over. He thinks I'm flaky and irresponsible." The tears fell faster.

Maggie hugged her again and then paused for a moment. She put her hands on Dahlia's shoulders and made Dahlia look at her.

"Listen. You are an awesome, creative, and kind person. If he doesn't like you for who you are, good riddance."

"But what if he's right? I should have told him about Wendy."

"Yeah, you probably should have, but you made a mistake. He needs to realize that."

Maggie was right. Dahlia sat up straight and dried the remaining tears. "And if he doesn't, maybe he's not the right guy for me. I promised myself I'd never change for someone ever again." She looked proudly at the few books left at the booth. "But I'm not the same person I used to be. I never thought I could run a bookstore, and now look at me. I might actually make this place profitable."

Maggie leaned against the table, playing with a leaf on one

of the roses. "You know, life is short." She glanced up at Dahlia. "I've seen you with Garrett. The way he looks at you is the way Brian used to look at me." Her eyes glistened and she looked fiercely at Dahlia. "If you care for him, don't give up so easily."

It was Dahlia's turn to comfort her friend, and she slipped an arm around Maggie. "Thanks."

Maggie cleared her throat. "I've got to get back home. My mom's watching Alex right now, but I promised I'd be home in time for dinner. If you're not going with Garrett now, do you want to join us at the fireworks tonight?"

Dahlia smiled. "I'd love to."

Maggie left and Dahlia gathered up the remaining books and stacked them in boxes. Garrett's words had hurt and she didn't know if there was any chance to fix their relationship. Although she'd grown in the last few months, she didn't know if she'd ever be the person he wanted her to be.

Her throat thickened at the thought of losing him. She knew what they had was special. He just had to forgive her.

She loaded the boxes into her car for the short ride back to the bookstore and slammed the door shut. Whatever happened in the future, she wasn't going to let it ruin Founder's Day for her. Instead of the romantic evening she'd planned with Garrett, she'd have a fun evening with friends watching the fireworks. Maybe that would take her mind off of him, at least for a few hours.

~

Bursts of bright oranges and blues flashed across the dark sky as Dahlia scurried across the grass to where her friends sat.

"Sorry I'm late," she said. "I got caught up at the bookstore prepping for tomorrow."

"No worries, the fireworks only started a minute or so ago." Maggie smiled at Dahlia, her hands resting on her son's shoulders. Alex gazed up at the sky in wonder.

Gretchen waved at her from the other side of the blue-and-red checkered blanket the three of them sat on, and motioned for her to sit down.

She leaned back on the soft flannel blanket to watch the light show, allowing herself to be caught up in its glory. Around her, families oohed and aahed over the display. The fireworks technicians set off the final round, a magnificent show that lingered over the water before trailing off beyond the inky horizon.

The attendees gathered their belongings as the last firework disappeared, the crowd abuzz with the excitement of Founder's Day.

"Well, that's it," Maggie said. "Alex, time to get you in bed." She turned to her friends. "I have to work the evening shift tomorrow, but do you guys want to meet for breakfast somewhere?"

Gretchen started to say something, but her response was cut off by a series of explosions behind them.

"What the—" Dahlia said, as everyone turned to look for the source of the noise.

From somewhere near the center of town, flames shot high in the sky and smoke billowed from the fire.

"The café," Maggie shouted. She shoved her son at Gretchen. "Can you watch Alex please?" Gretchen nodded.

Maggie took off running, with Dahlia close behind her.

When they got closer to the café, they saw that the fire was further up Main Street. Maggie stopped and Dahlia almost ran into her.

*Please, please, don't let it be To Be Read*, she thought.

The chances of it being another building grew slimmer

the closer she got. Sirens filled the air as the town's only fire truck forced its way through the clogged streets. Dahlia pushed through the crowds. The fire truck had entered the short alley behind the book store and was spraying the dumpster behind the store. Flames had crept up the side of the building.

Where was Wendy? Garrett had said she'd gone home with a migraine earlier in the day. Dahlia looked around frantically for her friend, but didn't see her. Then someone grabbed her from behind.

## 22

"Dahlia, thank goodness you're okay," Garrett said. "I was taking a stretch break outside and saw the flames." He scanned the crowd. "Where's Wendy?"

Dahlia stared at him, her eyes wide with fear. "I don't know," she whispered. Fiery orange flames licked at the upstairs apartment. An icy chill shot through her body. Was Wendy still in the building?

Garrett ran over to the firefighters, shouting at them. Dahlia followed close behind him. "My mother, she's inside." His eyes were wild.

The firefighter relayed the information to his team. Garrett tried to bolt for the building's front door, but the firefighter held him back and directed them to stand on the other side of the street, at a safe distance from the scene. She put her hand on Garrett's arm, her fingers digging into his skin as they waited together.

Just then, a firefighter in full battle gear burst out of the front door of To Be Read cradling Wendy in his arms. He carried her over to an ambulance, where the EMTs immediately began assessing her.

No one could keep Garrett and Dahlia away. They waited until the EMTs had finished and then they circled around Wendy.

"Mom," Garrett said. "I was so worried about you."

Wendy reached out for him, pulling him close. Whether from smoke or emotion, his eyes filled up with tears.

She pulled off the oxygen mask and croaked out, "I'm fine." She smiled weakly at them before replacing the mask.

"We're going to need to take her to the hospital in Haven Shores for observation, but I think she'll be okay," the EMT said to Garrett as they loaded Wendy onto the ambulance and shut the door. The crowd parted for the ambulance, which pulled onto a side street to make its way out of town.

"We can take my car to Haven Shores." Dahlia tugged at Garrett's arm. "It's right over there." She gestured at her car parked next to Wendy's truck. She closed her eyes for a second. *Please, please, let Wendy be okay*.

Garrett looked at her for a moment as if not really seeing her, before he snapped out of it.

"Dahlia, wait. Your store."

They both looked over at To Be Read. The firefighters had controlled the fire and only embers flickered now on the roof. Smoke hung heavily in the air.

"It can wait. Me being here doesn't change anything. Hold on." Dahlia found Gretchen, Maggie, and Alex standing at the periphery of the crowd. As she neared them, they started talking in a jumble of words.

She held up a hand to silence them. "I've got to go to the hospital with Garrett. Can you please talk with the fire department? Let them know I should be back in a few hours. You can give them my cell phone number if they need to reach me before then."

Maggie squeezed her arm and said, "We will. Give Wendy our best."

Dahlia thanked them and returned to Garrett.

"Okay, let's go." They followed the ambulance's path out of town, riding in silence most of the way. Dahlia couldn't help but wonder if Wendy's stalker had anything to do with the fire, but she didn't mention her theory to Garrett. That was a can of worms that didn't need to be opened.

~

After arriving at the hospital, they had to wait for a while before being allowed to see Wendy. Once she was evaluated and checked in, the hospital staff permitted them to enter her room. Two nurses were getting her situated in a bed.

"How is she?" Garrett asked a doctor writing in the chart outside her door.

"She inhaled a lot of smoke, so we're going to continue with our treatments and keep her overnight for observation. She should be feeling better by tomorrow, although her throat will be sore."

"Thank you," Garrett said. The tension in his face eased.

The nurses left, and Garrett and Dahlia crossed over to Wendy's bedside.

"How are you feeling?" he asked softly, leaning in to give his mother a kiss on the forehead.

Wendy smiled, although she looked exhausted. Then she coughed and said, "Like Santa Claus caught in a chimney fire."

Dahlia smiled. Wendy would be okay. "You gave us quite a scare." She reached for Wendy's hand.

Wendy squeezed it, looking from Dahlia to Garrett and

back again. "You two came here together. Does that mean your silly argument is over?"

"How did you know about that?" Dahlia asked.

"Do you know how many phone calls I got from the Ladies after you were seen arguing in the park?"

Of course. Good gossip traveled fast.

"So did you make up?"

Garrett didn't answer, but he had an odd expression on his face.

"Garrett?" Wendy nudged.

"Sure," he said, nodding. He turned to Dahlia. "I think Mom is settled in here. You can get back to the bookstore now if you'd like."

Wendy groaned. "Dahlia, I feel awful about the bookstore. I never thought he'd do something like this."

"You mean your stalker?" Garrett narrowed his eyes at Wendy. "When were you going to tell me about him? You could have been killed. I'm going to make sure the hospital stations someone at the door to your room. This has gone too far."

"You know?" Wendy cringed.

"Yeah. Adam told me. Not you, and not Dahlia. I had to hear about this from a guy I barely know."

Wendy patted his arm. "It's just a little problem I've been having with someone I used to date. I'm sure he didn't mean to hurt me."

"This isn't some little thing. Do you realize how bad this could have been?"

She shrank into her pillow. "I know." She reached her hand out to him. "I'm sorry. I should have told you, and I never should have made Dahlia keep it from you."

"Maybe I should leave you two alone," Dahlia said. "Garrett's right, I should probably get back to Candle Beach, but

I wanted to make sure you were okay." She shifted her weight between her feet and shot glances out the door. Wendy and Garrett had a lot to discuss and it was better done without her present. Although the fire had brought them together, she still wasn't sure where she stood with Garrett.

"You're welcome to stay, but I understand if you need to leave," Wendy said.

"I can come back in a few hours and give you a ride home," Dahlia said to Garrett.

"I'm sure I can find a ride home, don't worry about it."

"Okay," Dahlia said. "I'll see you tomorrow, Wendy."

She left the hospital more confused than ever over her relationship with Garrett.

$\sim$

In Candle Beach, the fire truck remained at the smoldering bookstore, but no active flames were evident. Dahlia parked next to Wendy's truck and approached a firefighter who was still there. He leaned against the back of the fire truck, completing paperwork.

"Hi," she said. "I'm Dahlia Winters, I own this building. Or what remains of it, I suppose."

"Oh yes, Ms. Winters. Your friends said you were going to the hospital." He checked his notes. "The final report won't be in for a while, but so far it looks like a clear case of arson. You should be able to go in with someone tomorrow and recover anything that survived the fire."

She took another look at the building. The exterior had looked bad before, but now she could see that much of the brick hadn't been harmed by the fire. Except for the blown-out window, the building itself was fine.

She walked over to the window frame and peered over it. The water damage inside, was another story. Soggy books lay strewn across the floor, bloated with liquid. There wouldn't be any books to save, but maybe some of Aunt Ruth's things had survived. Ironically, all of her remodeling efforts had been in vain. Insurance would probably cover the building and contents, but what would this mean for the terms of Aunt Ruth's will? At least Wendy was safe. Books could be replaced, people couldn't.

It seemed like years ago that she'd been at the summer market, intent on selling as many books as possible, although in reality it had only been a little over eight hours ago. As quickly as the bookstore had come into her life, it had literally gone up in flames.

She finished answering the firefighter's questions around midnight and drove home, exhausted.

She tore off her smoky clothes and showered as soon as she entered the house. The water pressure rinsed off the long day and made her feel moderately better. After a cup of tea, she headed for bed, but she tossed and turned for the better part of an hour.

*This is ridiculous*, she thought. She got dressed in yoga pants and a sweatshirt and grabbed her house keys and a flashlight.

On the way down the hill to the beach trail, she passed Garrett's house, noting that the light was on in his kitchen. He'd apparently found a ride home.

Her flashlight cast a small beam of light on the beach trail, but ahead, the moon illuminated much of the beach. She walked down to the surf, mesmerized by the foam glowing in the moonlight. Had it really been only a few weeks since she'd made the decision to stay in Candle Beach? Aunt Ruth's legacy of To Be Read didn't exist anymore, and things with Garrett were up in the air. Was it worth staying?

~

Garrett's deep voice interrupted her thoughts. "I thought I'd find you here."

The pounding of the waves had disguised his approach, and she jumped when she realized she wasn't alone.

"Sorry, I didn't mean to frighten you." He moved to within a few feet of her.

"How'd you know I was here?"

"I saw you walk down the hill," he said. "I couldn't sleep either."

She nodded and shivered a little as cold air off the water blasted through her sweatshirt. "How did you get home?"

"I hitched a ride with the police officer who came to Haven Shores to interview Mom."

So he was calling her Mom now instead of Wendy. That was an interesting development.

"What did the police have to say? Did they catch the person who burned the bookstore and almost killed Wendy?" She shivered again, this time with fear that the arsonist was still on the loose.

"They caught him," Garrett said. "Apparently he was in the crowd at the fire." He laughed at the irony. "That's the benefit of small towns. Even with all the tourists, any strangers stand out to local law enforcement."

"Was it the same person who left her the threatening note and vandalized her truck and booth?"

Garrett mock glared at her. "Yes, it was. And it would have been nice to know about those earlier."

Her shoulders slumped. "I'm sorry. I almost told you so many times, but we kept getting interrupted."

He put his hands on her shoulders, holding her an arms-length away. He looked directly into her eyes. Even in the soft moonlight, his gaze was intense. "Dahlia, it wasn't your fault. My mother is a force of nature. It wasn't up to you to tell me. She should have said something." His hands slid lower on her arms, eliminating the chill she had felt. "I can understand why she wouldn't have told me though. I haven't always been very open to hearing things from her." He stared out over the water. "Or from you," he added, looking into her eyes again.

"Garrett, I don't—" she started to say, before he put a finger on her lips.

"Let me say what I need to say first."

She nodded, and he pulled her closer. "I know you're not like my mother. She never would have stayed like you did, even after everything Agnes put you through."

Dahlia tilted her head to watch his expression as he spoke.

"I've loved you ever since the first time I saw you, standing there at the overlook."

"Do you mean that? You really love me? I didn't think you'd even noticed me that day." She was almost afraid to breathe. "You barely acknowledged me in the parking lot."

"Yes, silly. I love you." He smiled. "Of course I noticed you. I thought you'd seen me taking your picture. I couldn't help myself." He sighed. "You looked so serious and beautiful as the wind blew through your hair. But you were staring so anxiously toward Candle Beach and I felt awkward about interrupting a private moment. I couldn't seem to get the words out to introduce myself." He brushed a strand of hair out of her face.

"Later, when we met formally, I got it into my head that you were a carbon copy of my mother and every other creative type I've ever known. I'd vowed to never get involved with anyone like that, but somehow you were always there, infiltrating my thoughts. I tried to push it away, but couldn't." He looked out to sea again. "And then when I saw the flames at the bookstore, all I could think about was your safety and my mother's. If I'd lost you..." He removed a hand from her arm and brushed away a tear.

Dahlia didn't think. "I love you too." She pulled his face toward her and kissed him squarely on the lips. Garrett moved his hands to her jawline and deepened the kiss. After a minute, they pulled away to stand a few inches from each other.

"You didn't lose me," she said. "And no, I'm not your mother." She grinned impishly and stood on her tiptoes to kiss him again.

## 23

*A* week later, Dahlia sat with her friends drinking wine in their usual booth at Off the Vine, being bombarded with questions.

"I can't believe we haven't seen you in a week," Gretchen said.

"I've been busy."

"Busy canoodling with Garrett?" she teased. Maggie slapped Gretchen's hand playfully, but then they both turned up their faces to hear Dahlia's response.

"No, not with Garrett." Dahlia stuck her face in her glass of wine, hoping to conceal the blush she felt heating her cheeks. "Okay, maybe some of that time has been spent with Garrett, but I've been working with the insurance company all week."

"A-ha, I knew it!" Gretchen looked smug. "Maggie saw you two snuggled up on a park bench together on Wednesday. She told one of the Ladies and now the whole town is talking."

Maggie had the decency to redden.

"The whole town?" Dahlia shook her head. Small towns.

"Sorry, I didn't think about it before I told her," Maggie apologized. "So how is everything going with the insurance company? We had a small fire at the café last year and it was a nightmare getting them to sign off on repairs."

"It's not as bad as I would have thought," Dahlia said. "Since this was a clear-cut case of arson, they've eliminated the waiting period for investigation, so I should be able to start interviewing contractors next week."

"We feel so bad for you," Maggie said. "All that work you did and then to have this happen."

"There's not much I can do about it. I could not rebuild To Be Read, and leave Candle Beach, but where would that leave me?"

"And there's Garrett to consider..." Gretchen said, for which she received a swift elbow to the mid-section from Maggie. "What?" A sly smile crept across her face.

"And you guys, and the town in general, and even Agnes," Dahlia said.

"Agnes?" Gretchen looked perplexed. "I would think you'd happily move as far away as possible from her."

"Well, I had the strangest conversation ever with her this week," Dahlia said. She ate a stuffed mushroom and sipped her wine, prolonging the suspense. Gretchen's eyes almost popped out of their sockets and even ever-calm Maggie fidgeted in her seat.

"Tell us!" Gretchen ordered. "What did Agnes say?"

Dahlia put down her drink. "She said that she never wanted to make me leave town. Before Ruth's death, she'd promised her she'd challenge me so I wouldn't get bored with the bookstore. Ruth suspected I'd want to sell it, and not want to be tied down, but she knew it would be good for me."

"You're kidding me." Maggie downed half of her glass of

wine in two long gulps. "All that was to challenge you? To make you emotionally invested in the bookstore and want to stay in town?"

"She may have taken it a bit too far." Dahlia laughed. "But she was successful. If it hadn't been for her meddling in everything related to the bookstore, I probably wouldn't have given Candle Beach a chance, and wouldn't be here today."

"Well then," Gretchen said, raising her drink for a toast. "To Agnes." They clinked their glasses together.

"And to Aunt Ruth," Dahlia said. They raised their glasses again. As the three glasses made contact, Dahlia could feel Aunt Ruth smiling down upon them.

～

"How's this?" Garrett anchored the arbor in place over the entrance to the path through Aunt Ruth's garden. He'd replaced some of the woodwork in the trellis and repainted it. The white paint shone in the sunlight, the perfect foil to the brightly colored flowers surrounding it.

"I love it." Dahlia pressed her hands together in front of her with the tips of her fingers against her lips. "It's perfect. Aunt Ruth would be proud of you."

He smiled. "I'm pretty proud of myself too. I always knew those woodworking classes I took back in Seattle would come in handy."

They'd whipped the gardens into shape together, with the refinished arbor as the last piece to complete it. She eyed the flaking exterior of the house. "Now I just have to repaint the house. Not looking forward to that."

"Well, at least you'll be here to enjoy it." He came up behind her, wrapped his arms around her, and rested his chin on her head. "You don't have any plans to leave, right?" he teased.

She elbowed him and turned around, planting a kiss on his lips. "You know very well that I have no intention of ever moving away from Candle Beach. This is my home now. And there's a certain guy I just might miss if I left."

"Oh really? A certain guy?" He kissed her and picked her up, depositing her on the porch swing. She laughed and pulled him down beside her on the flowered cushions.

"Yes, a very handsome guy who I happen to love very much and intend to spend a lot of time with in the future. That is, if he can tear himself away from his romance novels long enough."

"Oh, I think that can be arranged. And who knows, the story of how we met and fell in love might work its way into a romance novel of its own."

She stared into his eyes, allowing herself to get lost in them. "You know, I think I'd like that. As long as it has a happily ever after."

"Of course it will. How could it not?"

She leaned against him and closed her eyes to enjoy the moment. With the warmth of the sun, the beauty of the gardens, and the man she loved beside her, she'd never felt such happiness.

**THANK YOU FOR READING SWEET BEGINNINGS!**

Want to spend more time in Candle Beach?

Gretchen's Story: Sweet Success
    See the next page for a preview of Sweet Success

Maggie's Story: Sweet Promises

*Available on Amazon and Kindle Unlimited*

## SWEET SUCCESS: A CANDLE BEACH SWEET ROMANCE

"They're sickeningly sweet together." Gretchen Roberts watched as the couple in a booth at the back of Off the Vine snuggled close against each other.

Her friend Maggie punched her lightly in the arm.

"Ouch." She rubbed her arm and glared. "I think you've spent too much time in kickboxing classes."

"Ha ha," Maggie said. "You're happy for her, remember?"

"Okay, okay. I'm happy that Dahlia and Garrett found each other, but I miss spending time with my friend. It's been weeks since the three of us hung out together."

"We've been busy too," Maggie reminded her. "With the mild weather in January and February, this was the biggest winter tourist season we've ever had in Candle Beach." She sipped her glass of Chardonnay and surreptitiously glanced at Dahlia, who was making gooey eyes at Garrett, then rolled her own eyes. "Okay, they're annoying. But I am happy for her. It's been ages since I went out on a date. And what about you? I've got a kid at home, but you're young and single. Why are you sitting here with me on a Friday night?"

"I haven't had time to meet anyone. And I have better things to do with my time than try to meet men." Gretchen grabbed an onion ring from the basket in the middle of the table and crunched down on it.

"Like what?" Maggie gave her a pointed look as she took the last onion ring and dipped it into ranch dressing.

"Like—" Gretchen started to say, but was interrupted by a woman tapping her on the shoulder. A man stood a few feet behind the woman.

"Gretchen? Maggie? I'd heard you were back in town, but what luck running into both of you here." The woman pushed back the artfully arranged curls that hung down her back and gave Gretchen's shoulder a quick squeeze. The scent of floral perfume followed her every movement. Gretchen stared at the woman, unsuccessfully trying to place her.

Maggie recovered first. "Stella, how nice to see you."

Stella beamed at her. "Girls, this is my husband Lance. I'm living on the East Coast now, but we were in Seattle visiting my family and I wanted to show Lance where I spent all my summers growing up. The Washington coast is so different than what we have back east."

They shook Lance's hand and murmured polite greetings. Gretchen leaned back in the booth to get a better look at Stella. Stella's family had summered in Candle Beach and the three of them, occasionally with their friend Dahlia, would spend hours playing together when they were pre-teens. Now, Gretchen hardly recognized Stella as the carefree tomboy she'd grown up with.

"So, Maggie, what are you up to these days? I heard something through the grapevine about a restaurant?" Stella looked around. "Is this it?"

"You heard correctly. But not this restaurant." Maggie smiled at them. "I bought the Bluebonnet Café a few years ago after my son and I came back to Candle Beach."

"And your husband?" Stella asked. "Is he here too?"

Sadness shadowed Maggie's face. "He was killed in Iraq. It's just Alex and me now."

"Oh honey, I'm so sorry." Stella leaned in to embrace her.

"It was a long time ago," Maggie said, with a forced smile. "We're enjoying being back here in Candle Beach and spending time with family. With my husband's Army career, I didn't see much of them for the six years we were married."

"Oh," Stella murmured. "Well, I'm happy you have your family for support." She turned to Gretchen.

"And what about you? What have you been up to?"

"A little of this, a little of that. After college, I moved back here and joined my parents at their company, Candle Beach Real Estate. With the increase in tourism over the last ten years, business has been booming."

"Oh. Well, that's nice for you. I'm sure your parents appreciate your help. I know my parents would love to see Lance and me more often, but with his career on Wall Street and my position at the law firm, we don't get to take much vacation time. I'm up for partner this year." She wore a self-satisfied smile.

"Wow, that's great. Congratulations." Gretchen's stomach flip-flopped. Stella obviously led a successful life and didn't hesitate to boast about it. Her old friend deserved to be proud of herself, so why did Stella's comments bother her so much?

Before she could stop herself, she blurted out, "Actually, I'm in the process of moving to Seattle. I'm branching out from my parents' business and plan to start my own real estate firm there."

Maggie raised an eyebrow, but didn't say anything.

"How exciting," Stella cooed. "Seattle has so much going on. You'll love it." Behind Stella, Lance shifted from foot to foot and looked longingly at an empty booth in the corner of the restaurant. He cleared his throat.

Stella looked at her husband and laughed. "We'd better get going. We've been driving all day and we're starving." She looked around Off the Vine. "This place is so cute. Who'd have thought there would be a wine bar in little old Candle Beach." He tugged at her arm and started to lead her away. She called over her shoulder, "It was nice seeing you, girls." She gave a little wave and allowed him to direct her to the empty booth.

When she was out of earshot, Maggie said, "Now that was a blast from the past. I haven't heard from her in fifteen years."

"Yeah, and we probably won't for another fifteen." Gretchen pushed her dark wavy mass of hair behind her ears and sipped the margarita. Over the top of the glass, she glanced at Stella and her husband, who were engrossed in the menu offerings.

"So what was that about moving to Seattle? Are you really thinking about it? Or were you just saying that because Stella was so full of herself?"

Gretchen shrugged. She'd come up with the idea on the spur-of-the-moment, but now the seed of a plan sprouted in her brain. "I need to figure out what I want to do with the rest of my life. I don't want to be a property manager for Candle Beach Real Estate forever. I love my parents and all, but working for the family business was never something I wanted for my future."

"So this is real? How long have you been considering this?"

"Yes, it's real." She looked toward the window. Outside, the light had faded and the street was empty. "I'm going to move to a bigger city and be a real estate agent. Maybe it won't be Seattle, but somewhere around that area. I want to help people buy and sell their homes and have more of a relationship with clients. I can't do that with the nightly cottage rentals to tourists." As soon as the words left her mouth, she felt a strange sense of relief, as if a weight had been lifted off her chest and she could breathe again.

Maggie put down her wine glass. "So you're really leaving Candle Beach?"

"Yes. I've got to get out of here. This town is suffocating me. The coast is a great place to visit, but it doesn't provide many career opportunities."

"What about being a real estate agent in Candle Beach?" Maggie fiddled with her napkin. "I'd miss having you around. You're one of the few people over the age of five that I hang out with. My parents are always busy and even Alex is so obsessed with his Legos right now that he doesn't have time for me." She smiled, but her eyes were bright with unshed tears.

Gretchen smiled gently at her and patted her hand. "I'd still come visit, and I'd only be a phone call away. Don't worry." Her mood darkened. "But if I stay in Candle Beach, I'll always be competing with my parents for clients. Or worse yet, working for them the rest of my life."

"Starting over somewhere else will be risky. Do you have any money saved for the move?" Maggie asked. "When I bought the café, it took all the money I had left from Brian's life insurance after setting up a college fund for Alex. Even after that, it seemed like every day brought more unexpected expenses. Do you really want to move somewhere without a safety net?"

As always, Maggie was right.

"I don't have much in my savings account." Her optimism deflated. "I guess I could rent out the house Grams left me and lease a smaller place to save money, but I don't really want to do that. I'm not much of a waitress, so working at the Bluebonnet Café wouldn't work, but maybe Dahlia would hire me for a few shifts at To Be Read during the summer tourist season."

"Okay," Maggie said slowly. "So what about clients? You'll be starting over in Seattle. Here, you know everyone. This town isn't all tourists, you know. Locals and new people need houses too."

"I don't know what I'll do about clients." She leaned back against her seat. This was getting more and more complicated, but she knew she couldn't stay in Candle Beach much longer without going crazy. Her face brightened as she thought of something. "Dahlia's mother is a real estate agent. I bet she'd help me make some connections. Maybe her company is hiring."

"Maybe," Maggie said. They looked over to the booth where Dahlia had sat, but she and Garrett were gone. A waitress was clearing away the dishes from the table.

Someone waved at Maggie from across the room. She waved back and nodded at two men. One appeared to be in his sixties, with graying hair and a jovial face. The other was closer to her own age. Both were dressed in the casual uniform of tourists—jeans and polo shirts.

"Who was that?" Gretchen asked. She'd never seen them before.

"Oh, visitors who came into the Bluebonnet Café today. I

took over Belinda's tables while she was on break and they were seated at one of them. Nice guys. I chatted with them for a while about some of the local tourist attractions."

"Oh, you mean like the old well house and the pioneer cemetery?" She waggled her eyebrows mischievously.

"Ha ha," Maggie said. "I mean things like fishing at Bluebonnet Lake, or the whale-watching excursions they can charter down at the marina. There's a lot to do in Candle Beach."

"If you say so." She gulped the watery remains of her margarita and looked at her watch. "I think it's time to head home. I told my parents I'd man the booth at the chocolate festival tomorrow."

"It'll be crazy with all the tourists in town for that. My pastry chef has been working like a madwoman to create new chocolate desserts to showcase." Maggie finished her drink and waved the waitress over for their check.

After the check arrived, they split the bill, waved goodbye and went their separate ways. Gretchen put her hands in her coat pocket and walked up the hill towards the house she'd inherited from her grandmother. She'd felt adrift after college and had moved home while she decided what to do with her life, but the years had passed faster than she'd like to admit. It seemed like yesterday that she'd returned to Candle Beach after graduation, but it had already been ten years. It was time for a change, but how feasible would it be to start over in Seattle? There were so many unknowns, from money and how to earn it, to how easily she'd be able to get clients in a new location. She didn't know many people outside of Candle Beach, so she'd be on her own.

She trudged up the incline and stopped in front of her

house. The lovely Craftsman with the partial water view had been her home since her grandmother died seven years before. She didn't want to rent out the house and move somewhere else, but if that was what it took, it needed to be the top item on her list of money-making ideas. As she contemplated renting out the house, her boxer dog, Reilly, must have heard her footsteps, because he pawed at the front window. She smiled. It was nice to have someone to come home to.

~

Cheers filled the offices of Gray and Associates as Parker Gray's co-workers raised plastic glasses of champagne to toast his brother, Graham. He raised his own glass in a half-hearted manner and chugged the bubbly liquid. The sweet and sour tang burned on the way down.

A woman put her hand on his arm. "Isn't it great how much business Graham's brought in?" she gushed. "And to be the highest seller for six months straight. What I wouldn't do to be in his place."

Parker gently removed her arm and backed away. "Uh-huh. It's great." He threw his champagne glass in the trash and exited the room. The cube farm where his desk was located was dark and empty with everyone else at the party. He leaned back in his swivel chair and picked up a rubber ball stamped with the Gray and Associates logo from a basket of them by his desk. A yellow sticky note on his computer informed him that Graham wanted him to research a possible new commercial acquisition. Parker hated commercial real estate, but his brother had decided that a Gray needed to be at the helm of the commercial division.

Light streamed out of one of the few enclosed offices in the building, drawing his attention. He stared toward the light. Out of three offices, one belonged to each of his parents and one to his big brother Graham, the golden boy. He tossed the ball in the air and caught it, over and over again. If he stayed at the family's real estate firm, he'd always be overshadowed by his brother. For the umpteenth time, he wished he'd been forward-thinking like his younger siblings and gone into another career field. But the truth was, he loved what he did. He just didn't want to do it at Gray and Associates.

The problem was, Haven Shores wasn't a big city. He wasn't sure if there was room for another real estate company. But he had to try. He didn't want to be stuck in his brother's shadow forever. Things usually came easy for Parker—jobs, women, money—and he wasn't sure why he was letting Graham's success get him down.

"Hey, Parker." A woman in her twenties approached him, her suit jacket barely concealing the not-so-professional low-cut blouse she wore under it.

"Hi, Angie." He threw the ball in the basket.

"Are you busy later? My dinner date canceled and I'd hate to be alone on a Friday night." She pouted her pretty pink lips.

He considered her offer for a moment. If he wanted to create a successful future, he needed to start taking himself seriously. No more women for a while. He had a shot at a big commission and he needed to put everything he had into making it a reality. It was the key to starting out on his own.

"Sorry, Angie." He grabbed his jacket off the back of the chair. "I've got a hot date tonight with some market research."

She pouted again and jutted out her hip. "Are you sure?"

"Yeah, I'm sure. Thanks for the offer." He brushed past her and exited the office. His buddies would never believe he'd turned down a pretty girl, but then again, he'd never been more serious about any undertaking in his life than he was about this opportunity.